BY THE PRICKING OF MY THUMB

By

V. E. Sullivan

This book is a work of fiction. Places, events, and situations in this story are purely fictional. Any resemblance to actual persons, living or dead, is coincidental.

© 2002 by Viva Sullivan. All rights reserved.

No part of this book may be reproduced, stored in a retrieval system, or transmitted by any means, electronic, mechanical, photocopying, recording, or otherwise, without written permision from the author.

ISBN: 1-4033-2461-X (e-book)
ISBN: 1-4033-4262-8 (Paperback)
ISBN: 1-4033-4263-6 (Dustjacket)
ISBN: 1-4033-4264-4 (Rocket Book)

Library of Congress Control Number: 2002092541

This book is printed on acid free paper.

Printed in the United States of America
Bloomington, IN

1st Books - rev. 9/5/02

Dedications:

In loving memory

Of a dear son and sister

Douglas and Kitty

With special thanks to

Karen Bulthuis

And Margaret Brooks

By the Pricking of My Thumb

Chapter 1

Blindly, she reached back, pulling the rough terry cloth towel she kept for drying her hair from the heated towel bar, and, wrapping it Turkish-style around her head, she tucked it in at the nape of her neck. Reaching forward, Suzette used the corner of her thick Turkish towel to wipe a circle clear in the steamed up mirror. She stared at herself, and the reflection she saw was a mixture of her handsome parents, Jason and Amelia Lang. She had her father's thick chestnut hair, her mother's large, green eyes, and lashes that weren't half bad either. She had the same wide, sensuous mouth and well-defined lips as her mother, and good, strong teeth, a product of good, wholesome eating. She guessed, all in all, she had just missed being really beautiful.

She rubbed vigorously for several minutes then tossed her head back and picked up her brush. Her thick chestnut cap fell into place like a shining helmet. Dropping the towel, she stepped on the scale. She decided the eight stones it read were not too bad. Robert and she had had a day on the town yesterday. Lunch at "Ces't Bon", after which they'd strolled around Portabel Road looking for antique bargains, mainly for cane-bottomed chairs to match the ones they already had. But bargains were getting very hard to find. People were becoming much more aware of what they had, and were selling them for hard brass themselves.

Suzette dealt in old rare books, and had worked for the old established English firm of Berkshire and Stilts. It had been established back in the 1800's, and it had stayed in the Berkshire and Stilts families over the generations.

Stop gathering wool, my girl, and get on with the day, Suzette scolded herself. Wrapping another towel about her slim body, she left the bathroom.

The phone was burring off the hook on the bedside table. Who in the world would be calling now? She looked at her watch. Six forty-five... must be bad news. Throwing herself across the old bed, she answered rather breathlessly "Hello?"

"Suzette, love, hoped I'd catch you before you'd left. I've just discovered- oh, dear, what a nuisance! Someone has just come into the shop and Ed's not here yet. I'll drop you a note in the afternoon post. Cheerie bye, love!" And the phone went dead.

Suzette rolled over on her back, looking at the instrument in her hand. So like Auntie Millacent, she thought. Shaking her head, she replaced the phone in its cradle.

Rising slowly, she dropped the towel and stepped over it. It had been almost two years since the early morning call had come from Paris, informing her that her parents had been killed in that tragic car accident on the little country road outside of the little French village where her grandmother had lived, in Provence.

Suzette was the only child of Jason and Amelia Lang, and she was 26 years old. They had distinguished themselves during the Second World War, and had given evidence at the Nuremberg trials. She remembered her father's diary had been given in evidence, mainly against one S.S. officer, a Colonel Heindrich von Heusen, and his lieutenant, Kurt Schreiler. Both had been convicted of cruel and lascivious acts against the Jews from Poland, to The Hague and to Paris, and Heindrich had been found guilty by the tribunal and sentenced to hang. As he was being led from the courtroom, Heindrich had threatened both Amelia and Jason. Suzette remembered now that an investigation had gone into the car crash after their deaths, with an inquest, but nothing had ever been settled. The case was neither open, nor closed, just gathering dust in someone's filing cabinet somewhere in Paris, she assumed.

Gathering dust! Yes, that's what you're doing, you big, daft thing! Get yourself going or you're going to be late.

She ran down the stairs and hurried across the entrance hall, catching her heel on the corner of a worn, Oriental rug, and pivoted forward, striking her shoulder on a corner of the dining room. Rubbing it vigorously, she said, "Damn! Got to get that thing fixed," and picking up her briefcase, she opened the door, and closed it soundly behind her, and so the day began.

Chapter 2

Millacent Lang replaced the receiver and made her way to the front of the shop tucking in stray strands of white hair that had escaped from the bun at the nape of her neck. She ran her hands down the sides of her work coat to smooth any wrinkles. For all her eighty years she was straight of back and had good eyesight. Only her hands showed her age, as arthritis had gnarled the joints of her fingers. She still had good use of them, anyway. Walking through the curtains, she saw a tall man standing with his back to her. She was about to say, "Can I help you"? When she noticed that he had not heard her enter the shop.

She watched with an uneasy feeling as he examined a beautiful old desk with inlaid wood of cherry and black ebony, delicately carved. He ran his hands over the surface and down the sides. He opened the drawer in the center and removed it, putting his hand in the cavity as if searching for something.

This was enough for Millacent and she gave a little cough. "Is there something I can do for you?" she asked. She saw his back stiffen as if caught in a wrong act, but then he relaxed, straightened his back, turned, and bestowed a cold smile on her.

"Wonderful, these old craftsmen. Not a nail to be found," he said, in a cultured voice just as cold as his smile. Steel gray eyes looked at her, one of them appearing twice as large as the other because of a monocle. She tried to rid herself of the uneasiness she felt under that cold gaze.

Smiling, she responded, "Yes." She hoped she wasn't conveying her uneasiness to him. Walking towards the desk where he was standing, she wondered where in the world Mr. Halley was. It was nearly nine o'clock, and he was never late.

"Do I have the honor of addressing the proprietor of this interesting establishment?" His voice carried a hint of sarcasm, which put her on her guard at once, and her trained ear caught a German accent. She instantly thought of her brother, Jason, and wondered why.

She drew herself up to her full height of five foot, two and, folding her hands in front of her, said as masterfully as possible, "You do, sir, and who might you be?"

Removing his hat and taking a step towards her, he outstretched his hand. "Heindrick von Heusen, madam." As he bent over her hand a cold chill ran down Millacent's spine and the hair on the back of her neck pricked.

Mr. Halley burst through the door, cap in hand. "By heck, Miss Lang, there's sommat wrong with her under her bonnet!" His words were drawn out as he looked with surprise at what he saw.

Millacent withdrew her hand and said, "That's all right, Mr. Halley. You'll find a list on my desk of today's work." She breathed a sigh of relief to know she was no longer alone with this man who filled her with anxiety. What was there in his looks that remind me with such pain of the past, of Jason's past, she wondered? Why did she feel this way? He was just another customer... wasn't he? I'd better see what's on his mind, she told herself. "Were you interested in a desk?" she asked. He was pulling a fine, leather glove off of his left hand. Handmade, Millacent thought, or I miss my guess.

"Well, yes I am," he said, as he slapped the loose glove to and fro in his gloved hand. "But not just any desk, dear lady." He swung around and hit the top of the desk with the loose glove with such force that it made her jump. "This desk."

Really, Millacent, get a grip on yourself, you silly twit. 'He's trying to ruffle you', she reproved herself. "Well I'm sorry then, because it's not for sale. To you or anyone."

The monocle dropped from his eye. "But surely you bought it to sell." For the first time there was not so much arrogance; he was not quite so sure of himself.

Good, Millacent old girl, you've stuck a nerve. "Well, when I bid on it at Millit's, I admit I was thinking of a sale. But when Mr. Halley brought it to the shop and I really saw the fine workmanship and the colour of the wood, I realized I couldn't part with it. It is only in the shop because it was delivered here, but it will be going to my cottage this afternoon."

"But surely, Miss Lang, you are open to a price." There it was again, that half sneer, half smile. He was so arrogant. As if I could be bought for a price. Her English blood boiled within her.

"I'm sure you will find this strange, Mr. von Heusen, but some of us haven't got a price. So, you see, you haven't got enough money to make me part with this exquisite piece. Good day to you, sir." She swung around and disappeared through the curtains leaving him standing there with a look of black thunder on his face.

"There now, Miss Lang, You don't look half put out", said Mr. Halley, hurrying forward to take her arm and assist her to her cluttered desk in the back.

"I'm quite all right, Mr. Halley. Quit clucking about me like an old hen and go and put the kettle on." He wheeled around and walked to the sink in the very back of the shop to fill the kettle. He turned and looked back at her. Strange, never seen old girl so taken aback. Bleedin' heck! Who was that geezer any road?

Chapter 3

Heindrick von Heusen stood for a few minutes, watching her retreat through the curtains, then turned and left the shop. He must get himself together. Get a drink and collect his thoughts, he decided. He walked briskly down the sunlit street and thought what the devil was she playing at? He hadn't followed that desk halfway across the continent to be outwitted by a sly little old lady. She was smart, he'd give her that much. Could she know? Don't be stupid, how could she know? You only found out a fortnight ago and you can't be sure of your own information until you get your hands on that desk. He returned to the hotel and tried to make contact with Schreiler. Yes, that was what he must do now. The sooner, the better.

Chapter 4

Standing outside her home, arms laden with groceries and doing a balancing act with her bag and keys and the mail, Suzette finally got the door open just as the phone rang. "Oh damn! Now, what?" Hurrying to get it she tripped over the same rug she had caught her heel on that morning. Everything went sprawling: eggs, wine, cheese and that beautiful torte. "Bloody Hell! This had better be good!" Yanking the phone from the cradle she half yelled, "Yes, 4789?"

"Hey my lovely, what's up?"

"Oh Robert! Only your dinner. There are parts of it all over. Tripped trying to get to the phone. Now don't tell me you're not going to make it?"

"No danger, darlin'. Only going to be about a half an hour late. And by the sounds of things you could use the time, love."

"Oh yes. Robert, would you please pick up another bottle of wine? This one seems to be making for my rug in many rivers. Got to dash, see you soon!"

She made for the kitchen and grabbed a towel, hurrying back to rescue the rug and pick up the debris. At least she'd have time to make a salad, set the table and freshen up a little. She wouldn't put the lamb chops on until Rob came and then they could have a drink and discuss the day.

While putting the finishing touches on a small, intimate table, she thought of Robert Nevil, of his strength, his gentleness, the ways he thought things through. There wasn't much hesitation. Things always seemed to be clear-cut to Rob. He had a keen sense of humor and was such fun to be with despite his job. He was a keeper of antiquities for the Victoria & Albert Museum in London. She felt so blessed to have him. It was Robert who had seen her through those tragic times in her life when she thought her world had come to an end at the death of her beloved parents, leaving her only Aunt Millacent. He had his gentle good looks. He was well over six feet, with fair hair that had a habit of falling onto his forehead, a smashing smile with white, even teeth, and grey eyes that could turn to steel when he was put off. He had the body of a well-put together scarecrow: all arms and legs, but somehow always looked impeccable. And she loved him dearly.

Chapter 5

Von Heusen set his fork down and picked up his wine glass, looking at it through the light. Not a bad little wine, he had to admit. The fresh trout with the very light sauce sprinkled with almonds, fresh asparagus and mushrooms were second to none. He had finished his coffee and was fitting his Turkish cigarette into a long holder when he caught his waiter's eye and asked for a brandy and a telephone. His table was set back in a corner, well out of earshot. Time to reach Schreiler. He had given the operator the number and there was nothing to do but wait.

He placed another cigarette in the holder. He held up the brandy and swirled it around the snifter. H'm, nice. The English, for all their boorish ways had some pleasant pastimes. This one was one of them. Too bad we had to lose the war. There was much they could have learned from der Fatherland.

The soft peal of the telephone brought him back. He reached for the receiver and heard a guttural voice. "Ja, ja. Nein, nein. Kurt, speak English. Yes, look I've got a job for you. Catch the first plane from Berlin and meet me as arranged. No, no. I'll fill you in when you arrive. Ja, ja. Schnell. Auf wiedersehn." A cold smile crossed his face as he replaced the receiver in the cradle.

He signaled the waiter, who asked him "Everything satisfactory sir?"

"Yes, just get my bill."

"Thank you sir."

Laying his coat over his shoulders he placed the homburg on his head, picked up his gloves and walked toward the door.

"Coo Blimie! He's a mean 'UN", said the waiter with a chill, taking the receipt to the cashier, a buxom blond behind the cashier's window. "See that bloke what just left, Rose? What you make of him?"

"Trouble" Rose said, "for someone. And be thankful it ain't us, ducky."

Chapter 6

Millacent Lang stepped down from the van Ed Halley used to deliver large pieces of furniture that customers could not take or handle themselves. She usually walked home from the shop in the village. She always enjoyed it and it wasn't that far, really, maybe six or so blocks with only a slight incline. The village was well kept and had won the award for "best kept" and "beautiful gardens" several years running. But today Mr. Halley had insisted she ride, as he was bringing the desk any road. And, say what you like, that bloke at the shop had upset her. And there was no arguing with him. Oh well, she was a little tired any road. Maybe she'd stay here for the rest of the day and help Dori Halley arrange the furniture to accommodate her beautiful new desk. And she did want to write to Suzette and catch the afternoon post as promised.

She stopped as she went up the walk to pick a dead head from one of the rose bushes, which lined both sides of her walk. As she plucked the dead head, she heard Dori, rather than saw her, coming towards her with the basket. Dori Halley wore a crisp house dress and a fresh white pinny, and her head was covered with a bandanna from which escaped bright, shiny, copper curls, and a beautiful, calm face with very large, round, blue, blue eyes.

"I've a kettle on for a cuppa, and I've just taken a fresh seed cake from the oven" she said, smiling as she handed the basket to Millacent to catch the heads. She enjoyed making potpourri for the shop with Miss Millacent. It looked like a bumper crop this year.

Millacent adored them, both of them. They fussed and pampered and looked after her and indulged her every whim. They were the closest people to her outside of Suzette. "Thank you, love. We'll get a lot done today. Wait 'till you see my beautiful find. But first, I'll enjoy that cuppa and a piece of cake. Feeling a bit peaky. Might even have a lay down for a bit this afternoon when we're through." In crossing the threshold into the shining hall, which was her habit, she stopped and opened the glass front of the elegant old grandfather clock and adjusted the hands on the lovely face. "We must have that hand fixed one day."

Ed and Dori were moving the old Welsh dresser to the staircase wall as Millacent stood with her head cocked to one side. "You know,

I quite like it there, Dori. Yes, I do. It's very nice. All right then, you can bring it in now. Do you need an extra hand?"

"Well no, we brought the trolley."

Ed brought it in through the wide front doors and wheeled it up to the wall. "Flamin' heck, Miss. Millacent. If it ain't just going to fit between these two leaded pane windows just fine!" Setting it in place, he slid the trolley carefully from under it, and stood back with the two women, looking at it. The late afternoon sun was streaming through the big bays directly across from the desk and playing it with delicate patterns as the light caught the diamond cut panes of glass. It was impressive.

"Oh I say, Miss Millacent. It is a real beauty! And don't it look a real treat there with the light an all? Can't wait to give it a good rubbin' with the linseed oil!" Dori, her face quite flushed with excitement and the exertion of moving the dresser, her bandanna all askew, left the room. Ed and Millacent smiled at each other.

"She's that excited, she is" Ed said. "I'll just take this back and mind shop the rest of the day. There's some windows what need fixin'.

Tell Dori I'll see her for tea at home." And with that he put on his cap and went out and softly closed the door.

Having given Dori the message, Millacent left her polishing the desk, and went upstairs to clean up and have a rest. Entering her big bedroom, she found Sultan, her black Persian cat. His enormous green eyes darted back and forth as the leaves from the tree outside her bay window made quick moving patterns on the Persian rug. She stooped down and picked him up. He instantly started purring. "Silly old stick," she said, cradling him in her arms and laying down on the bed.

It was sometime later she awoke and the sun had almost set and Sultan was sprawled on his back in the window seat soaking up the last rays of the warm sun. She rose slowly. My goodness! Must have taken more out of me than I thought, and she walked over to the dry sink where she kept a huge white bowl, delicately painted in a pattern of roses and leaves. A matching pitcher stood in the middle of it over which was a little lace doily, the edges weighted down with pink beads.

She poured some of the water into the deep bowl and, washing her face and hands, discarded the water in the receptacle behind the door

By the Pricking of My Thumb

of the old sink, which also held a bar and a towel. The bowl and pitcher were a favorite old piece that had belonged to her mother and she cherished them. She could see her delicate little mother washing after a rest on a hot day much the same way as she had done. And tucking the last of her loose hair into her bun at the back of her neck, she thought, *my house is still.* Patting her hair, she said "Ah, that's better," and made her way down the curved stairs to the landing, calling out Dori's name as she went.

Getting no reply, she walked into the front room. The fire was laid in the hearth and the tea trolley was set with a cold supper lifting the corner of the teatowel she found: a fresh green salad, slices of thick white crusted bread and butter, a nice slice of pork pie with piccalilli, a piece of stilton cheese and a small dish of trifle. And it did look inviting! As she pulled at the large white towel that had covered it she found a note.

"Miss Millacent, thought you needed the rest, love, so didn't wake you. Tea things set out in the kitchen. Just set a spell to the fire and it should be fine. Call if you need me. If not, see you in the morning. Cheerie bye, Dori."

Smiling, she lit the fire and turned to go into the kitchen. She saw the desk polished for the first time. It fairly glowed, as if it was lit from within by it's own fire. It was a delight to behold. She could hardly wait for Susette and Robert to see it. If she wrote right now, she could just make the post. Then she and Sultan could enjoy that lovely tea.

Settling herself in front of the fire, she was happy to have got that letter off. It was a bit of a dash to catch the post. But now, Sultan, we can enjoy our very own tea. Sultan sat cleaning himself and purring loudly on the hearthrug. She settled herself in her chair and proceeded to eat. How delicious. Must remember to tell Dori just how thoughtful it was.

She leaned back with her teacup in her hand and gazed at her newest possession. It really was lovely now that Dori had oiled and polished it. Every delicate piece of inlaid wood glowed with its own fire. As she sat basking in its loveliness her eye caught something on one of the carved ebony roses.

She set her cup down on the trolley and walked towards it. Probably just threads from Dori's polishing cloth. She stooped to remove them. "My they are caught fast," she said. And twisting the threads around her finger, she gave a quick jerk. There was a faint click. "Oh dear, Ed is going to have to mend this now." Her hand went to the loose piece of ebony wood and to her utter amazement it came away in her hand. It had been a part that concealed a compartment. It was approximately six by nine. How very clever it was! She put her fingers in and they touched something soft. She caught the corner of a soft cloth and drew it forward. It was just the same size, about two inches thick.

"I say, who's the clever girl, Sultan? It's heavy. I wonder what it is." She took it over to the fire, and crouching on the old milk stool, she laid it carefully in her lap and started to unfold it. Sultan got up and came to her singing loudly and rubbing his massive head on her leg for attention. The last fold was lifted. Sucking in her breath she said "Sultan look at this!"

There in her lap lay the most exquisite icon she had ever seen in all her years of dealing, and she had seen a few. But none came up to this caliber. Such perfection. Gems danced in the firelight. "Oh Sultan! I have never seen anything so perfect and lovely in all my life." It was covered with a sheet of gold and inlaid silver and encrusted with precious gems, some large, some small rubies, diamonds, emeralds, and sapphires. Some she didn't know what they were, but she knew that they were real. It was a Madonna and Christ child. Very, very old, she was sure of that. What on earth was it doing there in this desk, itself quite old?

Setting the exquisite piece down and walking back to the desk, she really examined the desk with a gifted appraiser's eye, and ran her hands over and down it, and with her tape from her pocket measured and re-measured. There was no doubt in her mind. The desk was built to house this exquisite piece of artwork. She found herself praying Susette would come with Robert this weekend and Robert would be able to date both pieces. Maybe I should call. No, it would be a lovely surprise for them. And picking up the icon and holding it carefully, she was enthralled with it.

Millacent hated to put it away, but that was the only thing to do. Lovingly, she rewrapped it and carried it back to its little vault and tenderly laid it in, pushing it back. Picking up the little piece of ebony wood, itself a marvel of workmanship, she studied the grain to see how to fit it back. There, there's that faint click. It was in place and undetectable. If Dori's thread had not caught, it never would have been discovered. And, try as she would, she couldn't find a way to open it again. "Surely," running her hands across her eyes, "I didn't dream this."

She started again, running her hands down the front slowly. She stood up abruptly. A picture formed in her minds eye of just such a scene that very morning at her shop with von Heusen. Was that what he called himself? He'd been searching for something in the same way. Was that why he had become so upset when she said it was not for sale? A shiver ran down her back and she let herself slip onto the desk chair. If he knew about it, well, it certainly must be true. And Millacent knew she would be dealing with him again. And that thought filled her with such foreboding.

And trying to remember where the thread had been caught in the ebony rose, Millacent moved her fingers ever so slowly over the rose. There it was, the tiny click. But one would really have to know just where to begin to look for it. It was very clever, very clever indeed. Rising slowly, walking to the tea trolley and pouring another cup of

V.E. Sullivan

tea, she sipped it slowly and said "Sultan old son, I'll be that glad when the children arrive. They'll know exactly what to do."

Chapter 7

Suzette woke slowly and rolled over on her back, opened her eyes, and saw Rob standing there.

"Here's your tea, sleepy head," and setting the cup on the bedside table, he sank down on the bed beside her. "Miss Lang, did any one ever tell you how lovely you are even in the morning?" She reached out her arms and he gathered her to him, holding her close and running his hands slowly down her back. "You are so soft. I never get tired of touching you."

"H'm. You smell so good, Rob. Your hair is still damp too."

"I know, my sweet, but I've got to make tracks. I'm meeting with the board. Look, I'll call you later. Maybe if you're free we can meet for lunch. There's a letter in the hall from Aunt Millacent." And with that he tipped her head back and gave her a long, sensuous kiss. "'Till later then, love." And was off.

Suzette lay there basking in the glow, her body still tingling from Rob's touch and his kiss. He always had that effect on her, like she was floating six feet off the ground. She smiled, pushed herself up, and reached for her cup. It was strong and sweet, just the way she liked it in the morning.

Tying her robe around her, she padded into the hall, yawning. She reached for the letter, and taking it to the table, poured another cup of tea as she opened it

Dear Suzette, just a note to ask you and Robert to come for the weekend if possible. I'm so excited about my newest find and know you will be also. I can't believe my luck. There's a rather irate gentleman determined to buy it. And, I'm just as determined to keep it. Just a hunch that's nagging at me, but, if your father's old war diary is at hand, could you bring it along? Please take care driving. Phone me if it's not possible. It would be wonderful to see you again, love. Take care. Cheerie bye, Auntie M.

Strange that she should ask for her father's diary. Suzette used to spend hours as a young child going through it. But since the accident, she hadn't had the heart to pick it up. It was in the bookcase. What on earth could Auntie want with it? And what about the man? All very interesting. It would be great going to York and then to Auntie's village, St. Gilliams on the Ouse, a sleepy little place about thirty miles from York. It hadn't changed over the centuries: cobbled streets, church towers with bells ringing, charming streets with little parks, green grocers, bakers that filled the streets with delicious smells, shops with soft wool for the looms, dress shops, chemists, and doctors' Surgeries, a library, and charming tea shops, everything one needs. The houses were all lovely cottages with bay windows and deep thatched roofs. She loved going there and so did Robert. Well, she would take the letter with her, and if they had a chance to meet for lunch, Rob could read it and make plans for the weekend. She knew she was free.

Chapter 8

Robert was waiting in front of "Ces't Bon." His coat collar was turned up, the wind was tousling his fair hair as it had come up, and it threatened rain. He looked at his watch; he was a little early. Glancing up the street, his heart gave a lurch as it always did when he saw her. Swinging along the sidewalk, her beautiful long legs made her walk graceful as she hurried on, her bag over her shoulder, her trench coat being flapped by the wind. My God! How I love her. How lucky he was to have her, with her soft feminine ways and easy laugh, so naive about her beauty. He saw her lift her hand and wave. And he waved back, all warm inside like a schoolboy waiting for his first date. By heck, if this is what it's all about he hoped that he would never lose the feeling. And then she was there, smiling up at him. He kissed her lightly on the cheek.

"Come on, ducks. Let's get out of this."

"Have you been waiting long, darling?" she asked as he took her coat.

"Not a bit. Come on, here's AmÂel and our table's ready." As they waited for their drinks, Suzette took the letter from her purse and passed it to Robert.

"Here my sweet. What do you think?" Rob took the letter and read it quietly as was his fashion.

Looking up, he smiled. "Sounds just the ticket, flower. I'll get the Jaguar served and the tyres checked on Thursday. How about going down early Friday morning and making a day of it. We both love York."

"Oh yes, please! And we can spend the day in the Shambols, have lunch and get to St. Gilliams in time for tea at the Hotel. Oh Robert, that's what I love about you. You're not all wishy washy, will we or won't we. It's all cut and dried." She crinkled her nose at him. "What do you make of Auntie wanting daddy's diary? Don't you think it's odd?"

Rob had his fork halfway to his mouth and decided to chew his salad before answering. "H'm. Well, we'll take it out tonight and have a go at it."

"Do you think it has something to do with her new find or that man she wrote about?"

"That, my sweet, remains a nice little mystery for us to solve. Would you like to eat out tonight and then pick up a bottle of the bubbly and we can have a fire and try to sort things out?"

"Oh yes, please. I have a hectic afternoon with old Mr. Berkshire uncrating some first editions Mr. Stilts bought. So, I won't have time to go to the shops before they close."

"Great. That's settled then. I'll walk you back and then I have some running to do myself. I'll get the bubbly. And, let's see, this is Tuesday, so, I'll stop by the garage and make an appointment for the Jaguar Thursday."

"Oh love, let's get going. I think it's starting to rain." And sure enough it was soon pouring.

Rob hailed a cab, put Suzette in the back, and gave her a quick kiss. "See you at tea time, love, take care." With that he was off, his long legs carrying him to the car park.

By the Pricking of My Thumb

Such a lovely lunch, and the evening sounds not too bad either. She was lost in thought and jumped when the Cabby opened the door. "Berkshire and Stilts, Miss."

Chapter 9

Rob laid the fire as Suzette changed clothes and he lit a spiller. It took and caught nicely. He turned the wine in the bucket and set the glasses on the tray. He straightened up and reached over to take Jason Lang's diary from the back bookcase. He'd known Jason and Amelia and they'd been beautiful people. No wonder Suzette had that beautiful serenity about her life. She'd gotten it from her parents.

Amelia Bonn had been a pretty twenty-two year old, working in the French underground since the invasion of France and doing everything from sabotage of the Paris rail lines to helping to get downed airmen back to Britain.

Jason Lang had been a top intelligence agent with MI5 counter espionage and had been dropped behind the lines in the French countryside to meet up with a remnant of the French underground who were being hunted all over France by the Gestapo black boots. Finally they met and fell in love and were married, and returned to live in England after the war. Suzette was a product of their love, and what a love! Suzette was named for Amelia's mother.

Gazing into the fire he relived those agonizing weeks over again when Jason and Amelia had returned to France to the country village of Sarlat after Amelia's mother's sudden death but were both killed in the car accident, leaving Suzette alone, except for Auntie Millacent.

So lost in thought was he that he hadn't heard Suzette come in and he jumped at the sound of her voice. "Who's the clever boy, then? It looks wonderful! Shall we open the bubbly, then? Rob, darling, I'm sorry. What ever is the matter?"

Smiling brightly, he said, "Nothing love, just gathering wool." He didn't want to go over thoughts of Amelia and Jason with Suzette, as they were still pretty painful to her. "I'll just put on another log and open the wine and we will get all comfy and give this old book a go."

She sank to the pillows in front of the fire and pulled back her caftan and wiggled her toes in front of the warm blaze. How dear he is, and good, thought Suzette. Life is wonderful. She would recall these words later.

Chapter 10

Millacent turned the key in the old fashioned lock on the shop door and heard the phone ringing. Leaving the front door open she hurried to the phone. Picking it up a bit breathless she said "Hello?"

"Auntie Millacent, are you all right? Whatever is wrong?"

Recognizing her niece's voice she said "Oh yes, Suzette, love, I was just unlocking the door when I heard the phone. That's all dear."

"Oh thank goodness. I rang the cottage and Dori said you were on your way. Wanted you to know Rob and I will be arriving Friday at teatime. Rob wants to take us to the Hotel Grand for high tea. Isn't that smashing, all those dear little sandwiches and goody cakes. Can't wait to see you Auntie. By the by, has that strange man been bothering you again and does he have a name?"

Millacent smiled. She could just see Suzette's large eyes all aglow with curiosity. Yes, my love, he does. Von Heusen."

"Not the Von Heusen of the war trials!" Suzette said. A hint of concern had crept into her voice.

"Well we'll soon see dear. I've run across the old clippings from the paper and I want to verify some things from Jason's diary. Did you find it?"

"Yes, Auntie M. We did, and we'll bring it along as planned. It's all rather exciting in a rather horrid sort of way. You know what I mean."

"Yes, my dear, I know exactly what you mean. I'll be ever so glad to see you."

"Yes, we are looking forward to it too. You know Rob, how he loves to come. He can't wait to see you and Sultan, Ed and Dori. Bye for now," and the phone went dead.

Millacent breathed a long sigh. So good to hear that the children were coming. Only one more day to wait to show them my find. Shivering, she returned to close the door, thinking, I hope I haven't made a mistake by not telling them before. If she had known what was taking place a few miles away, she would have thought better of her hesitation.

Chapter 11

Von Heusen had taken particular care not to be seen with Kurt Schreiler. As for what he had in mind, he wanted to have it clear he never had been associated with this man.

This thick headed, low mentality Oaf. What ever made him think he could possibly be one of mein Furher's master race, das dummkopf? Just because he was blond and blue eyed. Any fool could see that the shape of his head was all-wrong. Arms were like an ape's. And those hands! Mein Gott! It turned his stomach to think of some of the things those hands had done. Nein, he was good for one thing only, fear and force. There were some things even he wouldn't dirty his hands with.

Not that he couldn't if he had to. But when you have a pet dog that will do anything you ask him to just for a word of praise from you, why bother? He smiled that cold smile that had struck fear into many an enlisted man. Ja, time is coming.

He put his cigarette into his holder, turned his head and watched Schreiler at the far end of the bar in the dirty little back street pub in Soho. He pulled himself up straight as if his magnificent coat might touch something. It was pure revulsion as he watched Kurt eat, his face almost in the dish. His mouth was so full that the grease ran from his bacon buttie and was running down the sides of his chin and the foam from his pint on his upper lip, now all being wiped in a disgusting manner by the back of his hand, which he immediately wiped on the side of his trousers. He had to get him away from here, had only an hour and much to explain before he caught a train back to York. And I must make everything clear to the dummkopf. They must not be seen together on the train. He had a first class ticket and Kurt had a second class.

He took a silver case from his breast pocket and slid out a thin pencil. Hastily he scribbled a note and, giving it to the barmaid, he left, happy to be out and getting a breath of fresh air. Taking shelter in the nearest doorway, he waited for Kurt to come along. Ja, here he comes now. Mein Got. If there were only another way, so I wouldn't have to use this oaf shuffling along, his big arms swinging like a Neanderthal man. "Hurry you fool, this way."

Kurt at the sound of that voice snapped to attention. "Ja, mien major."

Chapter 12

The afternoon had passed swiftly for Suzette. She had just finished unpacking the last of the crates of books and was washing her hands when Tillie the tea lady came by.

"Ready for your cuppa, Miss?"

"Oh yes please, Tillie," and taking the big crockery mug, she made her way to her office. She just had to tell Robert what Auntie Millacent had said. She could wait until teatime but Rob would be a bit late. He had to get the Jag from the garage and make his way through traffic. And he would like to shower and have a drink when he first got home. They had their plans mostly made for tomorrow's trip to York. And, anyway, she couldn't wait.

She dialed the number and asked for Robert Nevil and was asked if she would hold as Mr. Nevil was on his way to his office and would be there any second.

"Oh, Mr. Nevil, there's a call for you." She could hear Rob say "Thank you," and open and close his office door. There was a click as he picked up the phone, "Hello?"

"Rob?"

By the Pricking of My Thumb

"Oh, Susette, my love. Everything OK?"

"Oh, yes, but I couldn't wait to tell you. Talked to Auntie this morning to say that we would be there and I asked about that man. And, Rob, she said his name was von Heusen." There was silence on the other end. "Rob, Rob? Are you still there?"

"Good, Lord, Suzette. You can't actually mean the man from the trials Jason wrote about!"

"She thinks so, Rob. That's why she wants daddy's diary. Oh yes, she said she has some clippings she had saved, and needs the diary to verify a few things. I must say she sounded relieved we were coming."

"Can't blame her, love. What would he be wanting with Auntie, and, what would he want that Auntie had? The plot thickens, flower. We are in for quite a weekend, I'll say." If only he knew.

Chapter 13

"By heck, Miss Millacent. You be in fine spirits all day. Sommat happened I don't know about?"

Gathering up her papers and clapping the old fashioned ink well shut she smiled and said "This time tomorrow night I'll be having high tea at the Grand with Robert and Suzette."

A big smile broke across Ed's face. "Bless me, Miss Millacent. Does Dori know? What a treat to have these youngun's here again. How long are they staying?"

"The whole weekend, Ed, and mind you and Dori are not to be late to Sunday tea." It had been a practice of long-standing to have Dori and Ed to Sunday tea and she did enjoy them so; the way they fussed. And any way, Dori did most of it. And after tea when cleaning was done and dishes had been put away, she and Dori worked on the potpourri baskets while Ed dozed over the paper with Sultan curled up in his lap in front of the fire.

"No danger. You know how much Dori dotes on that young lass and her young lad. She will be baking half the night and getting out her best jellies and pickles."

"In that case, Ed, why don't you go along? I've a few things I want to do and I will enjoy the walk home. The air is lovely tonight and it will help me gather my thoughts about me."

"You sure Miss Millacent?"

"Oh yes, I'll just see you out and draw the blinds over the door. You sure the back door is locked?" Ed nodded as he pulled on his cap. "Good, see you in the morning then. Give Dori my love." She stood in the doorway and watched Ed get into the van and drive off.

Strange, she thought, how empty the street was. But then it was getting on to teatime. The setting sun was casting long shadows on the narrow cobble streets. And the windows in the high street were all winking and blinking at each other as the last rays of the sun danced on their panes. She had loved the village of St. Gilliam, its people, those wonderful, hard working, honest as bread, Yorkshiremen.

She sucked in her breath as out of the shadows stepped a figure of a man she had never seen before, huge and fair. He had long arms and huge hands. Wonder where he's come from. She started to close the door when he raised one of his arms and placed one of those huge hands flat on the door. It was like pushing against a block of concrete.

"See here, young man. What do you think you're on about? We're closed."

"I've come about the desk."

"What desk?" Oh really, this had gone far enough. "I told you, you'll have to come back in the morning. I told you, we're closed."

"Nein. Not in the morning. This evening. Major said to tell you. Seven o'clock. Your place."

Feeling quite upset and a little uneasy, Millacent said, "Major? What Major? I don't know what you're talking about!"

"Major von Heusen. He said seven o'clock your place, and he'll be there." And he was gone as fast as he had come, slipping into the shadows.

She was really shaking now, as much from anger as from fear. She quickly closed and locked the door and pulled down the blind. So it was he. The same heartless beast from Jason's diary. And the thought of meeting him face to face again was very unsettling to her. She switched out the lights and went through the curtains into the back of the shop. The thought passed her lips, *by the pricking of my thumb, something evil this way comes.* And evil, it was. It surrounded

By the Pricking of My Thumb

her like a thick wet blanket. She struggled against it. Why, oh why, was I such a silly old twit. I should have told the children long ago. Now I'll have to face him alone. Dori will be at choir practice and Ed with the bell ringers, practicing his changes. Serves you right you old fool. Any way, he doesn't know about the little secret catch. I will have to put on my best performance and make believe I know nowt. And it's just a beautiful old desk that I don't want to part with because of the excellent workmanship. And besides it belongs to me. I came by it quite honestly. Unlike that Hun who has so much blood on his hands. While there is breath in my body, he shall not have it.

No time for work. She had planned to do the bills. That Inland Revenue man would just have to wait another day. She pulled on her coat and jammed her old hat on her head, picked up her worn handbag and made her way out of the shop. Poking her keys into her pocket, she hurried up the street towards her cottage. She made quite a sight. Her appearance was always so proper as was fitting a lady of her years but tonight, her hat set all right angles, her coat was misbuttoned and she had that expression on her face that said she was oblivious to anything around her.

Chapter 14

Constable Simms was doing his rounds and had stopped under the lamppost because the light was flickering. He thought, looking up, and staring at her as he tipped his helmet back, by heck! What's got into the old girl? She looks like the devil was after her. He raised his hand to wave as he had done so many times in the past and for the first time since he was a boy he got no response. Sommat's up. That's not like the old girl and that's not her way. She must be really upset. He was about to get on his bike and catch her up when his eye caught the clock in the village square. And it had gone six. His sergeant would have his guts for garters if he didn't check in, and the thought of that red-faced bull of a man shouting down at him pushed all other thoughts from his mind. He would have time to reflect on this later with much regret.

Head down and pumping faster than usual to reach the call box, the wrath of his sergeant was all he could think of. He took the corner and coming toward him on the wrong side of the road was a big black Daimler. "Bloody hell!" He was up onto the sidewalk and over the handlebars. Dazed he got to his feet only to get the last three numbers,

By the Pricking of My Thumb

885, of the plate. He took his pad from his breast pocket, wrote it down and picked up his bike, only to discover his front tyre had a puncture. Nothing for it but to leg it to the call box. Hoping as he hurried along that the sergeant had had his tea. By heck his knee didn't half hurt and he could've murdered a cuppa himself.

Chapter 15

"You stupid fool," shouted von Heusen, "can't you stay on the left? I told you and told you. Gott in Himmel, you oaf. You'd better pray that person is not badly hurt and they didn't get our license plate. Slow down and stay on the left."

Kurt never took his eyes of the road but the colour rose in his face. Got, he thought; he is still in the army, shouting and demanding. He'll push me too far one day. He thinks I'm nothing. Stupid, a dummkopf he calls me. But, I'm dumb like a fox and one day it will be my turn to call the tune. His hands gripped the wheel so hard his knuckles turned white. He must conceal his hatred of this man. He hated everything about him. His looks, his elegant clothes, his manner of speech, and the way he had with the freuleins, but, most of all his wealth, his wealth that Kurt and others had accumulated for him. And he, Kurt, was the only one left. The others had all met with fatal accidents. And playing the dumb clod, the willing trained dog, he had stayed alive, like a dog, faithful to the master. But the day is coming, and this master will find his faithful dog has teeth. And, maybe tonight will be the night.

Von Heusen sat shaken by the close call. It will be over soon and it will all belong to me again. I must calm down, this crafty old woman will not be able to resist my offer. And if she does I have this big oaf with me, that's all he's good for. He doesn't know what's at stake, but when it's over I can pay him off and send him back to Berlin where I've already arranged for a nasty accident. Poor Kurt. The palms of his hands began to sweat and his mouth was dry. Must pull himself together. After tonight he would not have need for another night like this night. Never again. His assets and some of his money from his Swiss bank account were already in the bank in Rio. Oh, the sun, the wine and all those beautiful young brown ladies. All were ready and waiting; just get tonight over with.

Chapter 16

Millacent Lang stood at the sink in the kitchen filling the kettle and trying to decide what she wanted to eat, if anything. Dori, as usual had left a lovely tea. But her stomach was churning. Dori would understand and she covered everything and put it into the refrigerator. She went to the pantry and took down a tin of digestive biscuits and stood looking at them. No, that's not what she wanted, maybe some oatcakes, warmed, with a little bramble jelly. Sultan sat on his little chintz covered stool in the corner of the kitchen, his enormous green eyes following her every move.

She took the tea pot down and poured a little of the boiling water into it, swirled it around, poured it into the sink and reached for the tea caddy. She put three in and one extra for the pot and filled it with the boiling water, covered it with the cozy and left it to mash as she heated the oatcakes.

Out of the corner of her eyes she saw Sultan sitting, staring at her. He always seemed to pick up her moods. He never made a move or a sound, just sat there. She took a plate down and put her oatcakes on it with a little dish of jelly, cream and sugar, cup and saucer. She put them all on the tea trolley. "Come on, Sultan, let's go in by the fire." He jumped down without a sound and followed her into the front room. "Oh Sultan, whatever am I going to do about this evening. He'll be here in an hour. I know all about him now and his cruelty to everyone who gets in his way."

Sitting her cup down, she walked over to her desk and picked up the yellowed newspaper clippings telling all about Major von Heusen's reign of terror from Poland to occupied France and of Jason's part of the war trials, testifying against him, and the threat he had made then against Jason. It was all so long ago and yet it was all so close now, like the walls closing in on her.

With shaking hands, she pulled at the paper and put it back in the desk drawer. "Come on, old love, let's get these things cleaned up and put away. By heck, he'll not get as much as a drink of water from me." And hanging up the tea towel she drew the blinds and locked the back door. With Sultan at her heels she started out the door just as the grandfather clock struck seven and a loud knock sounded on the front door.

Chapter 17

Across town at the Halley home, Ed was just coming downstairs after a wash up and changing for his practice. Pulling the changes was one of the biggest delights of his life, next to Dori. It filled him with such pride and humility. He always looked forward to it, and a pint afterward with his mates at The Old Lion and the Lamb, his favorite pub. As he rounded the bottom of the stairs and headed down the little hall, strains of Dori singing "All things bright and beautiful" came to him. It was a real treat to hear Dori sing. She had a lovely pure, soprano voice, full of quality and control.

He opened the kitchen door and stood to listen to her as she put the finishing touches on the beautiful torte for tomorrow when Suzette and Rob would come. They'd never had any children of their own and Suzette came as close to being their child as possible. It would be a real treat to have them at Miss Millacent's all weekend. Maybe Rob and he could get in a bit of early morning fishing before they headed back to London.

He slipped up behind Dori and slid his arms around her waist. She gave a start, and turned in his arms and said, "Well what are you looking at you big daft thing?" There was a touch of flour on her chin and her copper curls poked out as usual under her bandanna.

"It's just that you always smell so good. And not just of vanilla!" She gave him a slap on the arm, not in anger but in love.

"Oh, posh, Ed. Now hurry, we must get a move on." But a look of pride and love was in her eyes as she gave him a quick embrace. "I have my fruit soaking in brandy. When we get home I'll put the trifle together." She untangled herself and started across the floor when she stopped in her tracks and a shudder ran from the top of her head right down to her toes.

"What's up, love? You takin' poorly?"

She turned, her face quite pale. "Oh, Ed! I just had the worst feeling come over me. Like someone just walked over my grave and a feeling of doom. My stomach feels like I swallowed a lead weight and you know what my old Gram used to say."

"Yes, Dori, my love. I know. And I also know what Reverend Dawson would say."

"But, Ed"

"No, dear, you listen to me. We both loved your Gram, but she was full of the old tales and superstition."

"But, Ed, there are those who have the second sight. Those God fearing people. Gram was one of them. And I feel that sommat dreadful will happen this night."

"Come, come, Dori. You'll feel better when you get to choir and start practicing. It was only sommat you ate. I wouldn't wonder." And putting his arm around her waist, led her from the kitchen. "Let's be off, love. Things will be all right, you'll see."

Chapter 18

Heindrich von Heusen stood facing Millacent across the threshold, as immaculate as always, Camel hair coat, Homburg hat, and those handmade gloves. The monocle was reflecting the light from the hall and for one horrid second Millacent thought he was winking at her. Standing just to one side of him, not quite behind him, she saw the man who had confronted her at the shop.

"May we come in, Miss Lang?"

Millacent hugged Sultan close to her chest as if to give her Dutch courage. "I told you before, sir, we've nothing to talk about. The desk is not for sale." She released one arm she had on Sultan and reached for the door. And for the second time that night, that huge hand came up to prevent her.

"Sorry Madam, but we do have something to discuss. You had better let us come in. Kurt, here is not too bright, and is sometimes hard to control." And with that he pushed his way in, stopping in the hall to admire the huge grandfather clock in the entrance way. "Lovely, really lovely," he said. "But that's not what I'm here for. I believe it's through here, Ja." She followed them into the front room.

"Really, Miss Lang. This is quite charming. Excellent taste, don't you think so Kurt?" And then that sneer. Millacent looked at Kurt who just stood there, his arms dangling at his side like a huge rag doll you might see as a prize at a jumble sale.

"Oh yes, there it is. Mein Gott, just look at it. The way the light plays on it, ja, ja. It is beautiful is it not?"

"Yes it is," Millacent said, "but it is still not for sale!"

"Now look, I'm prepared to make a very handsome offer. One that would keep you handsomely for the rest of your life."

"My tastes are quite simple and my shop provides for all I need. I have no need of your money. I've told you before, there are people you just cannot buy and I'm one of them. Now, you'll have to excuse me as the Halley's will be here after choir practice."

She put Sultan down on the hearth and turned to show them out. Kurt stepped in front of her. "Please, madam," von Heusen's voice dropped a note and Millacent found herself trembling and the palms of her hands were damp. "I must appeal to you and your better judgment. You are an intelligent woman." He was pulling off those gloves and putting them in his hat. He removed his coat and scarf and laid them across a chair. Kurt pushed her back into a chair.

Really, this is too much. I must think, I've only got to keep them talking for forty-five minutes and the Halley's will be here.

"You see, Miss Lang, I've been tracking this desk, for I believe it to be mine. You know, after the war things got mislaid and sent to the wrong places. Ja, they were bad times then. I hope I'm not boring you." He didn't wait for her to answer, but went right on. "I'm sure you won't mind if I examine the desk for verification of ownership. If I find it, I'm sure you would want the rightful owner to have it, Ja." And that cold smile crossed his face and he turned to walk toward the desk.

Must do something. Millacent, you silly twit think. And before she knew it, it was all coming out. She hardly recognized her voice. "Oh yes, von Heusen. I know about you all right, and rightful owners. But you, sir, I know all about your hounding poor innocent people to their deaths, your plundering, your stealing. Your hands are covered with the blood of innocent people. The Jackal. Isn't that what they called you?"

He swung around, a look of pure hatred on his face. She knew she was going too far, but she just couldn't stop.

"Who are you? Just where did you hear that name?"

Her hands were trembling so; she quickly grabbed the arms of the chair. "Oh I know many things about you and your exploits from Poland through France."

"Mien Gott in himmel. It can't be, but Ja, Lang. That's it isn't it? Jason Lang. That schwein-hund. Ja, I see it all now. The same look in the eyes. The tenacity. But he and that French whore he called his wife got what was coming to them on that country road in France. Fitting, don't you think that they should die in the country they fought so hard to free?"

Millacent sprang from the chair so fast she caught him off guard, and dug her hands into his arms. "My God, you can't mean, you couldn't mean, it was an accident! The gendarme said so."

He threw back his head and laughed a hysterical kind of mad laugh. "It was an accident planned by me. I swore to even the score. Not quite cricket, what? As you English would say."

"Oh my God! You really are a jackal. A mad animal preying on people in a coward's fashion." He grabbed her by the shoulders. She could feel the steel grip of his fingers biting into her flesh. He started shaking her. His monocle dropped from his eye. His eyes were wild and his hair tussled.

"Shut up!" He looked like a terrier shaking a rag. So violently was he shaking her, her feet were off the ground. She dug her fingers deeper into his arms. He was shouting something but she couldn't hear. Everything was distorted in her head and she couldn't see anything but a dark haze.

Quick and quite suddenly, Kurt heard a snap. Like someone had stepped on a twig. She went limp. Heindrich was purple with rage. A bit of saliva had gathered in the corner of his mouth, all frothy. Quite mad, he is, thought Kurt. Things were moving too fast. Von Heusen threw her from him. She pitched forward and hit her head on the corner of the hearth. No one was watching Sultan and like a streak of black lightening he sprung at Heindrich growling deep in his magnificent throat and had ripped von Heusen's face with his claws. Heindrich let out a stream of oaths and threw Sultan across the room, and taking a handkerchief from his pocket, started to dab gingerly at his face.

"Schwein of a cat. Probably get an infection now." He didn't seem to realize there was a crumpled lifeless form at his feet.

He was still straightening himself out when he heard a totally strange voice behind him saying, "My, my. How the mighty have fallen."

He froze for a second, almost afraid to turn around. And when he did, his jaw fell open in disbelief. Kurt was standing there. He looked a good foot taller, very straight. And that voice, so refined. Mein Got! Was he going mad? What was going on?

"Oh, yes, Major. It's me. Your faithful lap dog as you thought. You see, while you were so busy being the Jackal, I was busy being the fox." He tipped his head forward and held up his cupped palm, and in a second, there lay in his hands a pair of opaque contact lenses and a set of very yellow and brown teeth. Heindrich stared for a second. Then he looked up into two very blue, intelligent eyes. His whole appearance was changed from a shuffling, long armed oaf into a tall, rather handsome young man whose long arms and big hands fit his frame. He couldn't believe it.

Kurt took a cigarette from his pack in his pocket. "Oh Major, modern technology is wonderful. You have no idea how long I have waited for this night. Now things will have to change, I'm afraid," and he let go a long stream of cigarette smoke. "I know you'll understand." He lowered himself onto the arm of the chair. "For example, what are you going to do about her? Silly old cow." And for the first time Heindrich looked down at the body at his feet. "And didn't she say the Halley's were coming after choir practice, which should be in about five minutes. Or she could have just have been saying that to get rid of you."

It was all moving too fast, and not at all the way he planned. Got to think, think. "Don't be a fool, Kurt. I'm a very rich man and know some very influential people. I could do a lot for you."

"Oh I know you can. And I also know you will. For you see, Major, I have taken precautions to protect myself. And I know so much about you all those years, Major. But this is not the time or the place and we will have plenty of time to talk later."

For the first time in his life, Heindrich von Heusen felt fear. This man could ruin him, his plans, his whole life. Everything was going marvelously. Where had he failed? His palms were sweating, his throat was dry. He needed a drink and time to think. There was no time. He turned and smiled that smile so familiar to Kurt, but it meant nothing to him now. He held all the aces.

"Quick, Kurt, move the car to the dark side of the lane and I'll turn out the lights and open the back door for you."

"Ach, you are thinking of the old Kurt, Major, who would have done just that, while you waited in the kitchen to garrote me. Nein, nein, you move the car and I'll turn off the lights and open the back door. I'm not going to do anything to hurt my golden goose, am I?" Heindrich stood looking at him across the space of about a foot and thinking, *a goose, that's exactly what I am, a goose*. His shoulders sagged a bit as he let himself out the front door. He could have sworn he heard Kurt laughing. But the lights went out and he walked to the Daimler.

Chapter 19

The break up of choir practice was always a noisy affair. Ed was walking back from the Old Lion and the Lamb to pick up Dori. He could hear them. Just like a gaggle of geese, he chuckled to himself. And then his brow puckered. He hoped Dori had lost that feeling of impending doom. The last time she had it, me old Dad died. Sommat be in it. Others may scoff. And he wouldn't admit to Dori how he felt. Better she think I thought nowt about it and any road, the lass would be here tomorrow. And that lad she was walking out with was a right'un. Made for each other they be. Any road. Tomorrow can't come soon enough. Oh there she be, my old girl. The light from the open chapel door cast a copper halo around her head. She was so wonderful. Far too good for likes of me. I'm lucky old badger, I'll be bound. And he hurried across to her.

They talked a bit of news and gossip on the way to Miss M's, which was how they both thought of her, with love, a pet name between the two of them. Neither spoke of the events of the earlier eventide. They pulled up in front of Miss M's cottage.

V.E. Sullivan

"By heck. She's an early one tonight. Shall we knock her up, love?" Dori leaned forward and looked at the quiet cottage. How peaceful it looked in the half-light. The roses were bathed in a glow of pink and white and the wire across the thatched roof winked and blinked like a bunch of busy fire-flies.

"No love, she'll have gone up early readying herself for the children. And I'll be bound if she didn't fuss about house all evening making some of her lovely fairy cakes. Let's be off. I still have that trifle to do."

Chapter 20

Sitting in the dark house with only the embers of the fire, each busy with their own thoughts, Kurt whispered across to Heindrich, "We had better find something for your face. Wouldn't want a nasty infection to set in, would we?" He said with a half chuckle. But his face did look nasty, three jagged tears down his cheek from cheekbone to jaw, red and puffy and still oozing blood.

"Ja, ja, I was thinking, Kurt. That old shed in the back garden. Bet the old woman kept some things in there. Bits of furniture and bric-a-brac. Enough to cause a nasty accident. It's big enough to store a lot. Let's have a look. Shhh, hear that?" The rumbling of a motor could be heard. "They're here. Maybe they'll think she's gone to bed and not bother coming to see her. Ja, good, there they go. Let's get to the back of the house and take a look at that shed."

Kurt let him resume the role of leader. Let him do all the work for a change. No sense rushing things. There was time. They got to the big old kitchen. Kurt lit his lighter and in the glow they saw the big old table with something white on it. The windows were all drawn shut with heavy chintz curtains.

V.E. Sullivan

"Find the switch, Kurt. No one can see back here. I want to find a torch to look around that shed." They began pulling out the drawers. Where would that silly old fool keep a torch?

"Here, Major." Kurt held a high-powered torch in his hand.

"Good, I'm going to take a look at that shed. We must move quickly before rigor mortis sets in." And with that he was gone.

He made his way down the back garden. Better not show a light, he thought, although the back garden was quite private with a high brick wall around and a locked gate at the end. He walked around a few minutes. His eyes had become accustomed to the dark and he found the shed. The door had a big padlock on it, but he had seen some keys hanging by the back of the kitchen door. Time was of the essence now. He ran back to the kitchen door and bursting through shouted, "It's locked. But one of these keys will fit it." Kurt was sitting at the table smoking. "Ach, you fool, get that old cow and bring her to the shed."

He was about to protest, but he wanted to be out of there and the Major was right. He was certain he was going to remove all traces of his own prints and the Major's. There was plenty of time to turn him in after he had made him squirm a bit. He made his way back to where Millacent lay and bent down and turned her over. Mein Gott, he thought. Her head had struck the corner of the brick hearth and there was a puncture wound in the forehead. Not a lot of blood but they would have to do a little cleaning up. Sultan was lying very close to Millacent, mewing softly. Kurt gave him a kick as he stooped to pick up Millacent. There was nothing to her. She was as light as a feather, rather like carrying a bundle of clothes.

As he carried her through and out the back door and down the path the Major had the door open and was busy looking about. Kurt walked through the door and said, "You're not going to like this."

"What is it now?" Kurt put her down and pointed to her forehead.

"It struck the hearth when you flung her down." Heindrich had that wild look again in his eyes. He was busy arranging things. He dragged her body across to the step stairs and arranged her to look as if she was knocked over backwards. He worked quickly, handling her like a mannequin. That's what it reminded Kurt of a window dresser he had seen in Berlin. Heindrich reached up and pulled a box. Several things came away including a heavy packing box with the metal edges, the kind that china comes in. He stood looking at the body, then, coldly, and with as little feeling as he might have had in picking out a tie, picked up the packing box and forced the corner of it into the puncture on her head.

"Ja, that is it." He stood back and looked at his work. "Ja, Kurt, what you think? It looks like she had a nasty accident, Ja?" He laughed that hysterical laugh again.

I better get what I'm going to get from him before he goes over the edge completely. "Ja, Major, looks quite nasty."

Heindrich was busy wiping his prints off of everything he had touched. "Come, come, we go now." Closing the door, he left the key hanging in the lock in the hasp.

They had finished with the house and making their way down the path when they heard someone whistling and bumping along the road. They fell to the ground. As Constable Simms came up to the gate he had thought he might have a natter with Miss Lang and find out what had been bothering her. And just maybe, just maybe get a cuppa. But it looked like he was too late. He threw his leg over the bike and rode off whistling "Land of Hope and Glory."

By the Pricking of My Thumb

"That was close. That bobby almost had us. Shut the gate now," and hurrying to the Daimler, they brushed themselves off as they went.

"Oh, Major. I think under the circumstances you should book me - or better still, let me book myself - into the hotel. I'm sick of those stinking, third rate flats I've been staying at. And now that I can afford it… well, you understand. We have much to discuss this night, ja?"

Chapter 21

Robert stood in the hall beside his small soft-sided case waiting for Suzette. "Come on, flower. If you want to spend the day in the Shambles we have to get going."

Suzette poked her head around the door. "Oh, love, just a half a mo. But you can get those."

Rob came around the corner and started to laugh. "By heck. I'll never understand women. We're not going for a fortnight. It's a weekend", as he picked up the two soft bags. He had educated Suzette to soft luggage as the Jag hadn't much baggage room and these soft sides give.

"Well darling, what if I spilled something or fell in the river. You do want me to look respectable, don't you? She said, with a teasing smile. "Rob, I'm so happy. Nothing can spoil this day. We'll have a smashing time in York and the Shambles. Let's have lunch at that super pub. What's it called? Something to do with religious orders, oh, 'The Trappists.' That's it."

"OK, pet, I'll take this down and leave you to check the stove, the fire place, windows, et cetera. Meet you downstairs. Don't forget our keys." He winked at her and was gone.

She quickly went through the place. Plants watered, everything in order, super. She locked up and dropped the keys into her giant shoulder bag and flew down the stairs. She stopped at the bottom and flung out her arms, twirled around, her soft gored skirt swirling around her knees revealing two very shapely legs. "Isn't it a super day, Rob? It's going to be a wonderful weekend, and to see Auntie Millacent, Ed and Dori, and good old Sultan. It's been a long time. It will be so good to sit around the cottage and have a real good natter. Who knows, we might even have a good old knee's up."

Robert closed the car door, laughing. It was good to see Suzette so happy not that she was wet to be around. She was always terrific company. But this was a fizzy happiness. Like watching bubbles on good champagne. He got in and started the car, put it in gear, turned and kissed her quickly on the cheek and said, "I love you, you daft old thing." And they were off.

Ed dropped Dori off at the gate of the cottage. "Wait up, half a mo, love, and I'll see if Miss Millacent wants to ride with you." Walking up the walk, she snipped a few dead heads from the roses and thought, what a lovely batch of pot pourri this year.

And Ed leaned across and smiling, thought, Come on Dori, love. Haven't got all day, work's waiting.

Dori slipped her key into the lock calling out "Only me, ducks. Want to ride with Ed?" Funny that, she thought, how quiet it was, and something missing. Why of course, no Sultan to greet her. Funny that, but maybe Miss Millacent let him out in the back garden. She went to the door calling, "Cooee," and Ed looked up. "She must have gone, love. Maybe you can catch her up on your way. You shan't miss her," and closed the door. And walking back towards the kitchen the house seemed unduly cold.

Why whatever was the matter with her? No tea things? Why it was unheard of. No matter how she felt she had her cuppa. Turning, she ran to the staircase, thinking, oh please don't let her be lying there sick unto death. Taking the stairs two at a time, she burst into the

By the Pricking of My Thumb

bedroom, her heart pounding a tattoo on her ribs. Oh, thanks be to God. The bed is made.

And a second unusual thing, her bedroom window was closed. She walked over and opened it and saw Sultan jumping up on the shed door. Silly old thing. Bet he thinks he's cornered something.

Smiling, she turned to the dry sink to empty the water from Miss M's morning wash, but stopped dead in her tracks: no water. She puckered her brow into deep furrows and shook her head. Then, shrugging, she thought oh well, maybe she had time this morning or didn't sleep well and rose early. These thoughts would come back to her later.

She had just reached the bottom of the stairs when the phone rang. She walked to the table opposite the grandfather clock and picked it up. "Look, love," Ed's voice came over the wire with a bit of strain."

"What ever is it, then"

"Well, she's not here. I've just come through after unlocking and she didn't do paperwork for Inland Revenue man either. And don't say I missed her, because I watched all the way for her and there's only one way she can come."

That heavy dread had come back to Dori, just like last night, a harried feeling of doom and despair.

"Dori, you still there, love?"

"I... I'm here. Maybe she has decided to get something for Suzette from the back shed in the garden. She's always on about the china she wants her to have. I'll have a look down there and ring you back straight away."

Dori replaced the instrument and felt suddenly sick to her stomach. You silly twit. Get ahold of yourself. What's she going to think when she sees you? She hurried through the kitchen and looked up to the key rack. Oh thanks be to God, the shed key is gone. She ran down the path calling to Sultan. "No wonder you're jumping. You have to stay outside. You don't want to be locked in there, do you? You silly old thing."

She jerked the door open, and trying to adjust to the dimness after the bright sunlight, she saw nothing at first but the mess. Then her eyes fell on the crumpled bundle. "Oh, no! Oh, no sweet Jesus!" She ran forward but all the while she knew it was already too late. Dear, silly love! She wanted to scream. Her throat was contracted in pain.

She could only fall on her knees and gather Miss M. to her as the tears rolled down her cheeks. "Silly, silly," she cooed. She rocked back and forth as if she was comforting a small child that had fallen. "How many times have we told you not to stand on those step stairs."

It was through her tears she noticed how strange her head was laying against her, and running her hand across her eyes to clear her vision, she saw the wound. She stared transfixed at the bundle in her arms. And laying her gently back to the ground, her body was seized with wracking sobs.

How long she knelt there rocking, she didn't know. But she slowly got to her feet. She hadn't noticed Sultan, but he was lying very close to his mistress making very distressed sounds. Poor old love. She gathered him to her and went out and closed the door. All the energy seemed to have drained from her body. And it was an effort to put one foot in front of the other. She knew she had to call Ed. He would be wondering what was keeping her. Sultan lay in her arms, as if he too were dead. He had probably been jumping at that door for hours, poor old boy. What ever would he do now? He would never be happy away from the cottage.

She couldn't ever remember the path being so long. She walked into the kitchen, set Sultan down on his stool and got his bowl, opened the refrigerator and got some milk. Set it down in his corner and walked to the hall with no more life than a robot. She picked up the phone and dialed the shop. She didn't seem to notice how quickly it was answered.

"Hello, Ed. I found her in the shed."

"Thank goodness for that. What ever was she doing any road?"

"Oh, Ed. You don't understand!" her voice broke. "She had an accident."

"Flaming heck. You hang on, old girl, I'll pick up the doc on the way," and hung up before Dori could tell him it was fatal.

She walked back to the kitchen, picked up the kettle to make tea. She felt as if she was standing outside her body as if in a dream watching this dazed looking creature performing menial tasks in slow motion.

Ed and Doc found her sitting at the table with a cold cup of tea in front of her. "What's the matter, woman. Why aren't you with Miss M.?

Doc Dundee took him by the arm, "Don't be daft, man. Get the brandy. Can you no see she's had a bad shock. Hurry man! Get on with ye."

Ed hurried from the kitchen to the front room and opened the lower door of the Welsh cupboard, took three glasses and the brandy. He crooked the fingers of his left hand around the stems of the glasses and picked up the brandy with the other and hurried back. He didn't dare let his mind think.

Striding into the kitchen, he saw Doc standing with his arm around Dori's shoulder and talking softly to her. Dori's face was buried in a very large white handkerchief that must have belonged to Doc. He stopped short, his face pale. No wonder Dori wasn't with Miss M, because... he couldn't make himself say it. He walked quickly to the table and set things down and poured three good drams of brandy and looking at Doc, his eyes must have asked the question for Doc just shook his head. Ed just tipped back his glass and swallowed the brandy in one gulp. He felt the brandy warm as fire, then slowly spreading like a flame through his limbs.

Doc took a glass and said, "Here, lass, drink this. No, not sip. Drink it down." All the while he was getting something out of his black bag. Ed saw it was a hypodermic needle. He drew some of the colourless liquid into the chamber. "Here, lad. Get around on this side and roll up her sleeve." He put the needle into Dori's arm and pushed the plunger. She gave no sign of being aware of anything. "Now Ed. Get her up to the guest room and into bed. Cover her with the eiderdown and close the drapes. She'll be out for a good wee while. And when she comes around she'll be over the worst of it, and the shock will be gone and she can take over. She says Miss Lang's niece is arriving around tea time."

"Oh, bloody heck!" Ed had completely forgotten. Oh dear God, poor lass. However will she take it? Doc was talking but Ed wasn't listening. He felt a heavy hand on his shoulder.

"Stir your stumps, man and do as I said quickly and then come to the shed in the back of the garden." Ed nodded his head and turned to Dori.

"Come on, my love, let's get you settled," and put his left arm around her waist and with his right arm under her arm he half lifted her from the chair. "Up now." Her head against his shoulder she let herself be led along and up the stairs. The last thing she really remembered was the softness of the eiderdown encasing her in a warm cocoon and then nothing.

Ed bent and kissed her on the forehead. He turned and was about the close the door when Sultan suddenly appeared. "Poor beggar." He knelt and picked him up and rubbed behind his ear. It was as if Sultan was unable to make a sound. He clung to Ed as a drowning man clings to a piece of wood. "There, there. You'll be all right old son. Dori and I will be here with you. Any road, naught will happen to you." Ed went back and put Sultan on the foot of the bed. He quickly curled up beside Dori's side, happy to be with someone warm.

Ed turned and pulled the door to and started to the stairs. He passed Miss M.'s room, the door was opened. Everything looked the same, except nothing would ever be the same again. Yesterday's roses on the dressing table were wilted and a few petals had fallen as if even the roses were mourning over her passing. He drew a large handkerchief from his pocket, blew his nose and wiped his eyes. Mustn't let Doc see me like this. Must try to stay together for Dori and

Suzette. Glad her lad will be with her. He'll be the best thing for Suzette, I'll be bound.

He hurried through the house and out the kitchen door half running. He almost collided with Doc who was coming back. "Ach, aye Ed, get her settled?" Look, I want you to go to the house and call Sergeant Littlejohn and tell him to bring the wagon and Corporal Simms."

"Anything you haven't told me, Doc?"

"Nay, nay. Looks like a clear accident but there will have to be an autopsy to determine the cause of death. Aye, looks like the poor lass lost her balance on those step stairs and pulled some heavy things onto her. But want to get things cleaned up here, and fast, before Dori comes around and the lass arrives. You want me to tell her Ed?"

"No, Doc, thanks. We'll be best at that. Only, may need you for Miss Suzette later, a sedative or sommat, so she can get through the night."

"Aye, well I'll be back early evening to have a wee look at Dori and I'll see the lass at the same time."

Chapter 23

"Come on, my lovely, or we will not get to St. Gilliams on time to take Auntie to tea."

Suzette turned, her eyes dancing. "Oh, Rob, it is just so perfect. Auntie's going to love it. We'll leave as soon as it's wrapped. I told the woman we didn't need a box. She shouldn't be a tick, darling. Oh, here she comes now. Yes, yes. Thank you so much. I'm sure it will be fine. We'll be careful. You've been very kind."

Rob was waiting by the door smiling. Suzette came up to him glowing with happiness hugging the package to her chest. "Cheers," he said, closing the door to that quaint little shop called The Seeker's Find in the Shambles.

They reached the car and both turned to look back at the shop with such longing as if this day of happiness would not soon come again. Rob put his arm around her waist, drew her close and looked down at her. Her eyes had clouded a bit and he kissed her on top of the head and whispered, "Suzette, love, it will always be perfect with us. You know that."

"You're right, Rob!" but her green eyes filled with tears and the sun caught the drops and turned her eyes into enormous emeralds.

"Come on, you silly twit. The copper on the corner is going to think I've given you a bash." And they laughed and got into the car and were off.

Touring along the countryside and chatting, Rob looked over at her. "Oh, go ahead and have another look."

"I really shouldn't but it is so lovely I'm going to. Rob do you think those four chairs we bought will be at the station when we get back? Really, imagine finding four more black ebony chairs with cane bottoms exactly like the two we have! Just think, now we can entertain at least without having to serve buffet style. We can all sit at our beautiful table. Oh, my goodness!" as she carefully lifted the last piece of tissue.

"Don't tell me we managed to break it before aunt Millacent gets it!" Rob said with one eye on the road and the other on Suzette.

"Don't be daft, Rob." Suzette said teasingly. "But if you don't watch this narrow road we might just do that. It really is quite lovely," said Suzette looking down at the exquisite doll in her lap.

It was a harlequin doll, sixteen inches long and with a delicate porcelain head, hands and feet. It was dressed in the traditional black silk two piece costume and a black skull cap was fitted to its delicate head. The ruff around his neck was a delicate horsehair lace. It reminded Suzette of a white ripple Christmas candy and its border was black velvet. It had a very fine wire in the hem so the top of it stood out from the body in a small circle and the black silk was so delicate. The white pompoms were little circles of white lambs' wool. His trousers were cut loose and ended at his ankles. His feet were encased in small black leather slippers with white silk socks. His face was a masterpiece. His soulful eyes were black jets that glistened and brimmed with crystal tears so real that you expected them to spill over and match the tiny single crystal tear on his cheek. A real craftsman spent many hours on this with loving care. "How old do you think it is, Rob?"

"Don't really know, flower. But I would think early nineteenth century."

V.E. Sullivan

"It's in perfect condition, Rob. And I never expected to find a perfect match to the one of Aunt Millacent's that got broken. She will be so pleased. I can't wait to see her expression when she opens it."

"I know," Rob said smiling. "It won't be long now, love."

Chapter 24

Heindrich tossed and turned in a state of semi sleep. Terrible nightmares plagued him. Giant cats with long claws and bulging eyes, shapeless figures all with vacant stares and twisted bodies, all clutching and clawing at him. He woke with a start to find his silk pajamas soaked with sweat. His face and head pounding, tongue thick in his mouth. Must be coming down with something. He rolled onto his side and it all came flooding back to him.

He lay there looking at the bedroom. He let his gaze travel around the room. His clothes were scattered everywhere. On the dressing table there was a half-empty bottle of cognac and two empty glasses. Kurt, ja. Something has to be done with him. I'm not going to have him hanging around my neck like a millstone sucking me dry like the leach he is. Oh no, I've worked too hard, sacrificed too much for that. But, I'm going to have to be careful. I underestimated him once and that was dangerous. And, I have given him the upper hand, something to hold over my head. Ja, ja, that was bad. But, I need him still. Must get back into that wretched house and get my hands on that desk.

I feel sure it is the right one. It has cost me too much and a man died very painfully rather than reveal to me where he had hidden the Madonna and Christ child. The sight of that battered body and those defiant black eyes flashed before his mind. He was shivering and the pain in his head was unbearable. Got to get a hot shower and shave and some breakfast and something for this head. I can think better and plan what must be done before I'm able to leave it all behind me forever.

Throwing back the covers, he got to his feet. Mein Gott. He was so dizzy and felt violently ill. He dashed to the bathroom and fell on his knees before the loo and wretched into the bowl. Couldn't remember ever being so ill. When it finally subsided he rose, shakily, to his feet and moved slowly to the sink. Running the cold water he cupped his hands together and threw the water onto his face. He gasped. The pain was unbearable. He raised his head and looked into the glass above the sink. The face that stared back at him had no resemblance to his own. Eyes bright with fever, the whole side of his face was swollen with three very jagged deep tears from the corner of his eye to his jaw. They were encrusted and very red and oozing a coloured fluid.

He took a soft wash cloth and filled the sink with warm water. Every time his heart beat the pain pulsated through his head. He must try to clean the wounds for already they looked infected. Damned cat. Several agonizing minutes later, tossing the washcloth in the corner and patting his face dry, not much better but they looked a little cleaner. And picking up his razor with a shaky hand, hearing a knock coming from the door, the razor clattered into the sink. Mein Gott. Get ahold of yourself. The knock came again, more persistent.

Wrapping a towel around his waist and calling "Ja, ja, I'm coming," he jerked open the door and Kurt strode into the room looking fresh and rested. How he loathed him. And for all that he might just have stepped out of a fashion magazine. He had replaced all the ill-fitting clothes with a smart tailored look. His butter soft leather jacket, tapered slim cut gabardine slacks, with beige cashmere pullover, a silk scarf draped around his neck, soft brown leather loafers and an Irish walking hat in his hands. So great was the change in his appearance no one who had seen him before would recognize him now.

"Mein Gott, Heindrich. What's the matter with you? You look like death. Oh, ja. I told you last night to stop by the chemist and get some attention for that face. But, no. the big Major had just wanted to get back here and drink his cognac. Now look what a mess you've got. Must see a doctor. We don't want anything to happen to you now that we are getting to know each other better, do we?" That half smile and sneer circled his lips. Heindrich could have killed him there and then, but he remembered he must not be goaded into anything. He must keep the upper hand and be composed and in charge of the situation at all times.

He turned and closed the door. "Kurt, order me some breakfast, just coffee and rolls, while I change. We can talk while we eat." He made himself stand tall and walk straight. He crossed to the bedroom, closing the door behind him. He staggered to the bed and fell across it. The bile was rising in the back of his throat and the beads of perspiration stood out on his forehead.

Twenty minutes later he came back into the room looking much better with the help of a hot shower and his elegant hand-made suit, in time to see Kurt sign for the breakfast trolley. He closed the door and wheeling the cart close to Heinrich he said "I took the liberty, Major, to order a little more. A little fresh fruit, two soft boiled eggs and toast. I have already eaten but will join you for coffee."

Perhaps Kurt was right. A light breakfast would be the right thing. Must not show him just how weak he felt. He had to keep this ungrateful dog in line right now. He should be at his feet regardless of his clothes. He must be made to take orders and to obey them for you can't make a silk purse out of a sow's ear. And he was still a schwein, the low life creature he had always been. And Heindrich wasn't going to be fooled by the clothes and Kurt again. No, never again.

Chapter 25

Dori willed herself to stay in the dark warm soft cocoon that surrounded her with images of happier yesteryears drifting past her, but try as she would the darkness was turning to light and she was floating up to it.

She left happiness behind with the knowledge that those happy days would live on in her heart. And now she had a job to do: to help heal the hurt for Suzette and Robert and even Ed. And she knew now that she would be given the strength from her Lord to see this through. And with that she opened her eyes and saw Ed sitting by the bed with Sultan sleeping in his lap. Poor love. He looks all done in, his chin resting on his chest. She was content to lie there and look at them. What a wonderful partner he had been and their lives seemed to mesh together, strong yet gentle, with the big giving heart and strong arms. He had sheltered her and kept her as best as he could from all that would harm her that day. And she loved him so much.

As if he knew she was awake, his head lifted slowly and their eyes met. No need to say anything for everything there was to say passed in the gaze. "Dori, love. How you be, lass?"

"Oh, if you get me a cuppa and a slice of toast, I'll clean up a bit and be right down."

Ed picked up Sultan and laying him on the foot of her bed, he came to her, bent down and kissed her forehead. Her arms encircled him and that strong embrace fortified him for what lay ahead. He held her close for a moment, then released her and walked toward the door. Then, turning, looking back at her, he said, "You'll be all right, Dori love, and we'll take care of Suzette, and Robert will help us bring her through this. You'll see, lass. All will be well."

She smiled and nodded and he went down to put the kettle on.

V.E. Sullivan

Chapter 26

Robert parked a few doors down from the shop and got out, swinging around the boot in time to open the door for Suzette. She swung her shapely legs out and he took her hand and together they walked to Auntie Millacent's shop. "No thrills here," Rob said as they walked up and gazed at the sign. Gold leaf, a little faded now, and all it said was Lang's Antiques. They both smiled, and still hand in hand, Suzette hugging her prize in the other arm, walked towards the door, still chattering like school kids on a holiday. They hadn't noticed the closed sign until they went to open the door.

"Funny that, Rob. We're not late are we?"

"On the contrary, flower, we're early." And as he turned he saw a strange look pass over her face. A face that a few seconds ago was radiant and flushed with happiness. Not quite pale and yet there was some uneasiness. Rob felt it in his own stomach. "Look, love," he said smiling, "the old darling just went on to clean and dress up for us." But even to Rob's ear his voice sounded hollow.

By the Pricking of My Thumb

"This is ridiculous. What could have happened? Where's Ed?" Suzette's voice sounded like it was coming from the throat of a frightened child.

"Oh, you know Ed. He just took her to the cottage. He wanted to be there with the girls. You know how crazy they are about you. Come on, love, you'll see. You're getting upset over nothing." Rob took her back to the car. She settled her skirt and hugged her treasure for Auntie M. so close to her chest Rob was afraid she would crack it. She looked up at him and the tears welled in her eyes.

"Robert, something's wrong. I can feel it. Just like I felt it before Daddy..." and the words couldn't come from her throat. Her eyes spilled over and rushed down her cheeks onto the package.

"Oh, darling. Don't go getting yourself and the doll all wet. You don't want Auntie to think you've gone dotty coming to take her to tea all red-eyed and damp. Or worse, thinking I've clouted you one." He kissed her wet face and smiled and hurried around the car, got in and started away from the curb thinking, oh God, not again. Don't let this be happening to her again. Millacent is the only tie she has with her

91

mother and father the only living one and if something were to break that I don't know how Suzette would cope with it.

Glancing sideways at her, he saw that her fingers worked nervously on the package and she was pale, terribly pale. But with all his bravado, he knew all the happiness of the day was over. A hard hurtful time lay ahead for her. He would have to be the strength for both of them. Thank God for Dori and Ed. What's the matter with you? You're a real wet thing. You don't even know there's anything wrong yet. But he did know.

"Rob, look. There's Ed's van. Do you suppose we're getting all upset for nothing? Not you darling. You're always a brick. I mean myself." And before he could stop her she opened the gate and ran up the walk, her coat and hair flying and the package dangling precariously in her hand calling, "Auntie Millacent," just as she had done as a child. The only difference was she was bigger and the package wasn't the rag doll she always dragged everywhere by one arm.

She reached the door and burst through, Robert hard on her heels. Dori and Ed were standing in the hall trying to look as cheerful as possible for the blow was about to fall. Dori was first to hold out her arms to her and was saying, "Suzette, love, let's have a look at you." She circled her with her arms and over Suzette's shoulder met Rob's eyes and the pain in them was almost unbearable. "Look, Ed. Look at our beautiful lass."

Ed came and gathered her in his arms. This did not strike Suzette as strange as this was the way it had always been and always would be. Ever since she was a child, this was the way it always began when she came to visit Auntie M. "Come through to kitchen," Dori said, "tea is all ready." She left Ed and Robert to bring Suzette through. The brandy was all set out on the counter with the glasses and the kettle on to boil. The best thing was to tell her, quick and clean. Not the easiest but the best.

As she turned around with the hot teapot in her hand ready to set it down on the table they came in, "Oh Dori, it looks so good, but Rob, don't you dare. We're taking Auntie to tea don't forget." She sank onto the chair and said, "Dori, wait 'till you see what I've brought for Auntie. What in the world is keeping her? Where is she?" She started to rise but Ed's hands fell on her shoulders. She looked around at the three faces she loved and she felt sick, dreadfully sick.

"Suzette, my love," Dori was saying, "there was an accident this morning and Miss Millacent," she looked up at Ed, not being able to stand the look on Suzette's face.

"She's gone, my love," Ed said as gently as possible.

She swung around on her chair, "Gone, gone? What do you mean gone?" Her voice was rising to a high pitch. "Gone where?"

But before they could answer she rose to her feet, threw back her head and half screamed, half sobbed, and crumpled into a small heap at their feet. Rob reached her first and gathered her into his arms and lifted her as he would a doll.

"There was no easy way, lad," Ed was saying as they led the way into the front room where the fire was burning bright.

"I know, Ed" Rob said as he laid her down on the Chesterfield. Dori was fast on their heels with the brandy. Ed was putting a pillow under her head and Rob was tucking her up in a throw Dori had placed there earlier. Rob was chafing her wrists. He didn't like her

By the Pricking of My Thumb

colour at all. Dori was at her side with a small glass of brandy. "What happened?" Rob said still trying to rub life back into Suzette.

"She fell off steps, poor dear, in the shed. We don't know much. Dr. Dundee took her away. Dori found her this morning and was in a terrible state herself. Doc put her out with a shot."

Rob looked up at Dori, his eyes misted and soft. "My gosh, Dori, I'm so sorry. Here you are running around looking after us. Ed, make her sit. I think we could all use that brandy."

"Yes, I'll get the glasses," said Ed.

Dori said, "Hush Rob, I'm all right now and I'm ready to take care of our poor lass, here. Try to pour some brandy between her teeth. I'm afraid she's withdrawn deep and we must bring her back quick. Dr. Dundee will be along soon to give her something."

Rob took the brandy with shaking hands and knew what Dori said was true. "Thank you, Dori, for being here with us. And that goes for you too, Ed. I don't know what I'd do without you both. We do love you, you know." His voice broke and he turned and put his hand under the pillow and raised Suzette's head.

She was so cold and white. In deep shock Rob thought. Come on, darling, just a sip now. He placed the brandy to her lips. Thank God it wasn't a delicate crystal thing but a sturdy glass. "Oh no, it's no good." It ran down the side of Suzette's chin. Rob looked up. He was filled with a cold fear. His whole body was feeling limp. Oh please God, I can't lose her. Help me to think. "Maybe a spoon, Dori. I could get it into her mouth further and pour a little at a time down her throat."

"We must get something down her and fast and bring her around. Then good hot tea with lots of sugar." My God, thought Rob, the Englishman's answer to everything, strong tea with milk and sugar.

Dori was there with the spoon, and once more Rob tried. It seemed to be working.

Ed, standing at the foot of the Chesterfield, said, "That's the lad, nice and slow. She's swallowing. Dori lass, keep chafing her wrists, I think her colour is coming back." Slowly, ever so slowly, Rob kept feeding the brandy to Suzette and he could feel the cold leaving her body and saw the colour coming back.

"Dori, love, get that tea. You know how."

"Yes we know, lad. We'll give you some time with her," Ed said and followed Dori out of the door.

"Oh, Suzette, my love. Please open your eyes and look at me. I love you so much, I can't bear to see you like this darling. Take my strength. Reach out for it. We can make it together like we always have done when things were bad. I need you Suzette, now and for always." He had finished feeding all the brandy to her. Her colour had come back but she hadn't. She was still in that dark place of despair she had sent herself where there is no pain, no memory, only darkness.

He must bring her back now or she might never come back, or if she did, might never be the Suzette he knew and loved. He encircled her and drew her to his chest. Her head fell into the hollow on his neck, so natural. Just like when she would fall asleep while they were driving. He stroked the shining head, so soft, and kissed her. When he could do no more the desperate tears filled his eyes, rolled down his face and fell on her upturned face. "Suzette, I won't let you go. We love each other too much and need each other more." He stopped rocking. He couldn't be sure but he thought he felt a shudder go through her body. He sat holding her perfectly still. Yes, there it was again. She was shaking and clinging to him. Great wracking, inconsolable sobs left her body. They tore at the heart of the three people that loved her, but they knew this to be the best thing for her and Robert the best one for now. Dori and Ed had witnessed the scene through the doorway and they knew their turn was coming, but right now this was the best.

After awhile the sobs turned to quiet crying. Cradled in Rob's arms, soon she would have a cuppa and with all the brandy and the exertion she would sleep and then Dr. Dundee would come and give her a shot to take her through the night. And by morning if he knew his girl, she would be ready to face things as she had done before. Only this time, she had almost slipped over the edge into a world of sub consciousness, escaping everything. Thank God she had fought back.

The crying stopped and she lay against him, her small arms embracing his neck. And, finally she opened her eyes. Looking at his tear-stained face she said, "Rob, I love you. You're my strength and my refuge. Don't leave me this night. Even if I sleep I need you near."

She sat up and held her arms out to Dori and to Ed who came to her and made soft clucking sounds, all sharing a grief too big for only one to share.

"Here's a hanky, Suzette, love. And Dori, has some tea here for you. It will help."

"Yes my ducks."

"Then upstairs for a wee lay down and a rest." Suzette's eyes grew large with anxiety. "No danger, love, I'll be there."

She kissed Dori and Ed and the three heads made a circle. "You're my family now, you know. You and Ed are all Rob and I have." Her shaking voice gave way to new tears and very tight hugs.

"No danger, Miss Suzette, you just try and get shod of us. Flaming heck. We're family, all of us now." And even with that he rose and blew his nose hard into a big white handkerchief and turned his back with pretense of getting tea.

But Rob saw him dry his eyes. Poor old darling. This had hit them for sixes and all and Rob knew that there were no greater people to stand by him or none he'd rather have than Ed and Dori. He felt drained of all emotion. His chest ached for them and himself. For he loved Auntie Millacent and the void would long be healing. But he must be strong for he had a dreadful feeling that this was only the first act of many terrible nightmares they were all going to have to pass through before they could be free in the sun again be really free.

"Look, love. Don't you think you should get upstairs and lay down proper like?" Dori said.

"You're right as usual, Dori. Our girl can hardly keep her eyes open." Rob gathered her up in his arms and bent to kiss her forehead. "It's up the stairs to that old room of yours with all your favorites, your four-poster bed and soft eiderdown and all your treasures. He disappeared through the door still talking to her.

Ed came and put his arm around Dori's waist. She dropped her head onto his shoulder, raised her hanky to her eyes. "Don't cry, Dori, love. Things will work out now that big shock is over and healing can begin."

She hugged him and said, "Oh, Ed. I hope you be right. We need nowt more to come, do we? Let's get this cleaned up. I need a fresh cuppa myself."

"Aye," said Ed, picking up the tray and moving to the door. "And I'm sure Robert could stand a strong cuppa. Poor lad, hasn't had nowt since he arrived."

"Oh Ed, you're right," and she went dashing past him towards the kitchen.

Chapter 27

"Where in the bloody hell have you been laddie? I've been trying to raise you for an hour or more." Dr. Dundee spoke over the line. His soft highland burr not covered by his anger in not being able to reach Inspector Pentecroft.

"Well I'm here now. What's all the flap about?"

"It looks like you'll be calling in New Scotland Yard, laddie. You've got a first class murder on your hands."

"Bloody hell!" spat Pentecroft. "First thing big that happens around here in years and I have to turn it over. Why? What did you find Doc?"

"She had deep discolorations made by thumbs and fingers on both shoulders. Someone was hanging onto her pretty hard and her neck was broken. But no pressure marks on her neck. My guess, laddie, is someone was shaking her by the shoulders. She was elderly and small, remember. A man could snap her like a twig, much like a mother could shake a bairn. Her bones were brittle with arthritis and by the looks of these bruises, the force of that shaking would've caused her head to whip back and forth and it just snapped clean. And we'll be lifting prints from her shoulders soon."

"By, gosh," Pentecroft said. "People in the village will be sore upset. We couldn't find a person who was loved by so many. Even those hard old farmers on the outskirts of the village thought the world of her. There'll be nowt for it, Doc, you know her as well as anyone."

"Aye, Ronald, aye. And a warmer heart, alas, you no could find. But murder it is. And there's something else. She had fibers of cloth clutched under her nails as if she had been digging into his arms. She had a puncture high on her forehead where he let go of her and she fell forward. Aye, laddie, and she struck her head on something sharp. There would be no much blood but there would be some. Did you no find anything in the shed where the body was discovered, laddie?"

Pentecroft cast his mind back to that scene. He remembered before Doc came, Constable Simms had said a small packing box with a sharp corner had been found beside her. There was dried blood on one corner. "Only that packing box your men took away with them."

"Aye, that sample of her blood matched the sample from the box. But, laddie, were there no traces of skin or hair? You'll have to start looking for it for it is certain she was not killed there."

A long sigh escaped from Pentecroft's throat. "Have you any idea of the time of death, Doc?"

"Nay, not for certain. I estimate the time to be early evening: not before seven-thirty and not later than nine but I'll know more when the tests come back from her stomach contents."

"Any idea, Dr. Dundee, how long?"

"I dinna ken, laddie. But I'll be working the wee hours and try to have a report on your desk by midday tomorrow," and rang off.

Pentecroft thought, that gives me forty-eight hours before the buckos arrive from London.

Chapter 28

Dr. Dundee called over to his chief assistant, "Be sure you go over all her clothes carefully, laddie. Vacuum everything and take scrapings off her shoes, the seams, heels and all. We have a murderer on the loose and we have the poor lassie here. We have been working hard but not as hard as we are going to. I want every jack man of ya on your toes, looking, and watching for anything. Ach man! This changes everything, the whole picture. We must start from scratch again. Bring the poor wee lassie back. She is the only one who can give us a clue or tell us anything, Michael! I want that bun undone and her hair combed into an evidence bag. Look sharp now. Aye, there is much to do. I have the inquest, the coroner's report and the Inspector's report to make by midday and I want to be ready. Oh, aye, we will all be burning the midnight oil here tonight. Well will you no get started and stop staring like a fish at me?" His freckle-faced, red-haired assistant rolled his eyes upward as if asking the Almighty for help.

Chapter 29

Inspector Pentecroft turned in his swivel chair, his fingers pressing hard together, and the palms flat. "Bloody hell! Where do I start?" A murder in St. Gilliams, my patch! Hell, there hasn't been anything like this for donkey's years, only petty stuff. I've got to dig up something before the hard nosed brass from London arrive and start pushing their weight around and treating me and my lads like country bumpkins. Got to get off on the right foot. Who knows what it might mean to my future if it worked. He wanted, in time, to leave St. Gilliam, but only if it came with a promotion. And besides all that, he liked the old girl and he felt he owed her his best effort to get this bastard.

He couldn't think of anyone in St. Gilliams who had that much malice to kill anyone. He rose, grabbed his hat off the peg and hollered through the office door "Sergeant, find me Simms and get a car around the front for me as fast as you can. Then get back here. I want you in charge of the scene here."

"Yes, sir!" The sergeant went down the hall to the duty room barking orders as he went.

By the Pricking of My Thumb

Terry Simms was sitting, staring into space. His hands were cupped around the crockery cup. He was so lost in thought that when the sergeant's voice came through to his thoughts he jumped, spilling the hot tea over his hands and onto the table.

"Flaming Nora, what's with you, lad? You got cloth ears or sommat? You'd better step lively, the chief wants you and me back at the desk in a hurry."

"What's up, Serge?" He said as he rose attempting to dry his hands and wipe off the table with the serviettes that were stacked there.

"I don't know, only we'd better get a move on. Leave that stuff to the housekeeper. And get your bleeding arse around here, now!" Pushing Simms ahead of him, he went running back up to the desk.

"Oh, there you are, Sergeant. Found him, good. Now listen, I'm only going to say this once and that's all the time I have for now. Old Miss Lang has got herself murdered. No, don't ask, just listen with both ears. Simms and I will return to the crime scene and Sergeant, I want you to move the big desk and the black board and the chairs into the duty room. From now on, that will be our incident room. Get pencils and lots of paper, files, file boxes, phones, you know what to do. You've had this end of the stick before, thank goodness. I want it all ship shape before the brass from London arrive."

"Yes, sir. You can count on me, sir." And with a half salute turned around and went down the hall barking orders. And in minutes the quiet little station house looked like an anthill that had just been kicked people everywhere carrying and fetching and running, "Good," said Inspector Pentecroft. He turned to Simms who looked like a storefront wooden Indian. Then it hit him. This was probably the lad's first taste of violence. He wasn't long from the training school at the police academy. And, as luck would have it, stationed back in his own village. And, of course, he would have known Miss Lang ever since he was a nipper. Well, the sooner he got his feet wet and really got into the case the better. A scared, nervous bobby was going to be of no use to him.

"Look here, Simms," he said taking him by the arm and leading him to the car that was waiting at the curb. Better keep the driver. He might need a third man once they got to the house." Then opening the door he shoved Simms into the back seat. "I know this is all new to you. And the first murder case you work on can either make you into a good useful policeman or keep you on the beat. Let's try and make it useful, eh?"

"Yes, sir." But he continued to look pensive and remained quiet.

"Look here, laddy. Is there something bothering you? Is there something you want to say? Better get it off your chest before we get there."

"Well, sir. I've known Miss Lang since I was a boy. I used to deliver her packages and run errands for her. I saw her on the night she was murdered and I know that she was that upset, she was."

"You what? You'd better tell me everything. Why didn't you come forward sooner?"

"Well, sir. When I saw her she was rushing home. All sixes and sevens, staring straight ahead of her. She never answered my wave and I was about to go after her when I heard the clock in the village square going six, and I hadn't called in. And you know the sergeant, sir." Taking a deep breath, he continued. He noticed the inspector taking a pad from his inside pocket. "I got on my bike and I had just rounded the corner when this big black Daimler almost took me out, driving fast and on the wrong side. Had to go up and over the curb. It punctured my tyre and bent my front wheel. Gave me quite a turn, I don't mind telling you, and tore up my knee."

"Foreigners, you say Simms. Interesting, did you get a plate number?"

Terry reached in for his pad in the breast pocket of his uniform. "Only the last three numbers, I'm afraid." He lifted the page. "Here it is, sir: 855."

"Good lad. We'll get someone on to the car rentals for foreigners from the continent not used to driving on the left. Remember anything else, laddie?"

"Well only that I was doing my beat that night and I went by Miss Lang's. I thought that I would have a natter with her and try to find out what got her so upset and maybe get a cuppa." Simms looked up sheepishly.

The inspector smiled. He remembered his own early days as a bobby on the beat on a cold night. "What time would that be, Simms? Can you remember? Just try as close as you can."

Corporal Terry Simms sat silent, then said, "Nine thirty, quarter to ten as best as I recall, sir. I completely forgot about it until I walked

By the Pricking of My Thumb

into the duty room and heard them all talking about poor Miss Lang's accident. She'll be sorely missed. Do you think if I had gone up to the house I might have discovered sommat? I can't get the picture of her rushing into the night..."

Before he could say another word, the inspector's strong hand came down on his shoulder, "Look here, laddie. There's nowt for it now but to get on with this bloody mess and find the one responsible. So put all of those negative thoughts from you and clear your mind. We don't want these brass nosed CID from London thinking we're clouts from the country do you? Let's concentrate on finding some pertinent information and good evidence out of the house and that shed. We also have the sad task of telling the family that it was not an accident but murder. And now there will have to be an inquest as soon as Dr. Dundee gets the autopsy report completed. That report should be on my desk tomorrow. Well, here we are. Looks like Doc's car is here. Hope he told the family. He knows them all so well. Understand her niece and her young man arrived today for a weekend. Nasty business, this... Benson, you stay here in the panda and keep your ears open for the radio. Simms, you know this property well and I want you to go over every inch of that back garden and shed and look twice at everything, no matter how dumb it makes you feel. I'll be over at the house."

Terry Simms turned and made his way to the back of the house to the back garden. He wondered if he would be able to remember how to open the locked gate. He reached his fingers through the knothole and felt around for the fine wire that would trip the lock at the hasp and let him in. His fingers found it and the gate swung open. By heck, it had been donkey years since he had done that and his eyes misted as he could just see her standing there as neat as a new pin, fresh white pinny on. And even way back then he was taller than she was by half a head. She always smelled of roses and lavender and even then she seemed older to him. "Now Terrance, if you be lockin' yourself out ever, just remember this, it will save you endless trips to the shop for the keys." Bloody heck. He passed his hand across his eyes and he hoped no one was looking out the back windows. You silly fool. Get on with the job and we'll get that old sod that did this if I have to work around the clock and all of my hours off.

He started up the walk. The well-kept garden looked the same and the small kitchen herb garden, all the flowers and the emerald patch of grass where Sultan used to sun himself while he weeded the flowerbed. By heck, it seemed just like yesterday.

He reached the shed. Might as well start here. He reached for the lock and saw long indents on the wooden door. He looked closer. They looked like scratches. Something he should be remembering about that. Come on, bucko. Get that grey matter going or you're always going to be the neighborhood bobby on the beat. Oh, yah. Sultan did that trying to get in. He hated to go in. He'd always remember her, his dear old friend, laying in the dirt and that awful hole in her forehead. Well, there be nowt else for it but to get on with it.

He opened the shed door and looked around for a rock or brick to hold it open wide, to let some extra light and air in. With the door held secure, he stepped in and let his eyes adjust to the changing light. Still might need his torch. He felt at the back of his uniform and pulled it out, switched it on and swung it around. Sure were plenty of boot prints all over. Government issue he'd bet, except maybe Doc's.

He let the light fall on the dirt. We didn't half make a mess of this floor. It will take a bloody genius to get clues out of this lot.

Well, he'd made up his mind he was going to find something and he dropped to his knees to get a closer look at where the body was found. He shone his torch. Flamin' Nora. What am I looking for any road? Something must be here even if Miss Lang wasn't murdered here. He was playing his torch on the spot where he first saw her body. First in a tight little circle and then ever widening ones 'till the light met the sunshine coming through the open door. Nowt. He brought the light back to where he knelt. We'll start again boyo. This time while he circled the torch he also put his hand down and ran it through the dirt, slowly, so as not to miss anything. After what seemed hours mucking about in the dirt, his fingers came in contact with something hard.

Carefully blowing the soft dirt away he realized he was looking down at a small, round, cloth-covered button. He was excited. He dropped his torch as he reached into his breast pocket for the note pad and pencil. It occurred to him as he tore the sheet of paper from the pad that he was holding his breath. And he exhaled the trapped air in

By the Pricking of My Thumb

his lungs and took his pencil and turned the button over in the dirt. By heck, there were little bits of thread and just a tiny piece of fabric about the size of a little pin. He laid the torn piece of paper beside him on the dirt and rolled the button onto it with his pencil. Terrance, my lad, you keep going, keep looking. Then his enthusiasm came down with a thud as he realized his precious find might have come off of her dress months ago. Maybe it had lain in the dirt all that time. But his training at the police academy was paying off. Treat everything at the scene of a violent crime with great care and overlook nowt. And take nothing for granted.

About thirty minutes later he was still on his hands and knees in the soft loose dirt of the shed floor when a shadow fell across his line of vision. He looked up. The inspector stood half in and half out. Oh heck, he must look a right wally on his hands and knees in his shirt sleeves, his jacket and helmet hanging on a nail. He got hastily to his feet, brushing the dirt from his knees.

"All right, let's be having it."

He sheepishly picked up the small sheet of paper with the collection of small articles on it. Inspector Pentecroft raised his eyebrows. "Well who's the clever boy then?" His lips curved into a half smile and he took a pencil from his breast pocket and poked at the object on the small slip of paper. "Well done lad. We won't know what we have here 'till Doc goes over them. But with luck we'll have something, eh? Run, laddie, and see if you can get Doc before he leaves." Simms was off like a scalded hare. There was something about his receding back that reminded Pentecroft of himself. He will have a good future with the force and he will make something of himself. He raised his eyes from the paper and watched Doc and Simms hurrying down the path toward him.

"Laddie here says you found something."

"He did that, Doc, take a look at this." Doc opened his worn black bag and took out a small plastic bag and a pair of tweezers. He proceeded to pick up each article: button, hairpins, and the strange piece of glass. Half of a round with something caught in one corner.

"Aye, would you no look at this. Oh, you're a braw lad, I've always said that." He sealed the packet and marked it with his initials for later. And beaming at the pair of them marched off humming an old Scottish air.

"We'd best be taking ourselves up to the house and take some statements." Simms turned and started for the shed to get his jacket and helmet. For the first time since he got the news he was beginning to feel better about the whole thing. "Don't you fret none, Miss Millacent. We'll get that bloody bastard what did this to you."

"What are you saying, Simms?" And he realized he was talking to himself.

"Nothing, sir, just thinking out loud."

"Well lets be havin' you. We have a lot to do before the bucko's get here from London and I want to be ready. And I don't want them thinking we still have the cornsilks behind our ears, do we?"

"No, sir." Simms was ashamed of himself but he hoped Mrs. Halley would offer him a cuppa and he couldn't half murder one. She and Ed must be that upset over Miss Millacent. And he was thinking of a cuppa. But the more he thought of that hot, steaming cuppa the worse he felt. Maybe a sticky bun. He hadn't eaten since morning. He was suddenly overcome with shame, once more he was standing in the back garden of a dear friend who had just been brutally murdered and her closest family and friends up at the house trying to put their lives back together again. Some policeman he was going to be when in the middle of a crime investigation all he could think about was his tea. Besides, if he was going to have to work with Inspector Pentecroft and these blokes from London CID he had better not get the wind up them by taunts of a cuppa and sticky buns. And his inspector was a constant smoker, which probably did a lot to keep his hunger pains at bay.

He suddenly realized he was being spoken to. "Come lad, stop wool gathering. I'd have thought you'd have grown out of that. Aye Terrance, you be same. A mite taller, mind, but always thinking. Come on both of you, as Dori will have my skin. She has her sticky buns just out of oven and a fresh pot of tea."

"Oh, God bless you, Dori Halley and I'll not miss chapel on Sunday unless I'm on duty, then I'll go to eventide!" he promised. And, taking his helmet off and tucking it under his arm wiped his feet and entered the warm fragrant kitchen.

Chapter 30

Kurt watched as Heindrich dabbed at his chin. God, what a mess his face is in. But he does have some colour back. Must take care, too soon to lose the goose that laid the golden egg. Ja, I could get used to this life, the clothes, and the silk next to my body and the smell of the leather. Ja, ja, no more seedier end of life for me. He was smiling at himself when he realized the major was looking at him, studying him almost like a kinder looking at some kind of bug. Ja, he hates me all right. Must be on my toes from now on.

Heindrich took a cigarette out of his case and inserted it into the cigarette holder. When he clenched his teeth on the end as he reached for his cigarette lighter he thought, look at him. How he sits, like a proud peacock with his plumes on display. Well enjoy it, you dummkopf for your days are numbered. I only need you for a few more days, then pouf, gone. And no one will miss you, you poor schwein. As he exhaled a cloud of smoke he looked at the tip of the burning cigarette held in the typical European fashion, palm up, and between forefinger and thumb. "You may ring and have the trolley taken and then there are some things I want you to do, Kurt, besides spend my money and make yourself noticeable. This is a small village. Don't you think you will be remembered spending that kind of money? No, don't say anything, just listen. I want you to go around to the Lang shop and see what's up, and if it's locked, have your lunch at the pub with the locals and keep your ears open. Pick up the latest paper and walk. I want to use the car, and I won't be back before tea. So, try not to be conspicuous and don't charge any more to me." A look of pure hatred passed between them. Kurt nodded, got up, called the porter and left.

After he had gone Heindrich forced himself up and walked to the bedroom. Got, how he was sweating and the nausea was returning. He must drive into York and find a doctor and get his face taken care of. The pain was all over the side of his face and head now. He found his wallet, looked at the contents, found he was short a hundred pounds. Damn, Kurt. He couldn't have purchased all that for a measly hundred. The shoes alone were worth that. His traveler cheques and one of his credit cards must be missing. He hadn't time to worry about that now as his energy was running low. Mein Gott, what did I do with my monocle? He tossed his disheveled clothes from last night

By the Pricking of My Thumb

frantically around. Nowhere. He knew it had to be there somewhere, but for now, he'd just get the extra one he always carried and be on his way. He took a last look around. What a mess. Well, let that cow-eyed maid clean it. That's what she gets paid for.

Chapter 31

As Kurt made his way out of the hotel, his thoughts were on von Heusen. He felt that his old major was on the border of a complete mental breakdown, and what had he gotten out of him? A wardrobe full of suits and shoes, hats, coats, and drawers with silk monogrammed shirts and socks and underwear, all to come from the tailor, all on that credit card and two packages of traveler's cheques, which wouldn't last for long. He had developed an unquenchable taste for the good life. Had to get more, lots more. Somehow he had to get that Swiss bank account number and rid himself of this mad dog. So intent was he on his thoughts that he collided with a man who had just come out of a doorway. He looked up and discovered he was standing in front of Lang's antique shop. "Excuse me, sir, clumsy of me I'm afraid. I was deep in thought."

Ed Halley looked up at the well-dressed gentleman. "All right, gov. Can I help you?" Even though Ed had never seen this bloke before, he couldn't mistake the cut of the clothes. The only brass, hard brass, Ed had ever laid out was his custom-cut suit for his wedding day. He'd eat his hat if that wasn't an outfit, jacket and all, from Mr.

Cuttlers, of Cuttlers and Son's of York. One of England's foremost tailors. Cuttler's had only two establishments. One in York and the main one, in London run by the elder Cuttler's son on Saville Row. But there was no doubt this was bought from Cuttler's. He was aware that the gentleman was speaking to him. "Sorry, gov? Lang's closed until further notice. I was just putting a sign on door and lockin' up."

"Nothing serious, I hope." Kurt tried to sound interested with just a hint of concern in his voice. Ed was about to tell him of Miss Lang's murder but for reason he couldn't explain, he didn't like this bloke.

"Nothin' that can't be cleared up in time." And putting on his cap he edged by him and made his way to the van. If Kurt hadn't been so full of himself he would have been aware of the suspicious looks in the eyes of the man walking away from him. He looked at the door of the shop and read: "Closed 'til further notice. All inquiries of sales to be handled by phone or mail." Its numbers meant nothing to him. He squared his shoulders and walked away toward the center of town.

Ed watched him in his mirror and thought, strange bloke, German I'd guess. At least it was the same accent used by that other bloke that was pestering Miss Millacent about the desk. Dressed the same way too, come to think of it. Strange, two well-dressed strangers in town, and both German, and both making inquiries from the shop. Why does that bother me so? He looked down at Sultan lying in his carrying cage. Poor old boy. I know, can't rightly believe she's gone from us either. Still, old fella, you'll be all right. No danger. Dori and I will see to that. But for now you need a vet to look at ye.

As he drove along he was thinking what a grand lass Miss Suzette was. Closest thing he'd had for a daughter and Dori and he had loved her from a wee one who used to follow him around and hang onto his work coat asking all kinds of questions. And last night, when they thought she would be lost to them for good, their hearts were near to breaking. Couldn't stand to lose them both. But Rob, bless him, staying so close. They were right for each other, no doubt. And this morning when Terrence and Inspector Pentecroft came to take her statement, how proud they had all been of her, looking so small and pale, but no more tears, and answering all kinds of questions, and giving good answers too. As he was leaving he remembered her opening her purse to give the inspector a letter and Rob handing over a book that looked like a diary or sommat. Oh well, Dori would fill him in on the blanks he'd be bound over lunch. "Aye, here we are Sultan, let's be having the vet look you over."

Thirty minutes later Vince Tuckwin was saying. "There's no mistake, Ed. Sultan has got the worst of someone's shoe or boots. Pretty vicious I'd wager. No wonder he isn't eating much or acting normal. He has two broken ribs and some pretty deep bruises. You were dead right to bring him 'round. But I'll tell you sommat for sure, he's got his licks into someone, I'll be bound."

"What ever are you on about, veterinary?" Ed said stroking Sultan's head gently.

"Well there's this here blood on his head behind his ear like. See? Feel, just here."

"Flamin' Nora," Ed said as his fingers came in contact with the matted hair. "I didn't reckon to him being cut."

"That's just it," Vince said, "he hasn't been. I've examined him six ways by Christmas and there's nowt wrong behind his ear and no broken skin anywhere. And there's another thing. His claws were all matted with wood particles and skin, and ash, and something from the garden. See here? I've got them here in a bag."

"Well I never," Ed said. "I knew about the wood particles. He got them jumpin' up and hanging onto the shed door and then sliding down. That's where they found Miss Lang and he had been trying to get in, Blimie! You don't suppose Sultan attacked this bloke, do you?"

Vince Tuckwin was silent for a few moments, then walked to the phone and dialed the station house and asked for Inspector Pentecroft. After a brief conversation he replaced the receiver and turned to Ed and said, "The inspector wants samples of the blood and the particles from Sultan's claws. And, he's sending Corporal Simms over for it. I think the best thing is to leave Sultan with me for a couple of days. He has had a nasty shock and does need constant attention and complete rest for his ribs. It's a miracle they didn't puncture his lungs. I'll sedate him for twenty-four hours and we'll see how he responds to treatment. He's a magnificent cat, isn't he?"

"Aye, he's that all right," said Ed, "and he's going to really miss old girl, but then we all shall. Nowt be the same without her." There was a catch in his voice and Vince came around the table and laid a strong arm across the shoulder of the older man and squeezed gently.

"Yes, rum business this. But he'll get his comeuppance. You mark my word, Ed. And I for one can't wait."

Chapter 32

Suzette was making a valiant job of trying to eat the tasty lunch Dori had prepared, but she could hardly get it past the lump in her throat, and the tears weren't far from her eyes. Rob reached across and took her hand and squeezed it gently.

"You were bloody marvelous today, my love, I was so proud of you the way you came straight to the point about this bloke. I really think that it was a stroke of genius, you remembering that letter."

She looked back, her eyes shining with tears. "What would I do without your strength and love? And Ed and Dori, aren't they darlings?" The tears were spilling now. "They have lost such a big part of their lives and yet here they are, clucking over me. I love you all so much."

"Go ahead, my darling, don't hold back. They say tears wash the soul clean."

She rose slowly from the table; her trembling hands went to her face. "Rob, where do they all come from? I didn't think I could shed one more tear." He had her in his arms. Her head was buried in his chest and he was stroking her hair.

By the Pricking of My Thumb

"It will be all right my love. You have suffered a great shock and a loss of one of the dearest souls we should ever hope to know. We all loved her. And, I'll make you a promise, Suzette, darling. I'll move heaven and earth to find the bastard, and no one will ever hurt you again as long as I have breath."

She raised her tear-stained face to his and said, "I love you, and I'll always love you. I know you'll see this through, and I promise I'm going to try to be strong like the three of you. My being soppy is a drag and from now on I'm going to be all right." And she smiled for the first time since they arrived and Rob gave a silent 'thank you' to the powers that be. She took his hand and said, "Let's go and look at that smashing desk and see what we can find in it."

As they made their way into the room, the sun was streaming in the bay windows and the rays were dancing off the delicate pieces of the inlaid wood. They stood there with their arms around each other staring at it, both were taken aback by its beauty. "Oh, Rob, it is a superb piece of workmanship. No wonder she loved it so. How old do you think it is?"

He ran his hand over it, as a lover would caress his love. "It is a real find. Not English. Our craftsmen are good, excellent, rank high among many, but this is a remarkable find. Can't put a date on it just yet. I have seen work like this once before and I believe it was made in Poland. Somewhere in a drawer or under one, somewhere, we will find the signature of the craftsman."

You think so, Rob? Let's start looking and maybe find something we can give the inspector that will help. I looked through her drawers and table upstairs for those old clippings. And Dori hasn't seen anything, and knows nothing about them."

"Well, my love, maybe we will find them somewhere in this old beauty. Let's start looking."

By the Pricking of My Thumb

Chapter 33

Von Heusen had been riding around York looking for a small out-of-the-way surgery that would be too busy to take notice of him. But he couldn't find one. His hands were clammy and he was slightly nauseous again. Have to find something soon. He couldn't stand the pain much longer. He could feel the sweat running down over his ribs. He pulled into a lay by and laid his head on the steering wheel. He was shaky and light headed. Ja, stay here for a few moments and it will pass.

He became aware of a gentle nudging on his shoulder. He raised his head and tried to focus his eyes but it was a blur of white and blue. "Are you not well, sir? I've been trying to rouse you for the past five minutes. No, don't move. I can see you're not in a fit state to walk, let alone drive." Heindrich started to speak in rapid German. "Their, there, sir. There will be someone here in a few moments. Don't you speak any English?"

Heindrich's vision returned, if not in focus, enough to horrify him. The blue and white turned into a round faced English bobby. Oh mein Got, what's the matter with me? The police. The last thing he wanted to do was to draw attention to himself, and here he was with a concerned policeman and a smattering of bystanders all gawking like he was some kind of prize bull muttering to himself. He tried to move, but he seemed to have no strength and his shirt and his pants were sticking to him. He was shaking like a leaf on a tree in late autumn. He could hear the sirens off in the distance. He pushed his way out of the car intending to explain and make his escape from this maddening mess. Instead he crumpled into a heap like a bag someone had let all the air out of.

"Blimie!" said the burly policeman just as the St. John's ambulance pulled into the curb.

Chapter 34

Kurt pushed open the door of the "Hooded Monk," his old pub when he was playing the fool. His heart was pounding as he wondered if anyone would recognize the new Kurt. It wasn't anything like he expected. The men who used to rub elbows with him wouldn't even talk to him and the gentlemen who wouldn't have even looked at him before were the only ones who would talk to him, and they were asking him all sorts of questions. What kind of work he was in, how long he would be in St. Gilliam's. He didn't know how to approach the subject of the murder. The locals would be the ones that would be the closest to her. These gents, though they would know her, would be far removed from her and their wives would be the clucking tongues.

Mein Gott, he would have to get away from here. Too many people to remember him, and the Major wouldn't like that. He would get the paper. There should be a big piece in it. Silly old bag of bones. He could still feel her in his arms. Like a feather she was, her bones all sharp angles. He gave a shudder and he gave his jacket a quick brush down the front as if to remove the memory of her pressure, downed his drink with one gulp and excused himself, glad to be out in the air and looking for a newsagent for the paper. Better get ahold of himself and do some thinking before the major got back. He'd want more answers than what he had to give him.

Chapter 35

"Look, love, its not very likely Dori would know about the clippings. She would never go into Auntie's desk and unless they were lying around she wouldn't have a clue. And, knowing Aunt Millacent, she wouldn't say anything until she was dead sure."

"Of course your right, darling," Suzette said, looking at a few folded sheets and looking through them. Anyway, all this would have to be sorted out anyway.

"'Allo, 'allo, 'allo? Who's the clever boy then?" said Rob, dangling the old faded yellow paper clippings in his fingers. I think we have something here." And that's the way Dori found them, heads together over the desk, so intent they didn't hear her until she spoke.

"Inspector Pentecroft to see you loves." They both jumped like startled children caught nicking from the cookie jar late on a Sunday tea. "Oh, I say. I'm that sorry I startled you loves."

"Oh that's all right, Dori. We were just reading these old clippings Auntie had in her desk. The ones I asked you about this morning."

"Oh, yes. Glad you found them ducks."

Chapter 36

"Sorry, Inspector," Rob said to the man who was cooling his heels, hat in hand, "but we thought along with the diaries this would add credibility to the story." He handed the faded, tattered clippings to the inspector.

"Thank you," Pentecroft said and looked down at a picture of a man in a Nazi uniform with armbands and sculls on his lapel and an iron cross at his throat. Faded as it was, he could see the cold eyes, the curled mouth. In his left hand he held a monocle half way to his eye. "Yes, this is very interesting. We will run this information and pictures through the computer and Interpol. Even though this picture is faded, faces like this don't change much more through the years. Just get harder and more defined. If he is in this country, or anywhere, we will soon know.

"And there is something else, those particles under Sultan's claws proved to be human skin. And, since Sultan doesn't prowl at night and none of you have claw marks, he's had a go at someone. And, judging from the amount of it, it is pretty deep. And the blood and the skin particles will help also to identify his attacker. The blood on his fur matched your Aunt's. We're keeping our eyes open and our minds. And another piece of good work done by young Constable Simms, are the things he found from the floor of the shed. We've identified all of them except for the odd shaped piece of glass. The pins matched the pins that came from her hair and they're less than a month old. And the button was torn from the back of her dress. We have made a fine start in the short time that we've had and the boys from London arrive tomorrow. And, by heck, I would have liked to have had a lot more to hand over to them. However, the diaries and the clippings and the things that we've recovered from the shed make a good start. And Dr. Dundee will have the inquest when they arrive. We'll ring and give you the time. Just wanted to put you in the picture. Thanks again, and we'll be in touch."

The three of them stood there and watched him leave, not knowing whether to be happy or sad at the quick turn of events. Dori suddenly put her hands to her flushed face. "Oh I say, whatever will he think of me letting him go to the door by himself? I'm that mixed up with all the goings on, I never even offered a cuppa."

V.E. Sullivan

Rob put is arm around her shoulder and laughed, "Don't you worry, flower, he'll be back and you can make him one of your famous seed cakes. But speaking of a cuppa. How about it, my lovelies. I couldn't half murder one, I'm that parched." And, arms about their waists, ushered them to the kitchen.

Chapter 37

Kurt Schreiler stopped by the newsagent's to pick up the latest edition of the paper and there it was splashed all across the front page of the tiny village news "Lifelong resident of St. Gilliam found murdered." There were long articles about her life, the shop, and her work for the guild of women at the local church, her long hours of volunteer work on Well's day jumbles. It was endless. And down at the bottom of the page, Kurt's eye caught the piece about the inquest and the big boys being brought in from New Scotland Yard CID. For once Kurt smiled. He was mixed up in it helping to destroy evidence and helping to move the body, but he hadn't done the actual killing. For the first time there was no blood on his hands.

Well, no use putting it off. He'd have to go back and face the Major with what was in the paper and what the old gaffer had said to him at the shop. That's all he had found out. Oh, people were talking about it; everyone was, but only to themselves, and not outsiders. Village life was like that, and these strong, hard working Yorkshire men and women didn't take much to strangers asking questions. It took awhile to win their trust, and Kurt didn't plan to stay that long in

Yorkshire or England. Get all he could get and maybe find the numbers of Heindrich's Swiss account, at least one of them and be off some night before he knew what hit him. Serves the old butcher right, the way he used his rank and power during the war and after. Holding crimes over the heads of his men even though at the time the crimes were committed they were in uniform. Ach, so many bloody crimes one loses touch. But not the faces, the same faces still haunted his dreams at night.

He found he was approaching the doorman of the hotel. He nodded his head and walked up to the desk for his keys. "Has Major... or Mr. von Heusen returned yet? And, are their any messages?" The pretty blond behind the desk flirted with him with her eyes and the swinging of her hips. And the sweater was about one size too small for her full young breasts.

"Here's your keys, Mr. Schreiler, sir," as she looked up at him through thick lashes and let her hand linger a second or two too long on his as she passed the keys. I'm afraid Mr. von Heusen is still out and there are no messages. If there is anything else I can do for you..." letting her soft voice trail off.

Kurt chuckled to himself thinking; two days ago she wouldn't have given me a second look. He smiled and leaned over the desk and grabbed her hand "Maybe later Schotzie."

She giggled, "What ever does that mean?"

"It means 'sweetheart'."

"Oh, I say. You are a caution. But, I get off duty at eleven-thirty and maybe if you're still around we could have a drink somewhere."

He winked at her and made his way into the lounge. It still hadn't quite sunk in what a difference his clothes made and the way he carried himself. Everyone bent over backwards to wait on him. He found a place at the end of the bar where he could see the desk and watch for Heindrich and also catch the girl at the desk in action. Not a bad bit of tart there, maybe I'll get a chance when I get through with the Major. She was anxious enough she'd hang around for him. He'd have to be careful because Heindrich didn't want anyone getting that close to leave a real good description of him. Their faces, of course, were seen everyday, but just fleeting. He must watch what he drinks. He had quite a few already. You know what they say, "loose lips sink ships," and he started to laugh.

The lounge closed, and still, no sign of Heindrich, but he had said he would be back by teatime. Where in the hell is he? He made for the lift, wondering as he did so, if Heindrich had run out on him leaving him to face everything. Wild thoughts ran through his head and mind and he began to sweat. Mein Got, the money he had left would hardly cover the bills, let alone what he owed Cuttlers and if he had to get out, how would he get his bags and new clothes past the desk, and he wasn't going to leave everything behind. Nein, nein, he had been through too much. He had this coming to him. Life owed him this. Waiting his chance and playing the fool all those years and now it was almost in his grasp. To lose now was unthinkable. He walked to the portable bar that was set up in the front room of his suite identical to Heindrich's with all the amenities. A separate bedroom and big bathroom, valet service and all. He poured a snifter half full of cognac and downed half of it in one gulp. With the snifter in one hand he reached for the phone and called Heindrich's room again. Still no answer.

He had to relax. He knew he was drinking too much but he didn't know what else to do. Suddenly, with an unsteady hand, he reached for the phone again and with the other dialed, the desk just in time to hear Peggy speaking. "Can I help you?"

"Ja, Schotzie, it's me, remember?"

"Oh yes. I thought you had forgotten me."

"No, I'll be right down." And slamming down the receiver and taking another swig from the bottle, made for the door.

Chapter 38

Ed parked the van and made his way into the vet's. As he waited, he couldn't believe how fast the time went. His thoughts were interrupted by Vince's voice, "Well Ed, are you ready to take Sultan home?"

"I am that and all," Ed said. "Cottage didn't seem right without him. We missed him and all."

"Yes. Know what you mean. We will miss him too, when he goes home. He is the biggest cat of his breed I've handled. He is such a love. What a personality. He seems to understand every word we said."

"He does that and all. I know," Ed said.

Vince Tuckwin was stroking Sultan's head. "I can see with his massive body and short sturdy legs, he would be capable of much damage. The person he attacked will be well marked. With all he had under his claws, ash from the fireplace, fertilizer from the garden, and some animal particles, small animals, shrew or field mice I suspect. If he doesn't keep it clean and tended to, he will be sick with a bad infection that will spread. Staph is deadly left on its own."

Ed thanked him and was off.

Chapter 39

Ed came through the kitchen door with Sultan in his arms. "Well what's all this?" Ed said looking at the three of them. "Aye, a man cannot leave his lass for an hour before some big shot bloke from big city tries to nick his best girl."

Dori flushed very attractively and said, "You great, daft sausage. You're that big a twit sometimes." But the verbal abuse in her voice was coated with much loving tenderness.

"And would you look at him and all." They were all over Sultan who was so used to the extra attention by now he looked like the proverbial cat with a saucer of cream and he was singing so loudly his appreciation they couldn't help but giggle. He looked so proud of himself, and right he should be and all. For he had marked their killer and played a big part in the way that they might pick him out.

Chapter 40

Heindrich fought to bring himself from the dark pit of murmuring voices into the shining light about him. The first thing he became aware of was the searing pain in the side of his face, as if he was being branded. The next from, still a ways off, the voices. "I think our friend is coming around at last. Mr. von Heusen? Can you hear me? Mr. von Heusen?" Heindrich opened his eyes to the blinding light and fought to sit up. "There, there, lay still Mr. von Heusen, we're almost finished here. I'm Dr. Fleetwood and you are in St. Peter and Paul's Hospital in York. You have a rather nasty staph infection and we have cleaned out the wounds and closed them up again. And we have given you some shots. Oh, nothing much. Just some antibiotics."

They eased him up into a sitting position. His head was reeling. He felt he was going to be sick. They had anticipated this for the sister was standing at the ready. "There now, sir," in her business like manner. You'll feel much better," and placing a cold clothe on his forehead, marched out and left him there.

He did indeed feel better, and if only they could give him something for the pain. If he could only think. Gott in Himmel. He had made a mess of things. They knew his name, his name. For the first time Heindrich noticed his clothes were missing and he was wearing a short hospital gown. Dumkopf. Schwein of a cat. This was all his doing. Everything had been going so well until two days ago. That fateful night at that old cow's house. And to add to it the complete change in Kurt from imbecile to cunning enemy, no longer to be trusted or left on his own for too long. Mein Gott. How did it all happen? He had escaped from the prison in West Berlin, faked his death, and was able to travel around Europe amassing his stolen treasures and selling them off and accumulating a fortune in Swiss banks, three to be exact. Some transferred already to Rio. He had even been able to pay off Jason Lang and that French bitch without it being thought of as anything but an accident, and then finally the last hurdle. He had found the desk. At least he was pretty sure it was the same one. Having to kill the old bag of bones didn't bother him. It was Kurt and that cat that had brought him to this.

He felt sick again. His head and his face were about to explode. He felt drained of all energy. Worse than a newborn kitten. Where in Gott's name were his clothes? His wallet? Mein Gott, where was the

By the Pricking of My Thumb

car he rented. The rented car, all he seemed to remember was trying to get away from the bobby and nothing else until he woke up here. What did he say? Think, you stupid dummkopf, ja, a staph infection, shots, antibiotic and cleaning the wound. He put his hand gingerly to his face. It came in contact with a large plaster covering his face from just below his eye to his jawbone. He had to get out of there and call Kurt to come for him.

Just as he was trying to raise himself Dr. Fleetwood came around the curtain that closed him in. "There, there, Mr. von Heusen. We have a nice bed waiting for you."

"But I'm not staying. I must get back."

"That's nonsense, man. You're still under medication and you wouldn't get across the floor without collapsing. There's a good fellow. Here comes the sister with the trolley. We'll talk about it in the morning. But for now it's bed for you. And when you're settled, sister will give you something for pain and you will sleep 'til morning. You may not think so, but never fear, you will," and they were wheeling him out.

He realized the doctor was right. He could hardly lift his arm. "One moment, doctor, just a couple questions. Where is my car? And may I make a phone call to my hotel?"

"Yes of course you can, old man. Your car is safe in the lot and if you're able the sister will assist you to get your number when you're settled."

Sister had his things in a large manila envelope and he found the number of the hotel and asked for Mr. Schreiler's room. The connection made, the phone rang and just kept ringing. He swore in German and weakly handed the phone to sister. She set the receiver in the cradle and wiped the sweat from his forehead and taking a hypodermic syringe from the tray, rolled back his sleeve gave him an injection in the vein in his arm. And, drawing the covers up to his chin quietly left the room. Heindrich slipped into semi-unconsciousness with the face of Kurt laughing before him.

Chapter 41

Sergeant Littlejohn watched Inspector Pentecroft pace the platform of the York railroad station waiting for the arrival of the morning train from London, which would bring the brass from New Scotland Yard. The sergeant was a veteran in the force and had quite a few years on Pentecroft. He was a huge man who put the fear of God into the lads at the station house, but they all knew that they could go to him if they had a problem. Soft as butter inside he was. As he watched his inspector he thought, too bad the lad couldn't have cracked it before CID boys arrived. But, still in all, he had done force a credit. Had first-rate station house running tightly and a good head start. They hadn't been sitting on their hands, he'd be bound. Too bad he had never been driven to be anything but a good sergeant in his own patch. He smiled in thinking I'm like my old dad: he was a credit to the force also, and he felt he would have been proud of him and all.

The sound of the diesel brought him back from his wool gathering to see the train slowly pulling in and his inspector straightening his shoulders as well as his tie. Well here we go, and he wondered if they would all hit it off. Chance would be a fine thing. But he would back Ronald Pentecroft all the way and the devil with the rest of them.

"Well, Sergeant, here they come. Would you credit it, London brass from top to bottom. Well let's get on with it. Look sharp now. Ah, there, they've spotted us." Striding towards them were two men, one tall and long legged with a solid build, no fat, just muscle. The second was shorter and about his own build. Both clean-shaven and well turned out. "Bloody hell. He wished he'd had his trench coat cleaned. He felt like looked like he'd slept in it for days. And, it wasn't far from the truth. He was short on kip all right. They were face to face now. The tall man had extended his hand and a smile broke across his handsome features.

"Inspector Pentecroft? I'm chief inspector Ashley Quest and this is my second Peter Rennie," who had to juggle his bag of tricks and his case before they could shake hands.

"Right, sir. This is my Sergeant Littlejohn. If you'll come this way we have a car and we'll drop you at the hotel in St. Gilliams so you can freshen up. Have you had breakfast?"

"Not as you'd notice. British rail, stale bun and tea. Do you have something in mind?"

"Well," said Pentecroft, "we could all eat at the Hotel Grand and go over things as they stand."

"Right then, let's be off, shall we?" Quest and Pentecroft set off leaving Littlejohn and Rennie to pick up the gear.

Driving the M-1, things settled into routine. Sitting at an angle, his back in a corner of the car, Quest reached into his breast pocket and brought out a gold cigarette case and opened it, offering them to Pentecroft. After they had lit up he said, "From all I hear, you have made a capital start on the case and you run a tight station house. I know how you must feel, the London boys charging in on your patch, but I'm sure we can work well together. A man in my position has a quick insight on his mates, and who will get on and who is going to rub you up the backside. I think we'll get on."

Pentecroft had been studying him through a thick haze of smoke and thought, I like him. Older than me, this bloke, his hair was turning silver at the temple. "Well sir, I think you're right."

V.E. Sullivan

Littlejohn had one eye on the road and the other focused on the rear view mirror on the two men in the back seat. Rennie saw the tension leave Littlejohn's big body and a smile spread across his broad face. Littlejohn looked at Rennie sitting beside him and Rennie winked. Well would you credit it, this might be a right old cracker after all.

Chapter 42

Kurt was coming up from some dark recess of his subconscious and a bell was ringing. It hurt his head. He tried to shut it out but it was getting louder and louder. He finally opened his eyes. Gott, he couldn't focus them and his head was like a cannon ball, thick and heavy, and that ringing, it came to him: it was the phone. Mein Gott, it was the phone. He picked up the phone expecting to hear von Heusen's voice. Instead it was a man's voice he didn't recognize. "Ja, yes, this is Mr. Schreiler. What? What's that you're saying? When? Oh my Got. Can you hold 'til I get a pencil?" After what seemed an eternity, he returned and picked up the instrument. "Thank you. Ja, ja, I've got it, thanks."

Returning the receiver to its instrument he quickly picked it up again and punched the button for the desk. "Could you send me up my breakfast? Yes, the usual." He hung up the phone and fell back on the bed, his hands to his head as if to hold back the pain. So that's what's happened to Heindrich. All this time. Well, thank Gott for that. He still had time to get at least some of the Swiss account numbers off him. Maybe he could go through his room baggage and all and pick up some more money. Last night had cost him all his readies and the rest he had charged.

He had a feeling he had talked too much last night. She had asked so many questions and drink was always his demise. Even though he had promised not to drink any more after he left the lounge, she had been worth it. She had matched his appetite for more than food. He laughed out loud. He would have to see her later, much later and find out how much she knew. Maybe, buy her a little trinket on Heindrich. Ja, life was going his way at last. But, time was running out on him like sands in an hourglass.

He quickly toweled himself dry. He was worried about Heindrich's stability. These terrible rages were coming on all too frequently since he had murdered the old lady and the next time may be his last, and the moment would have passed him by. He knew what the Major was capable of. His cruelty was second to none. He had seen it all too often. Ja, the Jackal. The name fits him. In the old days, he stank of blood and death, and a shudder ran through him as he was stuffing a cream colored cravat into his silk shirt. A knock on the door made him jump. He swore under his breath, and said, "Enter." It was room service with his breakfast. He signed, adding a generous tip. Why not? Heindrich was picking up the bills. Even if he didn't realize how many.

He laughed to himself and pulled up a chair when his eyes caught sight of a small, white envelope with the neat small handwriting, "Mr. K. Schreiler." He picked it up and turned it over. Sealed, he ripped it open and read the same neat writing, "Kurt, darling, last night was smashing. I remember everything you said. You're a smooth one; a caution, with such thoughts and plans. See you tonight after I get off." It was signed "Peggy."

He let the note drop and thought, What in hell did I say to her?, but nothing came back. He had to move fast if he wanted to finish his breakfast and get the train to York and recover the Major. Gott only knows what he's been blabbing about. Especially if they have given him anything.

Wiping his chin he threw down his serviette and grabbed the leather jacket, slammed his door, and ran down the stairs and out the front of the Grand just in time to see a taxi that had pulled up into the space behind a dark car. It had just dropped off two men and was gliding away from the parking area. He raised his hand to the cabby and the next moment he was off.

Chapter 43

They had been sitting in the old fashioned canvas backed chairs placed very close together, hand in hand, basking in the sunshine since lunch. Neither had spoken a word for several minutes, both lost in their own thoughts. Suzette turned her head and studied Robert's profile. He had been her salvation. He'd never left her side. He'd given all his strength and love to her. He looked like he was sleeping. His chest was moving like the tide, washing in and out. God knows he needed sleep. The dark shadows showing under his eyes were proof of that. Tears stinging her eyes, she thought Darling, you'll never know how much I love you, what you have given to me. My life now more than ever has purpose, and strength and more sense to living. My world would be meaningless without you. Please God, protect my love. My heart and mind would never heal if anything should happen to him.

Dori and Ed were her surrogate parents, and her love for them ran deep. She knew that they would always stand beside her. Oh my God, had it only been three days since this nightmare started and still so far to go. The inquest, then Auntie M. could be laid to rest. But thanks to Dori and the ladies guild they were taking care of all that. Then to find this mad thing that had struck her down, and for what? The desk? Suzette was sure they were missing something very important there. But what? Such a beautiful piece of workmanship. And just as Rob had thought, he'd found a signature under the middle drawer. In the desk in an inconspicuous corner lightly burned in bold script: "Josef Solomunovich." That was no surprise because Rob knew the workman was Polish. But what was a surprise was what was written in an odd shade of red under his name: "Polish Jew." Strange! Was it put there as a way of identification? Surely there couldn't be another, not to equal this desk? For it was not put there by Josef. His name was burned into the wood and this was not written in the bold script of Solomunovich. They were still trying to figure that one out. But that was the only clue the beautiful old desk had yielded to them.

She watched as Dori hurried up towards them, wiping her hands on a large white pinnie. Dori signaled her by raising her free hand,

and Suzette put her fingers to her lips. No need to wake Rob unless it was necessary, and she was about to find out.

Oh my ducks, it is good to see the lad having a rest, thought Dori. She whispered, "Inspector Pentecroft called and will be around at teatime with Chief Inspector Quest from Scotland Yard."

"Thanks, Dori, we'll let Rob sleep a bit, there's plenty of time."

"Aye, love, you stay here and try to sleep yourself. There's nowt to do any road. The rest would do you a world of good."

Suzette smiled and nodded in agreement. Dori bent and kissed the top of her shining head.

Chapter 44

The taxi pulled up in front of St. Peter and Paul's Hospital. The cabby slid the glass portion back and said, "Here you are, mate."

"Ja, thanks." Kurt got out of the taxi and shoved some pound notes into the cabby's hand.

"Want me to wait, squire?"

"No, no thanks. Don't know how long I'll be."

"You've got some change, gov."

"Keep it."

"Ta, thanks mate." And he watched the receding back take the steps to the hospital two at a time. Coo Blimie. I bet this is his first baby. No wonder he said not to wait, the cabby thought as he pulled away.

Kurt pushed open the door and walked to the huge desk and asked the very efficient and starched sister where to find Heindrich von Heusen. She directed him to the room. He thanked her and hurried away towards it.

Rapping lightly on the door, he waited and was surprised to have it opened by another sister. "Ja, I'm Mr. Schreiler. I came for..."

"Oh, yes, Dr. Fleetwood will be finished with him in a few minutes. Won't you come in? I know he is anxious to see you."

I bet he is, thought Kurt.

"Oh there you are, at last. Where in the devil have you been?"

"He is a bit testy," said the sister with a condescending smile. The look from Heindrich would have frozen any man, let alone a woman. But, Sisters were a breed unto their own, and no doubt she had dealt with others just like him.

"Well, Major, I had to be notified of your whereabouts, then, as you had the car, I had to catch a train and then a cab. But I haven't made too bad time have I?"

There he goes again, making me a fool. thought von Heusen. I'll wipe that damn smirk off your face. Ja, you schwein-hund, your turn is fast coming, so enjoy your time in the limelight.

Not bothering to answer Kurt, he said, "Doctor, is it absolutely necessary to wear this heavy plaster? It pulls on my face and adds to the pain."

"Well, Mr. von Heusen, as I told you, you already have a very bad staph infection and we wouldn't want anything to get at you and add

By the Pricking of My Thumb

to what you already have, do we?" Another scathing look. "It is all here in the report I made for your doctor in London. Funny, thought I knew all the lads in private practice in Kensington Square. However, so many young chaps coming on the scene, it is hard to keep up. Well, there we go, you have your pills. And remember your doctor must see you again tomorrow. If not, I cannot be responsible for the outcome of what else it might lead to." And before Heindrich could answer him he turned to Kurt, "You will see he takes these, Mr. Schreiler, every four hours and he will run a fever. It is normal with the infection in advanced stages and he is still weak. I would prefer he stay another day but he insists he has pressing business in London."

Heindrich's look was pure hatred. They were acting like he wasn't even there, and, what was worse, like he was a child who couldn't take care of himself. He had squashed hundreds, yes hundreds, just like them before. And, mein Gott, if he didn't get out of here he'd lose all self-control and likely to give the whole show away. His mind was far from clear and he felt like he was floating down. He was all clammy again and needed air. The smell of the disinfectant was overpowering and it brought back smells and pictures of camps where so many things had gone on. Stop! Stop! His inner voice was screaming, and get out of here!

"Kurt," he half shouted. Kurt started, and almost snapped to attention for a second. That same terror filled him, but not for long. He had never held the winning hand before but he did now. He turned slowly and looked at Heindrich.

"Yes, what is it?"

"Find the car. I'm anxious to be off. There is much to do."

Kurt grinned and nodded to the doctor and the sister, "Yes, quite testy," and made his escape before Heindrich could say anything. He walked toward the front desk and saw the porter talking to the same sister. He asked and was directed to the back lot were the cars were held and kept for patients who were there longer than just emergency care. Kurt walked towards the big black Daimler not knowing what to expect. He walked around it: no scrapes, no broken headlights, and no dents. But why did Heindrich come to so public a place for treatment unless he was worse off in mind than Kurt thought? Got to make my move fast before all is lost. Better not keep him waiting. Maybe he will give a logical explanation of his movements the last 24 hours.

By the Pricking of My Thumb

But then, he will put the screws to me. Oh well. Better humor him for the time being.

He pulled the Daimler up to the hospital entrance just as they were wheeling von Heusen out. And by the look on his face, his disposition hadn't changed any. After he was settled Sister gave him the manila envelope containing his possessions, and the doctor's report for his fictitious London physician.

He pulled slowly away. As soon as they had cleared the hospital grounds, Heindrich reached up and tore the plaster from the side of his face. Looking out the corner of his eye Kurt saw large beads of sweat standing out on Heindrich's forehead. He could only see the good side of his face and the monocle winked in the sunlight. Kurt drew a deep breath and cleared his throat. "In light of what Dr. Fleetwood said, mein Major, do you think it was wise to remove that plaster?"

Heindrich's nerves were at a raw stage, what with the pain in his face and his forced stay in the hospital, and Kurt's strutting and presuming ways. He snapped. He turned around to face Kurt. He spat out the words. "Don't be more stupid than you already are. I might as well wear a sign around my neck saying 'I'm Heindrich von Heusen, war criminal at large.'" And with a string of oaths, he continued his ranting and raving about why he put up with him and his stupidity until Kurt wished he hadn't said anything at all. He knew it was only the beginning. He'd start on where he was last night and then what he'd found out and how little information he had for him and the old girl's murder. He almost wished he'd stayed in Germany. Then he caught the scent of aftershave and knew he had made the right choice.

He'd shut Heindrich's incessant talking out of his thoughts when he was suddenly and unexpectedly brought back to the here and now with a sharp blow to his shoulder and Heindrich shouting, "Well, what about it?" and Kurt hadn't any answer for him because he hadn't a clue as to what he was talking about. Well, in for a penny in for a pound.

He turned his lips down tight, making a white circle around his mouth, "For God's sake, about what? And don't ever strike me like that again." He still could feel the blow through his jacket.

Heindrich's eyes were blazing and he had the look of a wild, untamed creature cornered and ready to spring. He could hardly speak; he was shaking with hatred and rage. He spat dapples of frothy saliva.

"You dirty little bastard, you pay attention to me when I am speaking to you. And you will drop all these arrogant ways. You are still a sow's ear no matter how much silk you wear."

Kurt couldn't speak for a second. Heindrich's face was a mess, quite swollen. And because the nature of the clawing it had been difficult to stitch evenly so a thick welt zig-zagged from the corner of his eye to just below the corner of his lower lip towards the jaw, pulling his mouth down and to one side, and his eye up at the corner. The monocle in his right eye made it look twice the size. No one would forget that face, he thought. You might as well wear a sign for it was lost now. How can we ever go around unheeded? He must get what he could and clear out and leave this mess to Heindrich.

The blaring of a car horn brought his eyes back to the road just in time to swerve onto the verge and miss an oncoming car by inches. He was shaking all over.

"You stupid fool! Are you trying to kill us? Get out. Get out of this car and let me drive." Kurt opened the car door and walked a little unsteadily around to the passenger's seat. Heindrich was dabbing at his face. He must have hit the visor as a few drops of blood were oozing from his face and it must have hurt like hell. He was quiet and sickly white looking and drawn, as much from fear as from pain.

"Where is that flask I told you to bring?" Kurt opened the glove compartment and brought out the delicate silver flask in its shiny case and handed it to Heindrich.

"Where are those damned pain killers?" Kurt was going to say he didn't think he should mix the two, but one look at Heindrich he changed his mind and drew the white envelope from his pocket and handed one to Heindrich who tossed it backward with about an ounce of brandy from the cup that made the lid on the flask. And to Kurt's surprise he handed him one also. He felt the fine brandy burn its way down and in a few minutes he was over the disaster and they drove off, each concentrating on the other's demise.

Chapter 45

Chief Superintendent Quest was standing in front of the fireplace looking at them over the rim of his teacup. "This is truly a lovely cottage. I've always hankered after a place like this, maybe to retire to. Some place quite away from the smells and hustle and bustle of London. Yes, truly beautiful, this."

They were seated around the room. Some, family mostly, were seated along with Sergeant Littlejohn, his pad and pencil at the ready. Quest setting his cup down on the table, walked leisurely around the room examining the beautiful little collection of miniatures that always nestled together on the delicate Queen Anne table to the exquisite set of fish plates that lined the shelves of the Welsh cabinet, so real in scale that one expected them to flip flop off the plates. He continued his inspection. All eyes were on him. They sat quietly, Rob and Suzette hand in hand. Ed behind Dori's chair, his hand lay gently on her shoulder. Pentecroft and Rennie were standing a little apart on the far side of the room. Littlejohn in one of the high wing back chairs, the only thing that looked like it would take his bulk, his pad resting on his knee.

Rob leaned into Suzette and whispered, "Why do I expect to find Mr. Mustard in the study with a knife?" She put her hand to her mouth to stifle a giggle. But in a way it was just like playing Clue.

He was at the desk and finally the silence was broken. "I know this has been a great tragedy for you Miss Lang, for all of you who loved her. She must have been a great lady, and a gifted one by the looks of this room so rich in colour and collectibles. Must get to the shop before I return to London, but that's beside the point. This being Saturday, there is little we can do 'til Monday. Then we will get the inquest over as quickly as possible. I gather all the arrangements have been made." Suzette nodded, all merriment gone from her lovely face and replaced by a grave look of concern and uncertainty.

Quest looked at her and pangs of guilt sprang up in him. It always did in cases like this. No real solid ground, a lot of good information, clues, and a hell of a lot of work had to be done still. But that bastard could be anywhere for that matter.

"Inspector Quest, sir?" Rob said.

"I was going to say it wouldn't be necessary for Miss Lang or yourself to attend the inquest unless you so wish it. No, only those

By the Pricking of My Thumb

with something to tell like Mrs. Halley and her husband, as it was Mrs. Halley who found the body. I know all this is extremely trying and we will try and be a brief as possible and the questions asked will be straightforward. And I believe you know Dr. Dundee personally."

"Aye, we do and all," said Ed.

"Well then, I will only keep you a little longer. There are some things I want to get clear in my mind."

Dori rose from her chair to bring in a fresh pot of tea and her seed cake would be ready and all. "So, if you will excuse me, Inspector."

"Of course, Mrs. Halley. It will be greatly appreciated." He watched her leave the room and turned and smiled at Ed. "I believe you to be a very lucky man, if all reports I hear from my companions are true, and I have no reason to doubt them, I look forward to that seed cake."

"I am that and all," said Ed, pushing out his chest with pride as he always did when anyone complimented him on his Dori.

"Well then, let's get these unpleasantries over with so we can enjoy our delicacies later. Now, according to Inspector Pentecroft, you and Miss Lang believe this senseless murder took place over this desk." They both nodded. "Also you gave the Inspector a diary and a letter from your aunt and some clippings."

"Yes, that's correct," said Suzette.

"Well, I have just scanned the diary but will read it completely tonight. The clippings have been sent through our computers and we are onto Interpol and waiting for replies, which we hope, will be here by tomorrow. Are we moving too fast for you Sergeant?"

"No sir."

"Good man. Carry on then. Miss Lang, you said in your statement that your aunt had been writing asking you and Mr. Nevil to come and to bring your father's diary and that she was excited over her latest find and that an irate gentleman was after it and that she was determined to keep it. Am I right so far?"

"Spot on," Rob said.

"Good, we'll carry on, shall we? I also judge that as this is the only new possession that Miss Lang had, and Mr. and Mrs. Halley agree that there was a man upsetting your aunt about wishing to purchase it, that I am also inclined to agree with you. Mr. Nevil, I am not an expert at the antique business but I believe this desk was worth getting excited about. It is indeed beautiful. Can you tell me anything about it?"

Robert got up and walked to the desk. His face took on a totally new look, eyes dancing and an excitement about him that was quite infectious. They all moved in closer; that is, all but Littlejohn. He had to remain seated for he needed his massive knee to write on. All eyes were on Rob.

"Well for openers, it was lovingly created by a Polish Jew at the height of the Nazi invasion." All eyebrows went up, with the exception of Suzette's, and her eyes were shining with love and pride in Rob. Besides, she had been with him when he made the discovery.

"Before you say anything," Rob said, "I have something to show you. I think you will find this interesting." He pulled out the drawer and carefully turned it over for everyone to see, it was Josef Solomunovich's signature and the strange signature of "a Jew" under it.

"Pentecroft, what do you make of this?" Quest said.

Pentecroft got down on one knee to get a closer look and was thinking, silently, Here you go, Bucko, don't put your foot into it for all to see. But he said, "Well, I don't think the signatures are written by the same person, and 'Jew' is in a strange colour."

"I agree with you mate, let's get some scrapings. Rennie, unless I miss my guess, this is not ink, or even paint."

Rennie got out a small plastic bag and a scalpel type knife and he began to carefully scrape some of the colour off. "Do you think it is worth dusting?"

"I doubt it, Rennie. You would probably only find Mr. Nevil's superimposed prints over many others. But then, you might try some of the more unlikely spots where it has been handled much less. We might just get something to run through our computers and it just might spit out something most interesting. Sometimes we overlook things, and we might have overlooked something here. Incidentally, what do you think, Pentecroft?"

"Well, it is a certainty that we won't find anything on surface or sides, the way Dori keeps it polished. But I agree the undersides are our only chance and who knows where it has been and how many hands it has passed through since it has been finished."

"Right then, shall we leave our men here to finish off. I would like to go over and see Dr. Dundee before the inquest. We can go together, eh Pentecroft? And your Sergeant can bring Rennie back with him to the station house."

"Right sir, I'll just go and have a quick word with Sergeant Littlejohn and we'll say our good-byes to the family on the way out."

Quest turned to take another look. It was indeed a lovely old cottage. One he'd give his right arm to come home to, in the evenings, years down the road yet. Even as far away as retirement and he knew it.

Chapter 46

Heindrich paced up and down the length of his carpet stopping periodically to look at his face in the mirror over the bar. Mein Gott, I will make them pay for this, all of them. Schwein-hunds, dumkopf. That once handsome face, was now disfigured for life by that schwein of a cat. Such hatred boiled in him. His brain felt like it was on fire. His heart was pounding. It was all ruined now. How could he walk the street or even fade into a crowd? He would stand out now, all eyes staring, staring.

As he looked at his face he brought his hands down on top of the bar with a resounding smack. It jarred his whole body and a shock wave rose to the top of his head. He held onto the bar with both hands as the pain and nausea and dizziness moved up and down his spine like icy fingers. It passed and he was left with a pulsating pain in his face and beads of sweat were standing out all over it. He could feel the trickling of it down over his ribs. He reached down into his jacket pocket and drew out a small white envelope that contained his painkillers. He dropped two into his palm and poured himself a large

By the Pricking of My Thumb

brandy and knocked the pills back in one gulp and stood looking at himself in the mirror.

It seemed to take forever for the pills to work, but now the pain was almost gone and he was bathed in a warm glow. He eased himself into a big easy chair and gently laid his head back. He felt like he was floating, not since he was in the hospital had he felt so relaxed. His mind seemed so clear for the first time since that night at that old cow's house. He could see things clearly now, he didn't have to worry about being seen, nein. Not any more. He could do everything from this room. And in the evening, after the light was gone, just once more, one small job for Kurt and then poof, out of his life forever.

The thought of Kurt lying lifeless at his feet. The schwein in his fancy clothes, his white silk shirt stained with an ever-widening circle of blood brought a smile to the twisted face. Ja, ja, he had a plan now. A good and solid, foolproof plan. One phone call and all his work would be finished and he would be off to Rio where some of the finest plastic surgeons practiced. And with his money, he could have any face he wanted. Ja, so clear, and he drifted into a deep dream-free sleep. The glass slipped from his hand, the brandy making a dark ever widening circle on the carpet. And that's how Kurt found him, the pills and the brandy doing the work for him.

He knelt and touched the stained carpet. Wet. Good. That means Heindrich's drugged sleep has just begun. He must be quick and find what he was looking for and he'd be back in his own suite when Heindrich woke. He had been taught how to search and where secrets would most likely be hidden. Ja, he had been taught by the experts.

Twenty minutes had passed and nothing. He was beginning to sweat. His gut feeling told him to quit and leave, but something else told him he was close to finding what it was that he needed. He was holding Heindrich's passport case between his fingers and was leaning forward a bit. He was absently swinging it back and forth when he thought he heard something. He glanced quickly toward Heindrich, his luck was still holding. He was still breathing deeply and evenly. What had he been doing when he heard what he thought he heard? Think, dumkopf. What was that sound? He had heard it before but couldn't place it. He glanced at his hands. The passport case.

He moved his hands again in a quick, twisting movement of the wrist, back and forth. There it was again. What was it? The case was empty, the contents spread on the table before him. Once again, he repeated the movement. Only this time, held it up close to his ear. Ja, there it was. He worked quickly now, his pulse racing and his heart beating so fast and loud he thought it would explode. The soft supple leather yielded up its secret. Kurt found the wire, so fine it was like a strand of hair, but very strong and supple. He pulled it out. He marveled at just how cleverly the craftsman had been. For what had appeared to be stitching in the leather was actually the wire. His hands were clammy and trembling. As he lay the wire down it almost disappeared into the colour of the table top.

He separated the leather and there lay one small sheet of paper of the finest onion skin and three rows of numbers, each with some letters after them. Some kind of code of Heindrich's. He didn't dare remove it in case he could not get it back in just the right place hence giving himself away to Heindrich that his secret was found out. He knew without a doubt these were not the numbers of the Swiss bank account. He kept those in his head he was sure. But these must be safety deposit numbers of banks in Rio, Switzerland and Gott knows where.

He quickly withdrew his small pad from his inside jacket pocket and carefully took down the exact numbers in the same sequence just as they were written. Another fifteen minutes and Heindrich's suite looked exactly as it looked when he entered it thirty-five minutes ago. Another quick look around, and smiling coldly at the sleeping figure, gently eased the door shut and barely heard the click as it came together. The passage was empty, so he was back at his own door without anyone seeing him. He felt quite giddy, almost like being intoxicated.

His key was in the lock when he heard his phone ringing. He wondered who it was and in his state of mind he wondered if it was ringing when he came up. He couldn't remember, better get in there. He picked up the receiver and found he was sweating. The voice he heard filled him with a new uneasiness.

"Where have you been? When I didn't get an answer to my note I called your room and have been calling ever since. Whatever is wrong? Darling, are you there?"

"Ja, ja, Peggy, I just got out of the shower."

A little giggle escaped from her. "Is it still on for tonight?"

"Ja, but it will have to be late. When are you through?"

"Not until eleven-thirty. Is that too late?"

"No, but listen, Shotzie. You know that the lounge will be closed. I don't want you having to wait in the hotel for me. So how about taking a taxi to the train station and I'll meet you there at the coffee shop they keep open 'till after midnight."

There was a little pause. "Kurt, I guess that will be all right, but, you will come around won't you? I don't want to sit around in there too long."

"I'll be there, just watch for me. Auf wiedersehn, liebling." and hung up before she could say another word.

Chapter 47

The three of them had sat around the cluttered desk of Dr. Dundee for the better part of an hour in deep discussion. They each had a small lab beaker glass in front of them filled with Scotch.

After a long silence, Quest raised his head from the sheets of paper and reached for his beaker and took a long pull and said, "I can see all that you were telling me, and under the circumstances, you have done a capital job and left no stone unturned. Capital, really capital. First class." He turned and looked at Doc, smiling.

"Aye, I'll no say it's been easy for me, and the laddies have worked just as long and hard as myself."

"As you say, Doctor, I don't presume to be that knowledgeable about these things but I have been on a few PM's in my time, devilishly hard to detect. I'll never understand how you chaps do it."

"Aye, well then laddie, Miss Millacent was the only one who could tell us what happened and the poor wee lass told us a lot. The time of her death is always speculative because the body lay for a while by the hot fireplace and was then moved to the storage shed in the back garden. And the body had been cooled at two different temperatures. She could have died an hour earlier or an hour later."

"I see" Quest said. "You are quite sure she had been moved and didn't die as first thought by the accident in the storage shed."

"Oh, aye. There are a few dirt particles in the wound on her head but there were also quite a few fragments of ash and particles from the fireplace. The same ashes that were in the grate also were in her hair, stuck in the upper parts of her clothing. Also, Inspector, her hair half undone, that couldn't have happened if she had fallen. She was dragged across that shed floor, poor wee lassie, and placed in that position. The particles from her shoe heels bear that out, and then that dirty, bloody, bastard deliberately pushed that corner of that crate into her head." His face was black with rage as he reached for his beaker and downed it all with one gulp. "Oh, aye, there's no doubt at all in my mind and I want that animal—for, aye, that's what he is, a crazed, cunning animal—caught and put away before he can strike again."

Pentecroft had sat silently with his open palms pressed together in front of him. "Are you in agreement with Doctor, Ronald?" He didn't speak for a few moments. It was as if he were pulling himself back from some far away place in his mind and when he did speak it was to the floor, or so it seemed.

"Right then, yes I do. And I also agree our men have done a fair piece of work when you consider we had now't to start with except for poor Miss Lang's body. And then young Simms and Vince Tuckwin—to say now't of all the hours Doc has put in here and his staff have worked around the clock to get these reports together. I'm damned proud of all of them and their professionalism." He paused and got up, picked up his beaker in his hand and walked to the window and stood with his back to his superior officer who was now in charge of the case. Well, that's torn it, you damned fool. Couldn't leave it, could you? He struck a match and lit the cigarette in his mouth. The silence hung like a wet blanket in the air.

Chief Superintendent Ashley Quest looked at the doctor who raised his shoulders and rolled his eyes back. Quest thought for another moment before he spoke. "Yes, quite right, Inspector. You have every reason to be proud of your men and their work and yours. It couldn't have been easy to turn your case over to outsiders. You have been nothing but cooperative and you've made my second and I feel welcome, which is more than I can say for many others I have worked with." Quest saw the tension ease from Pentecroft's shoulders and the heavy sigh that escaped from Dr. Dundee. "And while we are on the subject of your men, do you think we could arrange to have Corporal Simms work with us for the remainder of this case?"

"Yes, I think that would be wise. Simms was born and raised here and the only time he has ever been away was when he attended the academy in London. Yorkshire people are warm and friendly but they don't open up and become quite clannish to strangers. No offense to you, sir. It's just the way they are. You can live here and serve them for years as the doctor here. And, though they respect and admire him, he's still considered an outsider. They only trust those who are really St. Gilliam village people and it will be very helpful to us to have young Terry on the case, don't you agree Doc?"

"Aye, laddie, it's all true. And they say we Scots are clannish and no trusting." He laughed and lifted up his beaker to his mouth to drink it and he realized it was empty and with a sheepish grin reached for the bottle. "And canna no top your beaker off for you before you're awa'."

Quest looked at his watch and said, "We have done everything here that we can do and I think that we've covered enough ground for today. So for one, I would say 'Thank you, sir, I will.'"

Doc didn't even have to ask Pentecroft, but knew he would appreciate a shot after this sticky few minutes he had been through. It could have gone quite differently, but thanks to Quest's clear head, all was at ease again.

Quest shifted the papers on the table in front of him and putting them back in order handed them back to Dr. Dundee. "I think we should go back to the station house and see if the telex or the computer can tell us anything. And then maybe both of you would care to have dinner with me tonight at the Grand and we can continue our discussions for Monday's inquest over a pleasant dinner."

"Aye, thank you, that'll be grand. Ma' housekeeper's awa' to her sister's and I hae no stomach for cooking mesel'. What time?"

"We should be finished in about an hour, say sixish in the dining room. How about you, Pentecroft, can you join us?"

"Yes, thank you sir, it would be a pleasure."

"Fine then, we will be off. If you're ready Ronald."

By the Pricking of My Thumb

"Right." Pentecroft finished his drink, put his cigarettes in his pocket and picked up his briefs. He smiled and winked at the doc, "'Til six then," and they were off.

Chapter 48

Kurt took the chance that Heindrich would not call the minute he awoke from his drugged sleep and took a quick shower.

He was toweling himself dry and wrapping it around his waist. He stopped to study himself in the mirror. His transformation from that slobbering dumkopf he had played for Heindrich's benefit and for his own safety surprised even him. His broad shoulders defined muscles formed his arms, his flat stomach and narrow hips. Ja, not so bad, he said to the handsome face staring back at him with alarmingly bright blue eyes. He ran his hand through his thick blond hair that was growing out nicely after an expensive trip to the barber, and his own white teeth were wonderful to see again now that they weren't disguised as yellow, uncared for, uneven brushed fangs. Ja, he was actually what Heindrich liked to call the true German. The ones that Hitler was trying to breed in all the brothels in those famous chalets that were baby factories where the officers with all the right connections and the breeding, the background and the colouring, the ones with the refined minds passing their seeds onto the same kind of women who thought it was their honor and their duty to have a perfect child for the perfect Germany, who lived in pampered, spoiled conditions, never lifting a finger, all fun and games, dining and dancing. And then the child at the age of five would be taken from their mothers by governesses and turned over to the youth camps and the mother was compensated by a substantial bank account for her child and herself in the Austrian Alps. So many children who never knew their fathers. And mothers that wove fairy tale stories of wonderful fathers when she herself was never sure who sired her child.

He laughed to think how much more Heindrich would hate him if he knew that he, Kurt, was such a child. A perfect child who knew everything except who his father was. Then, he thought, the time had come when he must make a quick call to London to an old friend of his in Soho who was keeping his little pet for him. Ja, well looked after, clean and ready to go to work for him and he knew instinctively that it must be soon because Heindrich's ways for getting rid of people were notorious, swift, quick, and out of nowhere when they were least expecting it. A shudder passed through his body and a cloud covered his eyes and he saw all of his old friends, Heindrich's prize unit of men, unquestionable in their loyalty and duty to him, orders followed to the letter no matter how insidious and despicable or vile they were. Young men, indoctrinated, brains worked over in youth camps to follow unfailingly or unflinchingly from their duty to their Fuhrer, his plan for an all-Aryan race—a perfect Germany with perfect people. Hitler, their savior, their all in all. His friends, all dead. Not by any act of war but by Heindrich's hands. No one could prove anything but anyone who knew of him, knew him to be a killer, ruthless, cruel beyond belief and lived in fear of him. And now Kurt knew his turn was coming to be hunted and tricked and struck down. But he would be ready for him, mein Gott. No wonder they called him the Jackal. Once on the track of something or someone he was relentless, ruthless, snarling and snipping and laughing. The closer he got the more excited he became, even salivating at the mouth. No wonder he put such fear in all who came in contact with him, even himself.

He shook himself from this black thought but the smell of fear was everywhere in the suite. He had to get out of there. As he picked up the brush he noticed his hands were trembling, need a stiff drink.

By the Pricking of My Thumb

Looking at himself in the mirror behind the bar, his years of training were coming through. His face was calm and showed no trace of fear, the eyes, maybe a little, but inside he felt like he was going to explode. He raised the glass to his lips and the phone rang breaking the silence like a jet going through the sound barrier. He spilled his drink all down the front of his silk shirt. The strain of all this exploded from him as he yanked the receiver from the hook, "Ja, ja."

"How many times have I told you to speak English, Kurt? Even my impeccable tailor can't change a sow's ear into a silk purse, eh? Once a dumkopf always a dumkopf." and the sarcasm drifted from Heindrich's voice. "I'm really going to have to keep an eye on you. You can't be counted on for anything. Get yourself here as we have much work to do."

Before he could say anything the line went dead. Kurt was furious with himself, letting himself be caught off guard like that and letting Heindrich get the upper hand. He poured another drink and downed it. Held his hands out in front of him at arms length. Ja, that was better, steady once again.

V.E. Sullivan

He tore off his stained shirt and threw it onto the bottom of the closet and took a fresh clean one out, put it on, glanced quickly in the mirror and was off.

Chapter 49

Ed turned and smiled at Robert. "Thank you, lad. These Inland Revenue papers were laying heavy on my mind."

"That's OK, Ed. I hope this will clear things up. She left good, detailed books so it was pretty straightforward."

"Aye, laddie, she was a right'un. Everything done proper like. It looked cluttered but she could put her hands on anything." He stood staring at the desk. His shoulders suddenly slumped. "I can't believe she's gone. I keep expecting her to come through the curtain with something that needs doing or telling me to put kettle on."

Robert came up behind him and laid his hand warmly on Ed's shoulder and squeezed it. "I know, Ed. This has been a beastly bear for all of us. You have been a brick through it all. I don't know how Suzette and I would have been able to make it this far without you and Dori. You must know how much Suzette loves you both and my own feelings go without saying."

"Aye, laddie, I do, and we feel same about lass and you, I'll be bound. I for one won't be half glad to get Monday over with. Dori will have to live it all again, poor lass. Wish there was a way I could spare her."

Ed's hand came down on the desk with such a force that the ink from the inkwell spilled over its side and fell on the back of an old invoice like drops of purple rain. "Bloody hell. Its all such a muck up and a waste!" as he quickly blotted up the drops and wiped the inkwell clean. "That bastard will pay and pay good. If I could get me own bare hands on him I'd make it a noose for blighter's neck and save police trouble."

Rob let him go on talking, pushing things here and there and straightening a few chairs and boxes. Best thing for him, poor devil. He had been holding it all in for the girls' sake, and now with only Rob here to hear he could get it all out in the open. It was like a volcano that had just erupted. His words like lava flowing uncontrolled for several minutes. His Yorkshire dialect so thick at times Rob couldn't make it out. And then, as quickly as it started, it ended with Ed sitting at the desk, his head cradled in his folded arms and sobbing like a child. Rob went over and laid both hands on the heaving shoulders. And, in the end, he didn't know how long it took or what he had said, only his own face was wet with tears and the two men were spiritually bound together and their souls intertwined as if they were but one person.

They could hardly move in the room it was so charged with emotion. And with shaking hands, Rob picked up the manila envelope and the tan papers and said, "Let's get a drink, Ed. We both could use one."

Ed put his large hanky away and looked at Rob. There was no need for words between the two men. Their souls were still communing. "Aye, laddie. We'll go to my pub, "The Old Lion and Lamb" landlord keeps Yorkshire best bitter in crock behind bar for lads like me and a shot of whiskey to go along will see us through heck as like and we'll be as good as new before you can say 'Bob's your uncle.'" And with arms linked, the tall and the short, the old and the young matched steps to the door.

V.E. Sullivan

Chapter 50

Quest looked around the room. Inspector Pentecroft was shifting all the papers in front of him as if to make some order of them. There were five of them in all gathered around the makeshift table. There were others working on machines and answering phones but the select five were: Sergeant Littlejohn, Corporal Simms, Inspector Pentecroft, Inspector Rennie and he made up the last of them, with Corporal Simms being the greenest of the bunch. But there was something in this young man: quickness, intelligence beyond his years. This was going to be a bugger of a case and he wondered if this was only the tip of the iceberg with more shock and horror ahead for the lovely English village which only crime had been before this one was an overdue library book or one that had gone missing later to be returned by a red faced youth loaded down with his guilt. He couldn't stand it. Would the village ever recover? By God he hoped so.

By this time he had all the papers in separate piles. He walked to the chalk-board, at the ready, and picked up the chalk, and with bold but legible script he wrote three names across it with a long line dividing them. "Now then, gentlemen." he turned rubbing his fingers in the palm of his hand, "Here is how we stand." All had their note pads out and were scribbling down the names. All but Pentecroft, who never took his eyes off this imposing man.

Under the first name, he wrote, "1) Found guilty of war crimes, atrocities against the Jews, priests, nuns, women and children in Poland and the Kizarra area of Yugoslavia. 2) Escaped," underlined twice, "killing two guards. Believed to have had outside help. 3) He has been sighted numerous times all over Europe but is still at large. 4) Is believed to have amassed a large fortune in paintings, artifacts, and jewels, that, over the years he has turned into hard cash. 5) Very dangerous, psychopathic, and believed by the doctor at the trial, to be half mad already. A man dedicated to self-preservation at any cost and has no conscience and little respect for life, human or otherwise. Totally ruthless and unbelievably cruel and will go to any lengths to get what he wants or to protect himself or what is his."

He looked at his watch and moved rapidly to the second name. "1) Served in the elite group of this officer's men and believed to be the last survivor. 2) Records show this man to have a cunning nature and somewhere during these years of service his personality took on a change. Uncaring, dirty, slow witted. Whether this is a mechanism that his brain put up because he couldn't stand any more we don't know. 3) He is also dangerous and the Major's dog body, and demented. 4) His crimes of brutality are also documented and he could well have been the one to help Heindrich escape. His slow wittedness is probably the only thing keeping him alive, as the Major seems to think that he has nothing to fear from this man. But others at the trials thought he was a force to be reckoned with."

Under the last name he wrote: "1) murdered by person or persons hitherto unknown. 2) Owner of a fine antique store, a village resident most of her life and well loved and respected by all. 3) Lived alone in a thatched cottage set back from the road with hedgerows. 4) Housekeeper and the only man employed by her at the shop were man and wife. Totally dedicated to her in every way and off the suspect list. 5) Only living relative a niece who lives in London and her fiancée, who was well known to Miss Lang and most of her village friends, also not suspects."

"Well gentlemen, this is where we stand. Now, according to the niece, her aunt asked her to bring along, when they came for that weekend, her father's wartime diary. She also said she had found some clippings and wanted to check them out. Some things were bothering her and she told her niece about a man, she didn't give the gentleman's name, who was irate and very determined to purchase this lovely old discovery she'd found. And her aunt was just as determined to hang onto it. Now gentlemen, that man's name was one and the same as our Major, Heindrich von Heusen."

There was a clatter as the thick crockery teacup hit the floor. All four men jumped. "Bloody hell, what's got wind up thee lad?" Simms stood staring at one of the sheets on the table as the tea dripped onto the toes of highly polished boots.

"Corporal Simms!" Sergeant Littlejohn's voice cracked like a clap of thunder. "Will 'ya quit playing silly beggars and answer me?"

Simms looked up, still not saying anything. But, before the Sergeant could shout again, Pentecroft said softly, "What is it Simms? Have you remembered something?"

"Yes sir, well, begging your pardon sir. You remember the night we went back to Miss Lang's?"

Pentecroft looked stunned for a moment, "Oh! Right, I do. You tell the story, Simms."

"Well sir, on the night of the murder I was going to be late for my report when Miss Lang went scurrying past me on the other side of the street, all sixes and sevens, she were. I waved but got no reply. She had sommat on her mind, no danger. I was about to follow when I heard the clock striking and I knew the Sergeant would have my guts for garters, beggin' your pardon sir." They all smiled and Littlejohn's face, quite pink, suddenly broke into a wide smile.

"We understand laddie, go on."

"Well, I was rounding the corner on my bicycle when this big black Daimler came out of nowhere on the wrong side of the road and sent me head over tea kettle, punctured my tyre and didn't half bung up my knee. I didn't get whole number, just last three, but they were foreigners, must have been, to be on wrong side of the road like. I got the impression one of the blokes was big and youngish, and now I see it on the paper here, 855." He flipped open his note pad and thumbed through pages. "Yes, sir. Here it is. I made a note, like, 855. And this paper states UNE855 black Daimler, rented, York. It had to be them sir, the same night I went by Miss Lang's on my rounds and stopped by the gate

I sometimes have a cuppa, but drapes were drawn and house was all dark and quiet. I knew she was having her niece. The whole village knew. We all knew. And most of us knew Miss Suzette. Miss Lang was that proud of her, she was. And to think I might have been able to help her had I gone through and knocked her up." He leaned forward and put his head in his hands.

"Look, Corporal, the Halleys feel the same way. They were there because it was their habit to drop by after choir practice. But as you say, the whole village knew her niece and her young man were coming. And the place was also dark when they drove up. They thought she might be having an early night. And to be honest, I'm just as glad they didn't, or you didn't, or things might have been a lot worse had you or they interrupted something nasty. One corpse is bad enough for St. Gilliams, but laying to rest three of its best-loved villagers would take too long for the village to recover its losses. Might put you on the map as a tourist attraction, but dare say the village wouldn't like that much.

"But back to the question at hand. We now know that the car that was rented to von Heusen in York was in St. Gilliam the day of the murder and several days before that. That gentleman is one for us because we can assume that the Major doesn't know that we are aware he is here. Now to find him and run him to ground before he is panicked into doing something else." Quest looked at his watch, five-thirty. "Still have time to run down a few more things. How much of this has the local papers got?"

Pentecroft said, "A large article about her life and work in the village and about the inquest."

"Good." Quest said. "He might just be conceited enough to want to be in on it. Thinking how good he was, but then he is pretty marked up by that cat, but then again, he might send his accomplice who would blend in more with the locals. Let's keep our ears and eyes open. Also on all hospitals and surgeon's surgeries and chemists checked here and in York. The bastard's face must be playing hell by now. Also, speak to Mr. Halley after the inquest, Corporal, will you? And see if he has remembered anything else. Oh, and one more thing, check the register at the Grand and all bed and breakfasts between here and York. Major Heindrich von Heusen has a reputation for his fine clothes and hand made accessories so someone like that will stand out in the village. Someone's bound to have seen him. He had to eat and drink and sleep somewhere. That's it then, gentlemen. I'll see you all here Monday morning before the inquest. Any questions? Right then, off you go. And, if you think of anything between now and then, no matter how small and insignificant it seems to you, get in touch with either Pentecroft or myself."

"May I have a word, sir?" Corporal Simms said to Pentecroft.

"Of course, Corporal. Excuse me, I'll be with you in a moment, sir." Turning away from Quest, "What is it Corporal?" Pentecroft said, knowing full well the lad was feeling bad about showing up his superior as he had neglected to tell Quest about Terry's report.

Simms looked down at his feet, and up at the ceiling, then finally full at his superior's face. "Sorry, sir, to drop you in it like that but I was that rattled when I saw that report. It all came flooding back and with the Sergeant shouting and all, well, I just wanted to tell you. I didn't let it out to make myself out like a proper big shot, it just happened before I knew it like."

Pentecroft's hand came down hard on the lad's shoulder. "You're a good policeman, Terry, lad. I know you didn't do it to show me up in front of my superior, and I appreciate you coming forth. And, as long as we are being straightforward about things, it went clear out of my own mind until I heard you, so the fault lies with me for not remembering. If it hadn't been for your quick eye, a valuable piece of this puzzle would have been lost."

Ashley Quest, standing a little away but in earshot was thinking, You're a good officer yourself, Ronald Pentecroft, and good with your men. I wouldn't mind having you at the Yard with me. He made a mental note of it for later as Inspector Pentecroft returned to say, "Let's go, then, we'd better rattle or Doc will think we're not coming."

"Right." Quest said. And they headed towards the door in deep concentration.

By the Pricking of My Thumb

Chapter 51

Heindrich sat back and looked at the clutter on the coffee table: papers, glasses, bottle over half gone, wads of balled up notes on the floor. Mein Gott, it was a mess, but at last he had conceived a plan, one with careful handling of all details to get his desk. He was sure it was the right one now. Too bad he couldn't keep it, but he would be moving too fast in the end and traveling light. And besides, he only really wanted what was in it. He had been in touch with his bank in Rio and in Switzerland and the wheels were in motion. Nothing must stop him now, no one. Kurt would be his last act as Heindrich von Heusen and that stupid clod would be left to take the full blame for everything. No one outsmarted the Jackal and lived to brag about it. Kurt thinks he has me where he wants me. Playing the big shot. Well, after Thursday, I will be long gone, back over the Channel and out of the country and off to a luxuriously new life, new face, wealth enough to live as a king for as long as I live.

He was sweating now, and very excited. He only had to wait a few more days and it would all be over and he would be free at last. He started to laugh, softly at first. But the more he thought of the look on

Kurt's face when his dream exploded in his face, the louder it became. He threw back his head in a roar of hysterical laughter. Then the pain hit him like a brick in his face and head from out of nowhere. It was so intense he could hardly move or breathe. He felt violently ill. The pain was coursing through his face and eye and the side of his head felt like it was going to explode.

He reached for his pills and his glass. He could hardly see for the pain. He knocked the glass over and the contents made a river across the tabletop. His pills rolled onto the floor. He started to his feet only to fall to his knees. He crawled a few inches and reached the bottle of pills. He was bathed in sweat. He opened the bottle and took the last two. Not bothering to reach for the glass, he raised the Cognac bottle and downed the contents and lay back on the floor waiting for something to take the pain away or for it to subside a little so he could function once again.

He lay there in a stupor for what seemed hours, only to know in the back of his mind that it was only a short while. Then slowly and shakily he got to his feet and made his way to the bedroom to change his clothes and freshen up. Couldn't let Kurt find him this way.

Chapter 52

Kurt walked briskly up the hall to Heindrich's door and hoped this wasn't going to be a late session. He had much to do himself and his toy was arriving on the late train. He would feel much better when he picked it up from the stationmaster. Then he must see Peggy. Gott, what had he said to the stupid bitch? He must find out exactly. He couldn't have her telling tales and bragging now, could he? And the sooner the better.

He was standing in front of Heindrich's door. A quick brush of his hands over his handsome head and off of each shoulder and he knocked. There was no answer. He looked up and down the corridor, no one was around, all down for dinner he supposed. He rapped louder and this time it brought back a rough, "Enter." Kurt opened the door and slipped in, closing it behind him.

"It is about time you got here."

He looked at Heindrich leaning casually on the bar but he knew at once that he was leaning for support. Mein Gott. He looked like the walking dead. That unhealthy colour, the cheeks flushed from fever, eyes far too bright, and under it all the skin was a pasty colour with the damp look. He had seen it many times in the war with soldiers whose wounds had gone unattended too long and infection was spreading through their bodies and mind like a spider weaving their web.

"Well, what are you staring at? Get me a drink." He walked to the big chair like a man walking on eggs, sat down and lay his head back slowly. Kurt didn't dare say anything yet. Better let him get this under his belt first.

"Brandy, all right?" He asked casually, as if he noticed nothing.

"Ja, ja. Order us up some room service. I only want something light. Been eating this heavy English food far too long." He looked at Kurt with hot angry eyes as if daring him to come back with anything. But Kurt was wise to his tricks.

"Fine." he said in the same casual way. "But I'm hungry. So you won't mind if I have a full dinner?"

"Ja, I should expect something different from you, dumkopf? When I'm paying?"

Later Kurt wiped his mouth on the serviette and tossed it on the table, picked up his cup and washed down the rest of his coffee.

Heindrich had hardly touched his food. He had talked as Kurt ate. Told him of his plans for the contents of the desk, not what was in it though? It sounded way off, too risky to him, but just far enough off to work if nothing unexpected cropped up in the middle. They should have a full hour. It would be good to be free of Heindrich and have some real money—not half, or even an eighth of what Heindrich had, but he could always put the touch on him in a year or two when he thought Kurt had died. But he had no plans of dying, at least not of unnatural causes. He was ready for Heindrich and all his tricks; at least after tonight he would be.

He realized Heindrich was talking to him. What had he said? Something about the hotel doctor. He looked across at Heindrich who was holding up his bottle, must be out of painkillers. Well if he keeps up this boozing and pill taking I won't have to do anything. Death will be his constant companion. He refused to find an off surgery or have his face cleaned up. Since he had torn that plaster off some of the sutures had pulled loose and there was much swelling and discolouration, fever, and a hard yellow crust had formed all along the wounds. In places the crust had cracked and was oozing something that when you were standing close to him smelled totally unhealthy.

With all he had to look forward to, Kurt couldn't imagine him letting it go this far. It was very unwise of him. Went against everything he had drilled into his men. Take care of your body. Any open wound, keep clean and disinfected. It will heal and so will you. So why was he doing this to himself or had the fever affected his thinking? And yet all these plans seemed to say otherwise as far-fetched as they were.

"Are you listening to me dumkopf?"

"Of course, mein Major," Kurt lied. "I was just trying to think of the best way to do this. Do you really want the hotel doctor involved in writing a prescription?"

"Why not? He's a simple country doctor with a small country practice. And when the original hotel doctor moved into York he was offered the job. A good living with high-class foreign clientele, a place to live, and someone to fetch and carry for him. Like you, my friend, it went to his head. He is far too busy trying to climb the social ladder to pay that much attention to a small prescription for pain."

Well, let's hope you're right. It's my neck in the noose as well as yours. But Kurt kept his thoughts to himself as he saw Heindrich was pretty strung out already. "I'll see if I can find him in his room or have him paged," and was out of the door.

He made his way to the elevator looking at his watch. It was six-thirty. The sooner this was finished, the sooner he could put his own plan into actions.

The doctor didn't answer the door so once again into the lift and down to the desk to have him paged. That meant having to see Peggy but he hoped she would play it cool. As luck would have it, she was at the desk. And except for the outrageous way she was flirting she gave nothing away. Kurt moved a little away from the reception desk and waited.

In a few minutes the bellboy came up to the desk and spoke to Peggy. He saw her smile and pointed him out. He made his way to Kurt. "Excuse me, sir. Are you the gentleman what's wanting the doctor?"

"Yes," was all Kurt said.

"Well, beggin' your pardon, sir. He is not pleased as he just got his dinner served to him. He says either you were to wait or he could see you at his table, but he wasn't moving until he had had his supper."

Bloody hell, thought Kurt. He thinks he's King Tut. But instead of saying anything he just smiled, bowed and held out one of his arms. The boy smiled, tipped his cap and said, "This way, sir," and had Kurt taken into the busy dining room.

Weaving through tables and making excuses, Kurt backed into a chair. The man turned, just as Kurt did and for a split second their eyes met. The hair on the back of Kurt's neck stood up as it always did when there was danger near. Just wanting to get away as quickly as possible he said "Sorry," and moved off after the bellboy.

He didn't like it, not one bit. For no other reason except gut instinct he knew this man was dangerous to him and he didn't want to look at him again. Only to get this bloody prescription taken care of and get out of there, avoiding that table of three.

Chapter 53

"Sorry about that," Pentecroft said. "It's a good job you were not holding a drink." They laughed, but both men turned and gazed at the retreating back.

"Well dressed bloke anyway laddies," Doc said, eyeing Ronald Pentecroft's disheveled suit and smiling.

"Yes, he is that," Pentecroft said, scowling at the doctor and pulling his chair closer to the table. But, he had the same gut feeling and by the look on Quest's face he was feeling the same thing.

"I wonder where he's going in such a hurry." They all looked in the direction of the receding back.

"Aye. It looks like it's going to be to the doctor's table." They looked at him. "Oh, aye. He's Dr. Stanthrope, hotel doctor. Took over when the other chappy left. Name escapes me for the moment," and Doctor Dundee launched into the explanation.

"Doesn't look too pleased," Pentecroft said, "at having his supper interrupted."

"No he doesn't," Quest said as they returned to their own sumptuous dinner. "If he's enjoying his half as much as I'm enjoying mine, can't say as I blame him. This is really capital. First class. Haven't enjoyed lamb like this since I can't remember when." And raising their glasses in a silent toast to the cook returned to their conversation about the inquest and the stranger was forgotten.

For Kurt, he felt that three sets of eyes were burning holes in his back and if this dumkopf of a doctor didn't quit his fussing and get on with it he felt he would bolt from the room. His palms were sweating and he reached into his inside jacket pocket for his handkerchief and as casually as he could, glanced back at the table at the three men. He was greatly and discretely relieved to see they were deep in conversation. Still, no use pushing his luck. He would go out the other end of the dining room if this doctor ever got through.

If only he'd ask me to sit down I wouldn't feel this conspicuous.

At last, "Sorry, old man. Can't be too careful, you know. These are quite powerful. What did you say was the matter with him?"

Kurt looked at the doctor for a moment. He wasn't prepared for a cross examination. "Oh, his tooth, terrible pain, abscess," was all Kurt could think of to say.

"Well, maybe I had better come and take a look at him."

"No, no, thank you doctor. If you can just tell me where I can get this filled at this hour I'll be grateful. If he's not improved we can call you down later."

The doctor agreed and told Kurt of a chemist that serves his patients. "He lives alone above his shop, just ring the bell. He'll take care of you." Thanking him, Kurt was gone without even a backward glance.

V.E. Sullivan

Chapter 54

Peggy had been fidgeting with the registration cards but her mind was not on her records or her work. Would the time never go by? Another hour to go. She wished she could get away a tad earlier to freshen up a bit, but she had been late reporting to work. After a night like last night, it was a wonder she had arrived at all. She had almost run into her father leaving for work and that hadn't half scared her witless.

Oh, and Kurt. Could all those things he told her be true? If so, she was one lucky girl. Making plans to go to Paris was one thing. Why, she had never even been to London. But then, to go all the way to Switzerland! But Kurt had made it all sound so easy. She had just turned twenty-one so she didn't need her parents' permission to get the passport. That was lucky, for they wouldn't have stood for it.

Coo blimie! If they only knew half the things she got up to. Her dad would skin her alive, lock her in her room and throw away the key. They didn't know she was on the pill. She had gone to York for those and kept them hidden in the toe of her best shoes as her mum called them. Wore them Sundays and holidays like. Anyway, she didn't have to face up to them. Leave them a letter. That was the best way. No tears, no recriminations, no fighting. Kurt had said they would call them after they had arrived and they would have had time to cool down.

She had stopped and had her picture taken and filled out all the necessary papers. It had meant no sleep and lying to her mom and getting the train to York that morning. That was why she had been late for work. No wonder she was fidgety and nervous and jumping every time the bell rang. What if he was having her on? Couldn't be. She put her hand down on her chest and felt hard metal nestled between her breasts. A ring he had given her last night. An odd ring, but he said it was his family crest. She hardly had time to look at it. Only briefly before she left this morning, putting it on a gold chain and slipping it around her neck. Kurt had said not to wear it as it was big anyway and she could get a diamond ring or anything else she would want as soon as they arrived in Paris.

Just imagine! Her, Peggy Collingwood, going to Paris to be married to a wealthy German industrialist's son. She didn't really know that much, only what Kurt had told her about his family and the vast fortune. It was all happening so fast. Her mind was going around and around like one of those little things in a cage you see in a pet store window. Endlessly, round and around. It must be happening. All would be well as soon as she was with him again, held tightly in his embrace. He would tell her once again and explain it all in detail.

The memory of last night's wild passion flooded her memory. Her body tingled with a thousand little jolts, like getting a shock from a faulty switch, only worse. She was on fire. She felt the rivulets of perspiration running over her ribs and down her spine and the hot flush of colour creeping up from the pit of her stomach, over her chest and throat and finally reaching her face.

The bell rang. The cards flew into the air. She felt like a right wally. She hadn't even noticed anyone approaching the desk, let alone to stand there in front of her so long they had to ring the bell.

"Now look what you've done, Bert!"

Peggy disappeared behind the desk, not only to retrieve the cards but also to compose herself.

Her head was just appearing over the rim of the reception desk when a voice came clear. "Miss Collingwood, what's going on here?"

Oh blimie. The cat's among the pigeons, now. Well, there was now't for it but to face up to the night manager, Mr. Clifton. The Captain Bligh of the Grand as he was called behind his back. He really was nasty. The crease on his pinstriped pants would have cut paper, and not a speck on his dark coat or a hair out of place. He was apologizing to the couple, who any one could see felt quite sorry for the girl not quite on her feet yet.

"Really, no excuse for this at all. Quickly, girl! Quickly. The cards!"

Finally Peggy found the card and handed it to him. "I'm ever so sorry," she started to say, but was interrupted mid-sentence by Mr. Clifton.

"Not now, Miss Collingwood. We will take this up later."

"But Mr. Clifton, I was just going to say-"

"Hush girl! You forget yourself. Wait in my office." And turning to the couple, "I'm so sorry. We do try hard at the Grand to please."

But this time he was interrupted. "Bert, you have started all this by scaring that poor girl half witless and causing her no end of trouble by this." She let her hand drop to her side in exasperation.

"Never fear, my dear. I'm sure he will not do anything rash. I'm sure we can expect to see the young lady in the morning. May we not, Mr. Clifton?"

It was his turn to look embarrassed and ruffled, a position he had never before found himself. Managing a slight smile and bowing his head in a quick nod, he rang for the bell boy.

Confound that girl! He waited until the couple were safely in the lift. He swung around and walked the few feet to his office and pushed the door wide. Peggy sat stiffly in the hard straight chair at the side of the huge desk.

"Well? What do you think you're playing at? Embarrassing me in front of everyone like that."

"But Mr. Clifton, if you will only give me a chance to explain…"

"Explain?" he roared. "Explain what? That you were almost twenty-five minutes late this morning. Explain the way you have been mooning around all day, jumping like a mad March hare every sound you hear? Explain the way you flirt with all the male customers?"

He was striding up and down in front of her and in spite of his anger she stole a look at her watch. Fifteen minutes until she was off duty. And the way he was winging she could be here another thirty. She must get away and tidy up a bit and meet Kurt. She wouldn't need this silly job for much longer anyway.

"And don't think you've got me fooled, not for a minute! With your pretty face and your big eyed innocent ways. For I know your type." He laughed. "Innocent you're not. By God you make me sick. Always skiving off early and making some excuse. You have the others fooled and wrapped around your little finger, but not me. Watch your step, my girl. One more performance like tonight and I'll mark your cards for you."

"But Mr. Clifton that's not fair." Peggy felt her face getting hot. "I've always worked hard and I've got on with everyone here at the Grand. You're the only one who has ever found fault with my work or myself."

"Don't get cocky with me, my girl. I'm sure my report carries more weight than yours."

Before she could say another word, he stood very close to her and with clenched teeth he said, "Clear out of here, and you had better be on time tomorrow or I'll see the back of you, I swear."

V.E. Sullivan

She went to rise but he was so close she couldn't. She sat there staring up at him with wide unblinking eyes until he stepped back and let her rise and leave the office.

Chapter 55

It was all settled then. The four of them sat around the remains of their supper, drinking the last dregs from the teapot.

"Are you sure you both are all right, my love?"

"Of course, Dori. You and Ed both have things to take care of at your place, and you both have been so dear. You know how much we love you. You deserve a good night's sleep in your own beds. If I'm not mistaken, Rob and I will wake to the smell of fresh coffee brewing."

They smiled at each other and Suzette rose from the table and embraced both of them.

"Right you are then. Sorry old son," Ed said to Sultan as he gently set him down.

"No danger, Ed. As soon as we've cleared things away he'll find the first empty lap and settle 'til bedtime. Isn't it grand to see him back to his old self?"

"Aye, it is that laddie."

They accompanied them down to the door and watched as they walked down the garden path to their van hand and hand. Dori turned at the gate and waved back. "See you in the morning, ducks. Have a restful night."

"And the same to both of you."

They had finished the dishes and Rob handed Suzette the tea towel to hang over the bar to dry. They walked to the cozy front room and as Rob lit the fire that was laid in the grate, Suzette sat staring at the desk.

"If we could only figure out what is so important about this beautiful old desk that Auntie had to die for it. There must be something we're overlooking."

Rob came and sat beside her and encircled her with his arm. She settled herself in the crook of his arm and rested her head. Just as they said, Sultan jumped into Suzette's lap and started to knead at her thigh.

"Look, if you're going to do that, you retract those claws of yours." Sultan looked up at her, his green eyes like saucers being slowly eclipsed by the pupils in the light of the fire. He was singing loudly now and was curling himself into a comfortable position and lay his head on one of his huge front paws and closed his eyes.

Suzette stroked his beautiful black silky head and said, "If only he could talk, we could have this horrible thing all settled. He's done his part, old girl, and paid the price for it. He must have marked up that bastard bad if the vet is right, and it seems to confirm with the reports that Dr. Tuckwin sent over to Doc along with all the clippings of Sultan's fur and from his front feet and even bits of fiber from his back claws. He is certainly a beauty." They both agreed.

They hadn't realized how long they had sat talking. So much to talk about. But really, things were pretty much in hand. Millacent Lang had left all of her property, house and shop to Suzette, her only living relative, and an endowment to the Halleys, with a provision that no matter what Suzette did with the house or the shop, Ed and Dori would always be provided for, no matter what.

The fire was all but out, just a few red flecks in the ashes. "Well, petal. That's it for the fire, and you can hardly keep your eyes open." He kissed the top of her shining head. She stretched and he lifted Sultan from her lap. "Good Lord, you're like a bag of cement, you are. Silly old thing." Sultan shook himself and stretched, hunching his back like a cat in a horror show or a Guy Fox might. They laughed at him as he nonchalantly jumped up onto a stool and started to wash his long silky black coat. "I've locked up the back and seen to the windows."

"I've wound the clock and turned out the lights and threw the bolt on the front door," Suzette said as she turned to meet him. He embraced her and held her close. Then slowly, hand in hand, they went up the stairs.

Chapter 56

Kurt found Heindrich pacing the floor, a drink in one hand, a cigarette in his holder in the other. Distorted with pain, he said nothing, just took the bottle. His hands were shaking so he couldn't open it. Kurt almost felt sorry for him as he handed the open bottle back. He looked like death, ja, even smelled of it. Poor bastard. It must hurt like hell, and he noticed Heindrich had increased his dosage and was taking twice what he was supposed to take. But then, he recalled all the unspeakable pain and intolerable suffering he had inflicted on others.

He remembered one case more, maybe, because he hadn't been with Heindrich's special unit that long and he wanted to prove to Heindrich he had what it took to be one of his special men. He would never forget it. He'd had nightmares for weeks, sometimes crying out in his sleep and waking up to find it was his screams and not that poor writhing, unfortunate Jew. Even hardened, unfeeling interrogators for the Gestapo found it hard to watch and to listen. He had remembered the brightness of Heindrich's eyes, his cold smile, the excitement he seemed to get as the strips of flesh were slowly torn from the man's bloody body. The Jew was incredible. Kurt couldn't figure out why he didn't tell Heindrich what he wanted to know. Then the final humiliation. Heindrich brought in that beautiful old desk and had him dragged across the floor. He was like a red mushy blob, no resemblance to a human left about him. Heindrich had walked the few paces to within inches of this poor wretched man, or what was left of him, and had spat into his face, and with a spotlessly clean, soft handkerchief wiped his own mouth of the drops of spittle that hung from his lips. What he detested about the Jew was that he could maim his already tortured body, and even kill him, but he couldn't extinguish the light in those dark eyes to win out over his tormentors. Be it the fever or the spirit, Heindrich did not know, but what he did know was that this Jew would win and he would lose, which led to the last humiliation, of Josef's life. Heindrich lifted the wretched head with his heavy crop and asked him something. Kurt was trying not to look and to keep his face free of all expression. He heard Heindrich laugh and saw him poke his crop into the man's bleeding chest which caused him to render a scream of pain that trailed off into choking sobs. As Heindrich bent with the bloody end of the crop, he wrote something in the upturned drawer, or somewhere. Kurt couldn't bear to look. Then all hell broke loose. Heindrich was kicking the prisoner, screaming "Schwein-hund, filth of the earth."

The guards had to pull him off and away from the broken figure on the floor. "Major, mein Gott, Major, he's dead."

"He can't be!" he screamed. "He hasn't told me what I need to know."

"With what you put him through it's no wonder. I've seen stronger men than this one broken long before it came to this."

Kurt looked up at Heindrich now, all pity he felt for him a few moments ago vanished like quick silver. His own blood running cold in his veins he said, "I think I will be off now," and he turned and walked quickly toward the door.

"Not so fast," Heindrich said. "There are still some things that we need to do."

"Excuse me, Major, but I'm tired and it's late and I think you need to go to bed."

"Don't tell me what I need you pompous bastard..." There was something he saw in Kurt's eyes that made him stop. He picked up his drink and said in slurring words, "Get out, go to your bed. You're getting soft and tiresome. Ja, get out of my sight. I'll call you in the morning and you had better be there."

The anger was raging in both men as they stood, eyes locked together. Get out, Kurt's inner voice was saying. Get out before you do something stupid. He jerked open the door and Heindrich started to laugh. He didn't look back, just closed it behind him and made for the elevator.

Chapter 57

Peggy was making for the ladies convenience just around the corner from the lounge and the last of the hangers-on were leaving. If she had not had her head down, looking in her purse for a comb and her lipstick, she would have seen the two men who were also deep in concentration. They were on a direct collision course and the next thing she knew she was spinning around, her purse was flying from her hands, and if Ronald Pentecroft hadn't caught her by the elbow she would have been head over kettle on the floor.

She was afraid to look back at the desk for fear Mr. Clifton was watching. "Oh no, not again!" she said as she bent to retrieve her things.

"Beg your pardon, Miss."

"Oh no, not you sir, me. It just seems to be one of those nights," and before the men could say anything she was through the doors.

"Pretty little thing, Ronald."

"Aye, she is that," he said with a quizzical look on his face.

"Anything wrong, Ronald?" Ashley asked.

"No, not a bit. Only think I should know her. Face looks familiar."

Ashley Quest smiled and said, "Chance would be a fine thing," and they both laughed and continued on their way.

Chapter 58

It was eleven-thirty when Kurt pulled the Daimler into the car park of the train station. He was pleased with himself having called Arnie and told him to put his baby on the last train out of London. In about five minutes he would have it in his hands. Still, got to get to the coffee shop before twelve midnight.

He reached into his pocket for his cigarettes when his fingers came in contact with the soft velvet. Nice touch, this, Ja, very nice. He lit his cigarette and opened the little box. There, nestled on the creamy satin was a delicate gold chain and from the end hung two beautiful gold filigree hearts entwined. Just to let her down easy in case he had overstated himself. A country girl as pretty as Peggy would soon get over him and marry a local farm boy and raise a dozen kinder. He smiled and could just see her shopping on the high street and pushing a pram all soft and cuddly.

But in the meantime, she was to fill his hours and satisfy his passion and she more than fit the bill. He closed the lid and giving it a little pat, put it back in his pocket. Opening the car door, he stepped out and crushed his cigarette under his expensive loafers and walked the short distance to the waiting room door just as the train was pulling into the station. Couldn't be better. He went to the ticket window and asked where to pick up a package that was on the train. The man directed him to the door at the far end of the waiting room.

By the time Kurt got to it, he could hear the train starting to pick up speed. Just slowed down enough to pass the box out the door of the baggage car to the waiting man on the platform. Kurt knocked on the door and waited a few seconds. Then, hearing no reply opened the door and stuck his head in. "Anyone here?"

"Aye, mate, be with you in a tick."

He came all the way in and found himself standing in a small room made even smaller by the counter that ran across from wall to wall with a steel mesh that came down from the ceiling on each side and left an opening for the clerk to pass packages and things through. Behind the counter there were rows and rows of shelves with deep, wide boxes built into them, each with a letter of the alphabet in front. The man was busy finishing up with the mail paper and packages from the canvas box that had been passed from the train. Kurt looked at his watch. He still had ten minutes and all he had to do was drive the car around the far end of the station to the coffee shop and pick up Peggy. It did the pretty little freulein no harm to be kept waiting. It just heightened their anticipation of what was coming.

His thoughts were interrupted by the voice. He looked up and the man was there at the opening.

"Help you squire?"

"Yes, a package on that train that just came in."

"Your name?"

"Kurt Schreiler"

The man turned. His experienced eye went right to the box. "Oh yes, here we are squire. Sign here."

Kurt obliged and was handed the package with plain brown paper. No return address. It was about the size of a shoebox and bound with heavy cord. Kurt tucked it under his arm and was off.

He reached the car. He was dying to feast his eyes on it once again, but better not. He put it in the boot away from prying eyes and curious questions. He'd have time to caress it and look at it in his own room. Better get this sorted out with Peggy first.

Chapter 59

He pulled up in front of the small coffee shop and she burst through the doors. Kurt had just enough time to reach over and unlatch the door on the passenger side.

"Oh blimie, darling, I thought you had forgotten. I'm that glad to see you, I am, honestly."

The soft, silk headscarf framed her face and her large eyes were shining. He was overwhelmed with desire and caught her to him and kissed her. The scarf slid from her head and lay in soft folds around her shoulders. Her blond hair curled softly around her face.

Kurt was looking at her through half closed eyes and as he released her slowly she said, "Oh, Kurt! Oh my love."

Ja, ja, I guess I'm glad to see you too. I want to talk to you. Let's park by the river in that little lay by, shall we? Nice and quiet, no one to disturb us this time of night."

"Anything you say, darling." She snuggled up close to him and let her hand fall softly on his inner thigh. She could feel a quiver go through him as she laid her shining head on his shoulder. "There, that's better, isn't it?" She said softly.

"Ja," Kurt said, feeling his palms go clammy. What was it about this girl that set his pulse and heart racing and beating like a tattoo on his ribs. He had known lots of girls, and taken a few against their will in his time, but not one of them had the effect that Peggy had on him. She felt the same way, he could tell. He couldn't wait to get her out of the car and onto the throw he kept on the back seat.

His desire was mounting as he parked the car and pulled her to him once more. She was breathless, trembling a bit in anticipation as he led her across the grass and down a slight incline, almost to the water's edge and spread the blanket and made sure there were no rocks under them. When he turned back to her she was standing in the moonlight. Her body was beautiful, bathed in soft light and the shadows of the river and the trees made strange patterns on her shoulders and breasts, like tiny fire flies.

"Oh Shotzie! Kommen zie here."

She held out her hands immediately. He took them and pulled her gently to the soft rug. The smell of the grass, the river, and her hair all played a part and so it all began.

Sometime later, she had no idea, but she didn't care, as she adjusted her clothes and snuggled up to him, relaxed and contented just to stay there.

Kurt said, "Oh, ja, I have something for you, Liebling."

He laid the small velvet box in her lap.

"Oh Kurt, what is it?"

"Open it and see for yourself."

She popped the lid. The delicate, intertwined hearts winked up at her. "Oh, darling, it's lovely! So lovely I'll wear it always. I'll never take it off, never!" She was opening the clasp and she encircled her neck with it. It felt so good against her skin, as only real gold can.

"There. How does it look?" she said looking up at him.

He smiled and bent his head and kissed the two hearts that lay on her creamy soft skin. He too was relaxed and strangely at peace with himself. He could almost forget he had to find out what he had said to her. He laid his chin on the top of her shiny head and said, "About last night..."

"Oh yes, darling. I want to hear it all again so I will know it was not a dream." He stiffened just a little. She was so excited she didn't seem to notice it. "Oh darling, don't tease me."

"No," he said, not letting her escape from his arms, "I want to hear it from your own mouth, Shotzie."

"Well you know, darling, about me going to Paris with you and then to Switzerland for our honeymoon."

"Honeymoon?" Kurt almost shouted the words. "What honeymoon? What are you talking about?"

Peggy started to laugh, "Oh Kurt, stop teasing me." She turned her lovely face up to Kurt and stopped laughing. All at once she struggled to free herself. In doing so her silk scarf escaped her hair and once more draped itself around her neck.

It was Kurt's turn to laugh. "You can't be serious! This was just a silly diversion. Something to fill the long hours of my boredom."

She made a quick movement, was almost to her feet, half crying, half screaming at him, "What do you think you're playing at?" she screamed. "There are laws in this country about playing fast and loose with young girls."

He made a grab for her and missed, but his hand caught the soft folds of the scarf around her neck and jerked her back to the blanket. He had to shut her up. He was half blind with rage. "Silly cow, do you think I'd tie myself to someone like you? A village girl uneducated in the social graces?" His voice took on a raw edge. "Where could I take you? Mein Gott. You've never even been to London."

Kurt didn't seem to notice Peggy was struggling to free the pressure of the scarf on her throat. Tighter and tighter, she couldn't scream or breathe. She clawed frantically on his arms and at the back of her head. She felt like one of those puppets in a Punch and Judy show, like someone jerking all the strings at once. There was a dark stain forming in the front of her eyes, getting darker and darker and then all was black.

The more Kurt thought about it, the tighter he twisted the scarf, around and around in his hands until he finally realized there was a pull downward. She was no longer struggling but hung limp from his hands. Suddenly he realized what had happened. He let go of the scarf and she fell backwards. Her head fell on his arms, her pretty face black. Her beautiful mouth was twisted and distorted with her struggle and her tongue was hanging from one side of it. Her once dancing eyes were lifeless and bulging from her head.

Oh, mein Gott, he felt that he was going to be sick. He threw himself from the blanket to the water's edge and on his knees he plunged his head into the cold waters of the river and shook it like a dog. Then sat back and let the water run down his neck. He could feel it soaking his silk shirt. Gott in Himmel, what to do? What to do? Had she told anyone else? Could she possibly keep something like this to herself?

Kurt rose slowly to his feet and turned and looked down at Peggy. He found he couldn't bear to look at her. He pulled the scarf from the back of her head and covered her face with it. "That's better," he said half aloud to himself.

He turned and walked briskly up to the car. This was a popular spot with young lovers. He wanted to be sure no one was around to have heard her or himself. Good, nothing in sight. He turned and walked back to where she lay. He couldn't really think things out. All he wanted to do was to get away from her. He forgot about everything else.

He took his handkerchief from his inside breast pocket and wiped his head and neck off with it, bent down and picked up Peggy's purse and wiped it clean and tossed it into a clump of bushes growing at the water's edge. The water would probably carry it down river. He bent and rolled Peggy in the throw and picked her up and laid her across his shoulder. The small velvet box escaped from the folds and fell soundlessly in the grass between his feet. He barely missed stepping on it.

He walked a few yards to the small footbridge. He stood looking down at the river as if trying to gauge the depth at this point. Then, lifting her from his shoulder he rolled her into the river Ouse. There was a loud splash, or did it only seem deafening to Kurt. He watched as she disappeared from sight, only to surface in a few seconds sprawled on her back like a rag doll some child had carelessly tossed into the river. The current caught at her and she started to bob and float down river towards the causeway he hoped. He stood transfixed, staring as it disappeared under the bridge.

He clasped the blanket to his chest and stepped quickly to the other side and soon wished he hadn't for as she came under the bridge the moonlight caught her face. The same moonlight that hours ago had turned her into a vision of loveliness now turned her into a grotesque sight. Her sightless eyes seemed to hold him in her power. The twisted mouth seemed to be laughing up at him.

He swung away from the railing and ran like a small boy frightened by an apparition. He stopped at the car and lay over the boot and let the cold damp night cool his face. He made himself stand up and straighten his clothes. He took a small brush from the glove compartment and laid it on the bonnet of the car. He carefully removed his jacket and shoes and socks and trousers and stood in his underwear. He brushed carefully and methodically at each piece of clothing and shoes until he had removed all traces of the sandy loam of the river's edge. Just as slowly he dressed again and outside of the fact that his shirt and the shoulders of his sports jacket were still damp you couldn't tell anything had happened.

He turned the side view mirror and combed his hair as best he could in the half-light and patted it in place. Replacing the comb in his breast pocket, he shook his large handkerchief and draped it on the bonnet. It would dry in a few minutes, enough anyway to place in his pocket. He then looked at the rug, picked it up and examined it carefully, then giving it a couple of quick hard shakes, folded it and returned to the back seat of the car, closed the door gently, got in behind the wheel and turned the key and it quickly caught.

He suddenly realized he was very tired. He looked at his watch. It would be at least two-thirty before he would be back at the Grand and in his own room again. Better use the service entrance to be safe. He was dying for a drink and he thought about the flask in the glove compartment. He started to reach for it but stopped. Better not. Better wait 'til you're safely in your room.

He released the brake and was slowly pulling away. He was almost out of the lay by when a flickering headlight appeared behind him in his rear view mirror. He slowed down to a crawl to see if he could make out who it was. It was growing bigger now, Ja, there it is, a bicycle. It had stopped and into the soft moonlight, the figure of a Bobby pushing his bike came into view.

Kurt was so shocked to see the uniformed policeman he jammed his foot hard onto the accelerator. The tyres spun onto the road and squealed as he roared away.

The bobby's head shot up. He could only see the taillights of the big car roaring off in the distance. "Bloody kids!" he said to himself. But he knew he wouldn't catch them. He would just burst a gut trying to.

He put the kickstand down on his bike and when he felt it was going to stand he made his way down the incline to the water's edge. He took a packet of fags from his tunic inside pocket and lit the lighter. A soft breeze blew out the flame and he turned his back on it. Cupping his hands around the lighter, he struck it again and gave a long pull. He was ready to close the lid when in the flickering flames he saw something on the grass. "Well, what is this then?" He put the lighter in his left hand and bent to pick up the object. It was a small blue velvet box. "By heck, so that's what the ruckus was about! A lover's quarrel." He opened the lid of the box, it was empty. "Oh well, it must have come to now't. There's no sign of a weeping girl."

He blew out the lighter and reached for his torch. He swung the light around in a wide arc and slowly brought it in smaller to himself. Yes, he was right, there was an area trampled down, as if two people had recently been there. Oh well, no harm's done. He pocketed the

V.E. Sullivan

little box. He would turn it in with his report in the morning. He carefully extinguished his fag, picked up the butt and walked back to his bike. He tucked them both into his kit bag. He'd throw the butt away later. He threw his leg over the saddle, retracted the kickstand and pushed off.

Chapter 60

Rob woke to the delicious smell of coffee. Then he lay thinking, can this be only Sunday? He felt that they'd been there for days, and days, and days. He turned his head and stole a long look at Suzette. She looked so peaceful lying in the half circle of his arm. He was still a little worried about her. She was still quite pale, but Dr. Dundee assured him she would be soon back to her old self. Rob couldn't wait for the inquest to be over. Then Auntie Millacent could be laid to rest.

He had talked Suzette out of the notion of wanting to see her one last time, knowing full well that that would be the last impression she would have. Then every time she thought of her aunt, the disfigured face and the broken body would be all she would see. This way was better. She would remember the smiling face and the dancing eyes, the well-groomed little lady that she always was.

As if she felt his eyes on her, she stirred, and like a cat, arched her back and put her arms above her head, clasped her hands and stretched. "Well, good morning sleepy head," Rob said and kissed her forehead. He was happy to see that her eyes were not so dark, the pain was not so prominent and that life was returning to those beautiful green eyes.

She smiled and said drowsily, "What time is it, love?"

"Half passed eight."

"Oh damn! Dori's here all ready. I can smell the coffee. I was going to be up and help with everything. It's time I stop letting people fetch and carry for me and pull my weight a bit." She was struggling to free herself from Rob's grasp.

"Hang on, hang on, my love. Don't rush. You know what she's like."

"I know, Rob, but she has already done so much for us. It was a big shock to her and Ed. They loved her, too. I don't want to be a soft old Nelly."

"Never, not a bit of it," Rob said. "We're going to be just fine. Give us a kiss, then you can go."

"Really, Rob. Who's the soft Nelly now?" and giggled as he drew her close to him.

"I think children are awake, I hear stirring upstairs. Hope they had a good night," Ed said as he lay early post on the tray.

By the Pricking of My Thumb

"Aye, love," Dori said, putting in some biscuits. "These should be ready when they come down." She was wiping the excess flour from her hands. "We'll wait and see what else they would want before church. I have a nice joint for teatime. Want Suzette to eat a good meal. She is going to need all her strength to get through next few days, I'll be bound."

"Aye, she will lass. Rum days ahead. But once we get Miss Millacent laid to rest things should be better all around. Tell her I'll pull the ropes on the morning change for her and Rob."

Dori smiled and came around the kitchen table and picked an imaginary spot from his dark jacket. "You look right grand, you do," kissing his cheek. "I'll tell them. She'll be that proud she will."

Chapter 61

Suzette sat with her white gloved hands tightly clutching her common book of prayer, straight back in the hard cool pew listening to the pull of the change on the bells knowing Ed was doing it for them, the old darling, just like him. Where in the world would they be without Ed and Dori. Whatever would they have done? She knew full well they never would have coped with everything. Rob would have tried but she would have given up. She knew full well it would have been her undoing without these three dear ones.

The sweetness of the bells rang out over the still fresh smell in the air. Auntie's favorite hymn, "Amazing Grace". She knew wherever Aunt Millicent was she was smiling. The tears were dangerously close now, filling her eyes and threatening to spill over and run down over her cheeks. Don't you dare cry! she said to herself, tilting her head a little backward as if forcing them back to where they had come from. She didn't dare blink. She felt the warm pressure of Rob's hands covering her own shaking ones. She stole a glance with her eyes sideways at him. She didn't have to move her head, only her eyes. He was smiling encouragement at her.

"You're doing just fine, my darling. It will soon be over."

She gave a weak smile back to let him know she understood. But would it soon be over? She didn't think this nightmare would ever end. She could see no light at the end of the tunnel, only darkness. A shiver ran down her spine. Was there more or would it all come together like a giant puzzle with only a few pieces yet to be found and placed and it would be finished? She prayed that's the way it would end but she feared she was wrong.

All of a sudden a deep rich baritone voice broke through her thoughts, "In the name of the Father, and the Son, and the Holy Ghost." Why, that was the benediction! She hadn't heard a word of the sermon but she must have knelt, and risen, and sung, but she had no recollection of any of it. Like a mechanical robot she had done it all, so deep was her concentration.

Oh no, dear Lord, don't let me shut off the world. If I'm ever to be my old self let me feel it all. The pain, the words and then your healing balm. Please God, oh, please.

Then suddenly she felt as if a weight had been lifted from her shoulders and a sweet calm filled her heart and mind and spilled over, washing her free. It was wonderful, and then it was gone. That was all right. God had answered her and she knew she would someday have it back to stay when this was all over. It would be someday.

She felt Rob's hand on her elbow, helping her up. She felt almost giddy, light headed, but she knew she was going to be all right and could face whatever lie ahead of them.

The bells rang ever so much sweeter as they stepped from the half-light into the sun. The vicar was there, standing in the door shaking hands. As they approached, he took her hand in his and covered it with his other and gave her his condolences. He was a good, kind-hearted man. Suzette knew him well and liked him, just as Millacent had done. She knew his words of comfort were sincere and it lifted a burden from her heart and mind to know he was going to do Auntie's service. There was no need to have to go to the parsonage with pertinent lists of her life and her work in the parish. All those years of unselfish work and her dedication to the village of St. Gilliam. He knew only too well, and she would be sadly missed by one and all.

Rob and Suzette were busy talking to village residents whom she had known since she had been a small girl and used to come to St. Gilliam with her father and mother on holidays in the latter years, and as a young woman with her young man. Dori came hurrying up to them.

"Sorry, love, but would you like to stay and come along in a bit with Ed?"

But Rob spoke up before Suzette had a chance, "You run along with Dori, my love, I will wait for Ed."

"Yes, I think that's best. I would really like to give you a hand in the kitchen, Dori."

She was beaming as she tucked her arm into Suzette's and said, "I'll be that glad of your help and your company," and the two women said their goodbyes and made their way towards the cottage.

Chapter 62

David Collingwood stopped on his way down the stairs outside of Peggy's door but all was silent. He hadn't heard the lass come home last night and he ran his hands over his hair and started down the stairs. He could smell the coffee. Oh well, she's a good lass and she works hard. So what was this feeling that he had.

Poking his head around the kitchen door, "Morning, Mother."

"Aye, good morning. Your breakfast will be ready in a tick. Sit down and have a cup of coffee, I will finish up here."

Pouring himself a cup of coffee he said, "Did you hear Peggy come in last night?"

"No, I was that tired. I think I was asleep before my head hit the pillow," she smiled over her shoulder at her husband and he smiled back. "Give her another few minutes and finish your cuppa, then you can knock her up. I can keep her breakfast hot on the hub." She was a good wife and mother and kept a fine home. Here, Sunday breakfast was the same every Sunday. A mixed grill, a favorite of David Collingwood and of Peggy. A bit heavy for her but she could take what she wanted of it and it never went begging.

She turned to ask him what his plans were, was he going to play cricket? He was the club's best bowler. Or was his shoulder still stiff and too sore? But he had gone to wake Peggy. She smiled. He was that proud of his daughter, and so was she for that matter. She had been a beautiful baby and never gave them a wakeful night as some babies do. They had taken great joy in watching her cut her first tooth, learn to take a step, and then to talk. They never slept much the first night before her first day of school. They had many a giggle over that as the years slipped by. And here she was a very beautiful young woman of twenty-one. Where had the years gone?

I suppose they were a bit old fashioned and set in their ways, wanting her to keep proper hours and not wanting her to go out with every Tom, Dick and Harry. And Margaret had been quite adamant and shocked when Peggy spoke to her about the pill and hadn't dared mention it to David. He thought of himself as quite a modern man but really he was just the opposite and would have gone starkers to think his pretty little girl even knew about such things as sex, let alone thought about doing it. He probably would have locked her in her room and met every young man who came calling with his cricket bat. Margaret chuckled to herself as the mental picture came to mind.

She was taking the plates from the warming oven when she heard David coming down the stairs. He came into the kitchen and the look on his face made Margaret put down the plates, remove the oven mitts from her hands and say, "David, what is it? Is Peggy ill?"

"No, Margaret. She's not there, and her bed hasn't even been slept in. It's just as you left it last night, lass. With her bed turned down and her robe at the foot."

She stopped dead in her tracks. "That can't be, David. You must be mistaken. She's never stayed out all night unless she's called us to tell us where we could reach her. And, any road, she worked late last night. There would be no place to go. No one to meet at that hour. She'd have no place to go but to come home. Oh my God, David. You don't suppose something has happened to her?"

"Nay, nay, lass. We would have heard. Everyone knows her and us."

"But David..."

"No lass. Come over here and have a cuppa."

All the while he was reassuring his wife, he had a nagging in the pit of his stomach. By God, he'd skin her alive when she did come in for scaring them half witless.

"Look love, there are a lot of reasons a lass like ours might not come home. Maybe something happened at the Grand and when it was settled she figured it was too late to call and went around to one of her mates and they talked half the night as lasses do."

"Oh David, of course your right."

It tugged at his heart. Peggy got all of her good looks from her mother and right now with her head cocked to one side and those large blue eyes shining with hope, it might have been Peggy herself sitting there.

"Look, you get on to her mates and I will go around to the Grand and see if there was anything going on last night and then I'll ring you up." He bent and kissed her and took a gulp of his lukewarm coffee and he was gone. No stomach for Sunday morning breakfast now.

He backed the car out and made for the Grand. He could have walked but this was quicker. He wished he could rid himself of this feeling of doom. Ever since he had stood in front of Peggy's bedroom this morning, he had known something just wasn't right. He couldn't put his finger on anything; just this lead ball in the pit of his stomach. Maybe he was hungry, or had too much coffee on his empty stomach. Aye, that would be it. Ah, here he was at the Grand.

He pulled into the first empty parking spot he could find and took the steps two at a time. Hang on, hang on. No need to draw attention to yourself, on a Sunday morning, You are not likely to be taken for a country gentleman with your baggy pants and rolled up sleeves. He suddenly felt very conspicuous in the wake of the posh tourists, and he felt more like a gardener, but the gardener wouldn't be using the front door would he? Not bloody likely. Hope there was someone he knew around. What was he going to say any road? If she had stayed over at a mates she wouldn't appreciate her father making a fuss. But, too bloody bad. Serves her right for not coming home and giving them such a fright. She'd think twice next time, maybe.

That lead ball was getting bigger and heavier in his stomach as he made his way to the phone to call Margaret. And soon he was waiting for the call to go through and the pips to stop. He prayed she would have some news.

"Hello, Margaret love."

"Oh David, what's taking so long?"

"Have you heard anything?"

"Not a dicky bird."

"She left all right. That's the last anyone has seen of her."

"Was she late leaving?" Margaret asked.

"No love. She wasn't. Seems she had some kind of a row with the night manager. No one seems to know much about it except he gave her a dressing down about her work."

"Well, would you credit it! No one works harder than our Peggy. Really! More than ready and willing to do her share." She sounded like one of those mothers who thinks her children can do no wrong.

"Well that might be as you say love, but never the less it happened. The night porter heard it. Look, I think I'll stop by the police station on my way home just in case there was an accident or something."

"Oh David, you don't think..."

"There, there, love. Don't go getting your knickers in a twist. It's just a precautionary measure, just to let them know she's gone missing like. Just an extra pair of eyes, love. Just extra eyes. Not to worry. I'll be right along, you'll see. All will be well."

But in his heart of hearts he knew all would never be well again. God help us. David felt suddenly cold and empty with a terrible ache in his heart. Tears sprang in his eyes and he longed to hold his beautiful daughter in his arms once again. And Margaret, what ever would they do? He felt that some of the sunshine had just left their lives, and a cold chill went down his spine.

He threw back his head and uttered a long sigh, clapped his knees and rose slowly. He made his way back to his car and headed to the station house.

Chapter 63

Terry Simms was bursting with pride as he neared the station house. He'd been sent to York Saturday to do some legwork and to take a circular around to the precinct. It was just a stroke of luck, that's what it was to be at the right place at the right time. He had been pinning a photocopy of von Heusen's last picture on the board in the York precinct house when a bobby, about the size of Sergeant Littlejohn, looking over his shoulder said, "Funny thing that."

"What is?" Terry said.

"Well maybe I've seen this bloke."

"What?" Terry spun around. "Where, when?"

"Well, let's be getting a better look, shall we laddie?"

Terry stepped aside as the police officer took a well-worn pair of spectacles from his pocket and adjusting them tilted his head back and took several minutes. Terry thought he would explode.

"Aye, that's him all right."

"Are you sure, sir?"

"Heck as like. He collapsed in my arms." It all came out.

V.E. Sullivan

What luck. He had gotten a written statement from Dr. Fleetwood and the nursing Sister and a positive ID on the car from the porter who remembered because he parked it and thought it was a right treat to drive the big black Daimler.

Terry looked at his watch and wondered if the inquest was in progress yet. Or, was it this afternoon? Any road, he would soon find out. He opened the station house door and stopped to straighten his tunic and remove his helmet. Tucking it under his arm, he looked down the hall and thought he recognized the man sitting on the bench. Never, it couldn't be St. Gilliam's favorite son, best bowler on the cricket team! It couldn't be this crumpled man hunched forward, arms on his knees, hands clasped before him and his head and chin resting on his chest. By heck, it was him. Maybe someone had stolen his lucky bat.

"Mr. Collingwood, sir?"

"What's that? Oh, it's you Terry lad. Have you heard anything?"

"Sorry, I'm not sure. You see, I've been in York on police business since Saturday and I've just come back. What's wrong Mr. Collingwood?"

"It's our Lass."

"Not Peggy," Terry said. "What ever is it? Has there been an accident?"

"Nay, nay, laddie. She's gone missing. Never came home Saturday night. We're about spare, Margaret and I. We asked everyone. No one has seen her since she left the Grand Saturday late."

Terry said all the right things he had been taught to say but he felt uneasy. He knew Peggy well, went to school with her. Even stepped out with her for a while. They were still good friends and he knew it had to be something important to keep her away all this time without a dicky bird to her folks. Not like her at all. He could tell David Collingwood felt the same way. With a reassuring word, Terry left to see what he could find out. He returned with a cuppa for David and told him he was welcome to wait and talk to Inspector Pentecroft but he didn't know when he would be in. He explained to David the inquest might take a lot of time and all.

"Oh, aye. Went clear out of my mind about poor Miss Lang. I'll wait a bit, if not in road."

"No danger, sir. But if you do decide to go home, I'll talk to my super and call tonight and tell you all I know."

"Thanks Terry. I'm that grateful, I am. You knowing Peggy so well. I feel it is more personal now."

"Not to worry, we'll do our very best."

"Aye, you will, I know."

Terry patted his shoulder and told him he had a report to file and was sorry he couldn't sit and talk longer.

"Nay, lad. You get about your business. Can't have you skiving off, can we?" But the words were flat and lifeless.

Terry turned to go. All excitement he had felt on his way in had been replaced with a kind of dread.

He sat at one of the makeshift desks, took his notebook out of his pocket and started his lengthy report.

Chapter 64

The inquest had lasted longer than anyone expected with the evidence of the police and the account of the discovery of the body by the Halley's all duly recorded. But it was Dr. Dundee's fine evidence of the scene and his expert eye to details that other pathologists might miss that put it all into perspective and left no other choice for the judge to make but murder most foul by person or person's yet unknown, or words to that effect.

Ashley and Pentecroft knew the real work for them must start in earnest before all traces of the criminals disappeared.

For the Halley's, Suzette, and Rob, remained the last act of laying Millacent Lang to a final resting place and then the rebuilding of their lives could take place however slowly or quickly only the good Lord knew. Nothing could really end this tragic nightmare until justice was served. And they all knew the wheels of justice ground ever so slowly sometimes. However, just getting her funeral behind them would be a big step in the right direction.

They had nothing to do but to show up thanks to the wonderful friends of the Women's Guild. She was so well loved and admired by the residents of St. Gilliam. There was nothing they wouldn't do so all arrangements were being handled and Suzette gave a silent prayer of thanks for she didn't know where to start. It was all too overwhelming. She couldn't give anything her full attention. She started to do things only to find herself drawn away to something else and was ever so grateful to those dear people who had loved her also and watched her grow up through the years that it would be handled right with love and dignity that her beloved auntie deserved. Not the hit and miss, it might have been had things been left to her to do.

Chapter 65

Ronald and Ashley had decided to take lunch with Dr. Dundee before returning to the station house. They spoke briefly to the family, after Dr. Dundee had spoken softly to them.

Ed and Rob about the release of Miss Lang's body for burial. He thought for the lass's sake the sooner the better. Both men nodded their heads in silent agreement. He patted both men on the back and turned away without another word to see his lunch companions each referring to their seconds about things they wanted done back at the station house before they got there.

"Aye, laddies, let's be havin' ya. I've got hours of work awaitin' me at the lab and no want to be burning the midnacht oil to nacht."

"I'm ready. Are you Ronald?"

"Right. Then, Sergeant, you know what to do."

"Yes sir, I'll be ready when you get back to the station house."

Then Inspector Pentecroft returned to the two men who were discussing whether to take two cars. Finally Chief Superintendent Quest and Inspector Pentecroft went in one car, and Dr. Dundee in his own, as after their lunch they would be going in opposite directions.

V.E. Sullivan

Chapter 66

As the cars pulled away, Ed and Robert stood a little apart from their women. They decided not to tell the girls about the release of Millacent's body, but Ed would make a quick call to the rector and let him handle it from the church rectory and he could call and inform them when the day was settled upon, thus saving both their women that they loved added worry and they wouldn't have to think about it on a daily basis. Both decided this was far the better way.

They started to rejoin the women when Ed stopped straight in his tracks. Rob turned to look at him. The black look on Ed's face prompted Rob to say, "What's got you lookin' like a scalded cat, then?"

"It's him," Ed said, jerking his head towards a young man who had just come out of the inquest and stopped to light a cigarette before going down the steps to the sidewalk.

"What about him?" Robert asked.

"Remember my telling you about a bloke, that foreign gent, that was trying to enter Miss Lang's shop? The foreign bloke!" Ed, getting a little testy about Robert's lack of a ready reply.

"Oh, oh, I'm with you now. What about him?"

"Well that's the very one, just lighting a fag."

Rob let his eyes travel to the face of the man who was putting his cigarette case and lighter away, and for a split second their eyes met. The man looked away first. Was he upset or was that his imagination? No, he was, and he was quickening his steps now as if he was trying to fade into the crowd. Rob decided that would be very difficult, for the cut of his clothes alone made him stand out like a peacock in a pig sty.

Ed interrupted his thoughts by saying, "Wonder what he's doing here any road."

"Could be morbid curiosity or boredom," Rob said. "A young man who dresses like that demands a lot out of his daily existence, London jet-setters or the continent. Not our quaint little quiet St. Gilliam."

"Indeed, I wonder."

V.E. Sullivan

Chapter 67

Kurt's reason for lighting the cigarette in the first place was to take a look over the flame and through the smoke to see if anyone was paying attention to him or not. He was happy to see that everyone was far too busy with their flapping tongues to pay any attention. They probably thought he had come down from London most likely anyway.

He was putting the cigarettes away when he felt a pair of eyes on him and he looked up and his eyes connected with a pair of all too knowing eyes. He tried not to bolt, but couldn't contain himself. He was moving too fast down the stairs and into the small groups that were on the sidewalk. Anywhere to get away from those eyes.

Ever since Saturday night he couldn't seem to settle his nerves and now this. Damned Heindrich. Wanting to know what was happening at this inquest. Anyway, the sooner he got back to the hotel the better and to get a big drink under his belt. He was getting as skittish as Heindrich. Every time he closed his eyes he could see Peggy's face floating past him.

He was being really stupid, a real dumkopf. As swiftly as she had been moving, she would be long gone from St. Gilliam. It would be days, even weeks before they could make a positive ID on her. Water changes bodies after they have been in it for a few days. It comforted him somehow to think that she was somewhere else. Just in case she had told some other girl about them and that he could be tied to her.

He realized he was back in front of the Grand. He hurried on in and made right for the lounge. He didn't look left or right, just straight ahead, as if he had on a pair of blinkers. He walked right past the three men and never noticed them.

Chapter 68

"'Allo, 'allo? What's this then?" Pentecroft touched Quest's arm.

"Aye, that's the chap we saw in the dining room being taken to the hotel doctor isn't it?"

"Aye, laddie. And I noticed him among the curious at the inquest all right."

"Strange, don't you think, Ronald?"

"Could be he was just bored and thought he'd kill some time after hearing the locals talk about it. There isn't much to do for the likes of him in a quiet place like St. Gilliam. When we get back to the station house, if Terry's back we should have him do some checking—find out who he is and what he's doing in St. Gilliam and if he is alone."

They all agreed and started going over the different notes they had had when the waiter came up to take their order.

Chapter 69

Terry looked up at the big clock. It had been three hours since he started and he wasn't through yet. It was a difficult report to write and there was so much to get down and keep straight and he didn't want to muck up. He knew he had done a cracker of a job and he was proud of his work, and yet he kept seeing that slumped figure of David Collingwood. Whatever was Peggy playing at? But he knew there was more to it than that. Peggy would never stay away like this without telling her father or at least calling him. He felt it went much deeper than that and something bloody awful must have happened. Better check and see if he was still sitting out there and if he was, give him another cuppa. He'd be that glad when the Superintendents would be back.

He glanced over the glass partition by the Sergeant's desk and was relieved to see that David had gone. He would find out all he could and go by the cottage and tell them. If time didn't permit that, he would call and reassure them as best he could that they would do all they could to find her. Terry himself would keep his ears to the

V.E. Sullivan

ground and the first dickey bird he heard he would get on to them and he could promise them that.

Chapter 70

Suzette and Dori sat on little milk stools surrounded by small baskets of pink rose buds, bay leaves and bougainvillea, small bowls of crushed cinnamon sticks, arrowroot, and little vials of rosemary and rose oil. The warmth of the fireplace was filling the room with fragrant smells. Sultan was stretched his full length in front of the fire and seemed quite content to be almost singed. Suzette thought it was good to have something constructive to do besides sit and think and eat and sleep however fitful it was. And she loved to help with the beautiful scent of potpourri and it was something that made her feel close to her beloved auntie.

Ed had stopped by the shop to check on things and had brought home the mail that had piled up on the floor beneath the mail drop. In going through it, found a number of orders for the potpourri from York and Lincoln and London. So, with their lunch things all cleared up, Dori and Suzette set about getting the things together so they could set it for a few days before the little cardboard boxes all decorated with the lovely coloured print of Aunt Millacent's charming thatched cottage and the rose gardens were filled.

The idea for the little boxes actually was Dori's, as they sat around the fire one night a long time ago trying to figure a fitting package for their lovely mixture. Millacent had started to sell it in her shop at first. Then when dealers and owners of different shops started to buy it all up to take it back with them to their shops it got to be hard to keep things going and before they knew it, they had another little business going that filled in nicely for the bleak times all antique shops go through. And that's when Aunt Millacent drew up the agreement so Dori would have a nice little added income without worry about the tax man. It was all done through the shop.

And now Auntie was gone, she intended for the potpourri business not to go begging. And even if they had to hire a girl from the village to help Dori fill the orders, so be it, as she knew she wouldn't be available all the time. And she was determined it would not go by the wayside. She made a mental note to talk to Dori and Rob about it. She knew they could work things out and could see no problem in the future.

Her instinct told her Dori was speaking to her.

"Sorry? What was that Dori?"

Dori looked across to Suzette and smiled, "Oh, it was nothing, love."

"Oh, I'm sorry. I was just thinking, Dori, that I don't want to lose this little business and I won't be here to help all the time. Is there someone in the village that we could hire to help you fill the really big orders?"

"Aye, that glad you thought about that, luv, as I would love to keep it going myself. Aye, there is a nice young lass that works in chemist shop who is always looking for piecework. I know she'd be that glad of it and we will keep her plenty busy. You could meet her before you leave."

Suzette started to laugh, "Oh Dori, you know I don't need to meet her. If you think she's the one, that's all I need to know. We will set up the paperwork before we go. Remind me to get Rob to do it."

With that settled, the two women set to working in earnest.

Chapter 71

At the last minute, Rob and Ed had decided to take the van. They had told the girls they wanted to do some work. Ed wanted to unpack some new items and Rob to keep the books in order. But both men wanted to use the phone out of earshot of Dori and Suzette, Ed to call the parsonage and talk to Reverend Dawson about Millacent's memorial, and Rob wanted to talk to the museum and to Mr. Berkshire and Mr. Stilts keeping them all in the picture. He didn't see returning to London before a fortnight anyway. But if they could, they certainly would.

He also had to get on to a mate of theirs and have those cane chairs picked up and delivered to Suzette's flat before they were lumbered off to the unclaimed baggage and sold. They had looked far too long to find them and he wasn't about to lose them through neglect. Not by a long shot, he wasn't.

They had arrived and Ed parked the van in the back and they entered by the back door so as not to arouse the curious and who would knock on the glass wondering when they would open again. It pulled on both their heartstrings as they entered, but neither man spoke. They went right about their chosen tasks.

About two hours later, with everything accomplished they left by the same way, no one the wiser. About half way home. Rob looked over at Ed. "I've been thinking..." and he grimaced a little sheepishly. "It's really none of my business but when are you planning to open?"

"Oh aye laddie. It's your business all right enough. Yours and the lass's really. But I'd say sooner. Longer it's closed, harder it will be to get back. And you saw for yourself the invoices."

"Yes, that's what made me bring it up. Some of those things will be coming next week and as they're prepaid, someone is going to have to be there to accept them."

"Aye, I got things ship shape for the things that we have. Miss Lang and I had intended to do together. But the old girl and I have been working side by side for that many years and know where and what to do with things. It's just so good to be back there and putting things right. I've really missed it. She will always be there lending her warmth to the premises. I'm not daft, ye know," he said, stealing a quick sideways glance at Rob. "A bit soft," he grinned, "but not daft."

"I know what you mean," Rob said. "I felt her there guiding my thoughts as I went through things. Quite nice it was too, I must say. Confound it, I didn't feel I was wrong in going over the books and entering the figures and doing the tax work like I thought I would."

"She thought the world of you, laddie. Never fear."

"Thanks, Ed. I loved her a lot myself. Will you be able to cope with everything when we get into the full swing of it?"

"Aye, think so. Might have to hire a deliveryman as I would rather be full time in the shop now that she won't be there. Feel more comfortable than having a stranger shifting things all about so's to suit them. It's not our way."

Rob grinned. "Right, I agree. It looks so inviting and warm now. No use spoiling things. Right you are then. After tea maybe we can all put our heads together and come up with the right answers." He turned and looked out the window to see the lovely cottage come into view. It really was a beauty, right out of an ad for Town and Country. They parked the van and both men sighed and got out.

Chapter 72

Kurt lifted the cognac to his lips with shaking hands. He even managed to spill some; difficult, one would think, from such a large snifter, and beads of sweat covered his forehead.

The barkeep stole a sidelong glimpse at him. Blimie, he's had a rough night right enough or the devil himself is after him. He recognized him as being one of the guests at the Grand. Flashed money around but always signed the tab for it to be put on his bill and always had the best in the house. His bar bill must be something. Would probably keep me and my Mrs. for a fortnight. Oh well, nowt to do with him what guests got up to. He was paid to keep them happy and to be a good listener, not to turn them into members of the temperance league. He laughed to himself. Wouldn't have a job then, would you bucko? He caught Kurt looking at him but then he was very good at masking his thoughts as any good barkeep would be. "Same again," Kurt barked at him.

"Right you are, Governor."

To Kurt's satisfaction his hands had lost their tremor, or some of it. He looked at the barkeep who, was standing with his back slightly to him but not out of sight of his peripheral vision. "Keep my glass full until I tell you I don't want any more, hear me?"

"Yes, sir." He gave a quick glance and nod of his head.

Kurt realized he was being much too surly and loud and making himself stand out as there were a number of the lunch time businessmen still in there and some had turned to look. They were unaccustomed to disturbances in their lounge and looks of disapproval were all over their faces, nodding their heads.

"Damned stuffy Englanders. Like to wipe their smug look off their faces." He had reverted to talking to himself in German. Mein Gott what's the matter with me? But he seemed to have no control over himself and he didn't seem to know what he was going to say or do next. He realized he was singing his old German song from the barracks days. He swung around on his stool, lifted his glass high and finished his boisterous, rough song and just caught himself before he let the snifter fly to the glass mirror that ran the length of the bar reflecting the fine bottles of old liquor and liqueurs. Get out, you stupid oaf. If Heindrich hears of this. Mein Gott, you have enough trouble. Don't you remember what you're after? Get out, get out!

He set his glass down and, still more surly than he intended, asked the barkeep for his tab to sign, asked for a bottle of the best cognac to be sent to his room and left with as much dignity as possible. But not soon enough, for he overheard one of the gentlemen say "Bloody, foreigners. More and more of them coming to St. Gilliam with their boorish ways. Puts one quite off the Common Market, eh, what?"

He stopped in his tracks, ready to go back and make that conceited, pompous Englishman swallow his words. He was worth three of him. He was pure Aryan, not like other Germans. The Fuehrer saw to that. He was perfect in every way

Dumkopf, you'll ruin everything. Forget it, and get up those stairs and cool off. Ever since Saturday night you have lost it. You have killed lots of people, yes, girls, women, children, old men. What was so different about Peggy? Silly cow. How could she expect me to marry a cheap little village girl with no real education? No social graces. He would never marry beneath him. It went against all that had been bread into him. Nein, nein. He must marry a pure German girl, high in morals and from the right family. And when he had a big chunk of Heindrich's money he knew what to do and how to do it and to keep it coming in. Never a common man he would be again. Nein, nein. He was laughing, loud, when he realized he was at his door.

He let himself in to his expensive suite and closed the door and looked around. Some more of his things had arrived from the tailors. There were boxes piled on the love seat that ran along the front of his bed and he could see them in the mirror that hung behind the bar in the sitting room where he was standing. Ja, this was what he was destined for. No more settling for second hand or second best as he had done in the past with Heindrich throwing him the odd bone now and again as you would to a faithful dog, obedient, well trained dog. Well, no more. He had tasted the other life and was never going to settle for less.

Somewhere in his clouded mind he could hear the phone. He never bothered to answer it but made straight for the bedroom. He opened one box after the other. His beautiful suits and his evening clothes, Opera slippers, silk monogrammed dressing gowns, smoking jacket, shirts, cravat, fine silk underwear, almost everything was here, all paid for by Heindrich. He was laughing uncontrollably and dancing around the room holding the luxurious dressing gown to him when he realized someone was at the door. He remembered ordering the bottle.

He called to them and they entered. He gave the young bellboy a nice tip, walked to the bar, hastily, ripping off the seal on the top of the cognac bottle, discarding them on the floor. It gave him such an air of self-respect to know no matter how big a mess, he didn't have to clean up after himself ever again. He took the bottle and the glass and headed for the bedroom and that's how Heindrich found him, sprawled across the bed with boxes, tissue and their contents scattered everywhere.

Chapter 73

Heindrich pulled, jabbed, slapped and cursed Kurt until his head was once again exploding in a raging ball of red-hot pain, going in waves across his eyes and up the side of his head. So violently were the waves of agonizing pain he was quite nauseated and had to run to Kurt's loo where he fell on his knees before the bowl and was violently sick again and again. He was ringing with sweat, his shirt and underwear clinging to him as if he had showered in them and the stench was awful. No matter how often he showered he couldn't rid himself of it. It oozed from every pore of his body as well as his face.

As he lifted the cool flannel from his face, he saw the wound had split open again and a thick yellow pus was oozing from it. So swollen was his face, flushed and discoloured he didn't even recognize himself.

He swung around, cursing and shouting at Kurt, "You'll pay for this, you filthy bastard. Ja, you'll pay, and sooner than you think.

He bent over the prone figure on the bed. Gott, he could hardly stop himself from killing him there and then. It would have been so easy, a pillow over that handsome face he had come to loathe—no struggle, nothing. It would be over. All he had to do was roll him over on his stomach with his face on the pillow. Passed out in a drunken stupor, they would say. Too drunk to save himself, a tragic accident.

But nein, he needed him once more and it would be over, over for Kurt that is. And then, the end of his pain. In Rio it would all be taken care of and he would be his handsome, debonair self again. The good life of wine, women and song would begin.

He looked at Kurt once more. All in good time, you will see my friend. You will see it all unravel before your eyes when all the things you thought you could weasel out of me vanish. Ja, you should know by now after all these years. No one can out think or out do the Jackal. I will always win. How many times you have seen others try and fail, even with my back against the wall. I have never been outwitted. Ja, you know you little dumkopf. No one but the Jackal wins and lives to do it again and again. Nothing changes, only time and place.

He swung around and had to steady himself from falling. He was so weak and try as he might he couldn't make himself step on any of the delicate fineries on the floor even though they were Kurt's. He hated the very sight of them and him. He had paid for them and planned to send them all back after Kurt had met his demise. He stepped gingerly around and over them and into the sitting room, made himself a stiff drink and took five of his pain killers.

Had to try and make them last. The bottle was over half gone. He sat down in a big leather easy chair and finished his drink. He left the glass on the little table and went back into the bedroom. Kurt had not moved a muscle. He left a scalding note for him where he was sure to find it, under the bottle on the bedside table. He was going to have a quick look around in Kurt's wallet and the drawers but the nausea was beginning to return. So he left it and moved quickly to return to his own suite before another exhausting attack overtook him.

Chapter 74

Ashley too, felt the tension in the air of the make shift crime room, like riding to hounds who had picked up the first scent of the fox. He had been in a hunt several times but it was something he never brought up at the Yard not wanting to alienate his fellow workers by thinking he was a toff. He looked across at Pentecroft. They exchanged glances and nods. He felt it too. He could see it in his eyes, the way he sat tense and ready. He had to remember, these were fine officers and well trained but none of them had ever been on a murder investigation, let alone the hunt. They were all ready to go, their adrenaline giving them that extra edge and brightness to their eyes.

So much had come to light with Terry's investigation in York; a damn fine job he did, he was head and shoulders above some of the seasoned men he had back in London. But he definitely wanted Ronald on his team and Terry was so young, his turn would come again. Not so with Ronald. Like himself, getting along in years, and the breaks at getting ahead were fewer and fewer. He had had his share, but Ronald living and working in the beautiful village didn't stand a chance to show his mettle. As quaint and beautiful as it was, a man like Pentecroft longed to cut his teeth on something besides broken windows and stolen bikes and little shoplifting. No, it was now or never, and he intended to make it now. Not only because he had come to respect and to like him, but because he was a very good officer and would be a credit to his branch. And it wouldn't go to his head and spoil him. He'd get on with the others; why even Rennie would ask his advice when he deemed it fitting. If you could win over Rennie, it was a piece of cake, as the Yanks would say. Yes, Pentecroft had to come back with him, no danger.

But first they had a crime to solve, all of them. With all of the new and pertinent finds up on the board, pieces of paper tucked here and there, they had almost a family tree. Only it wasn't. It was a detailed outline of two very dangerous and cold blooded killers, and fascinating little details. That odd shaped piece of glass Terry had found that first afternoon in the shed dirt, turned out to be a small fragment of a prescription lens, and the black threads in the corner were black ribbon. After much study and speculation it proved to be that of a monocle. The rest of it had yet to be found and it would take two officers on their hands and knees working simultaneously on the shed floor. Pentecroft and Quest were sure they would find it, if luck and the god's were with them, they would. Both men felt pretty sure their men were Heindrich von Heusen and Kurt Schreiler, but the way of running them to ground and proving it without a shadow of a doubt was quite another matter, however they were well ahead of the game now, and had a lot more clues and facts to work on than they'd had twenty four hours ago. It was exhilarating. It was spreading like a fire through the room.

He said walking over to where Pentecroft stood, "Gentlemen, you all have been given your orders by the Inspector and myself and if you come across anything, anything at all, get it to Inspector Pentecroft or myself day or night. And at the expense of sounding old fashioned and in the words of the world's most famous detective, fictional or otherwise," he winked at Ronald, lifted his hands in the air and said "Gentlemen, the game is afoot." And to his total surprise everyone knew who he was talking about. But then he shouldn't have been, because there is not a schoolboy alive in England that hadn't read the adventures of Sherlock Holmes. And packing their note pads and whistles in their proper places, each talking to their prospective partners, they picked up their helmets and were ready to go.

Chapter 75

There were still several hours of daylight and Terry and his partner were getting ready to leave for Miss Lang's place to go through the shed once more, when Terry asked his bobby to wait by their bikes as he had to ask their superior something.

Terry walked up to the two men deep in thought and conversation about the days events. They were very surprised when Terry cleared his throat.

"Oh yes, Corporal. Remember something else? And by the way, a capital job in York. Well done."

"Thank you, sir. But Inspector Pentecroft, sir, it's about Peggy Collingwood. Her father sat here the best part of the morning waiting to talk to you about her going missing."

"What's this about going missing?" He hadn't had the time to go over his own everyday paperwork and incidents report for a couple of days.

"Yes sir, she never came home Saturday after her late shift on the desk at the Grand."

"Hmmm. How long have you known her Corporal?"

"We were in school together, sir, and we were stepping out for awhile, but we're still very good friends."

"I gather," Quest said, "this is not a natural thing for this Peggy Collingwood."

"No sir, it is not. She would never put her folks through anything like this. She is very close to both of them, a good respectable girl. Something has gone wrong, somewhere, for her to pull this, no danger. And I promised Mr. Collingwood I would stop tonight, time permitting, and tell them anything I could, just to let them know we care and are trying, sir." He lowered his eyes and his head.

"All right, son. We all know the family, and a fine one at that. David Collingwood is somewhat of a celebrity here in St. Gilliam," he said to Quest. "He is our star cricket player and the best bowler, mighty fine, I might add. I watched a match or two and a trial match between York and St. Gilliam and we won hands down thanks to David's sterling bowling and he is not slow at the bat either."

"Sounds like you know the family pretty well, Ronald. And do you agree with Corporal Simms, here?"

"Well, I don't know them in a social way, but yes, I know them and I can't say about Peggy, but I'm sure Terry knows, and not just letting his feelings get the best of him. I'm sure of that, better I can't say. Look, Simms. Go and finish off at the Lang's cottage and report back. In the meantime, we will see what we can turn up on Peggy, start an investigation anyway."

"Thank you, sir. I know they will be ever so grateful." He turned and left.

Pentecroft turned and looked at Quest. Both men were thinking the same thing. They must pull a man to do some legwork but they couldn't spare Terry. He was too vital to this investigation because of his sterling work in York and his long association with the Lang family. But they could check with Sergeant Littlejohn as to what he knew as to dates and then they would decide what to do.

After deliberation with Sergeant Littlejohn, Pentecroft and Quest decided to let the Sergeant delegate a man to do the tedious questioning and legwork. They decided to pay a call to the

Collingwoods, check out the scene at the home to reassure both parents that they were on the job and that their daughter's disappearance was important to them. It was a traumatic time in a parent's life when their child goes missing, no matter what that child's age might be, and they wanted the Collingwoods to know they were sympathetic to their feelings.

On the way over, Ronald filled Quest in a little on the family and to put him in the picture a little more. "It has been a spell since I've seen Peggy, you understand. She was always a pretty lass. The best of both parents and that's not bad. You'll see for yourself. Never has been in trouble to my knowledge. I feel Terry's right when he says they are a close-knit family. And the child, pretty and clever but not spoiled. She would be disciplined, but with love. I am sure there is nothing amiss between the three of them that would cause her to bolt."

"I am sure you are right," Ashley said, "but talking to them will at least give them assurance we are here and on top of things and they are not alone in this matter. It has been almost forty-eight hours or longer since they have seen her so something is afoot."

"Aye, well, here we are." Pentecroft pulled the car into the drive that ran along the side of a neat, well kept garden and lawn that surrounded the clapboard and mortar Tudor home of the Collingwoods. Before either man could reach the front door, it flew open and a very pretty woman with large blue eyes and a handsome dark haired man came bolting through it, colliding with the two men.

"Oh I'm so sorry," Margaret said as Quest caught her up in his arms to keep them from toppling onto the gravel walk. Quest looked down at the pretty face, upturned to his own and saw the tension drawing fine lines across her mouth and eyes and those eyes were so full of pain and worry he couldn't help but feel the pangs of uneasiness that swept through them.

He thought, Oh God, I hope this turns out well for this family. By the look of both of them, they couldn't stand too much more.

"That's all right then," he said smiling, and released his grip on Margaret.

David came up and put his arm around her waist. "I'm sorry, we're just about at the end of our wits with worry."

By the Pricking of My Thumb

"No need to apologize, Mr. Collingwood. Shall we step inside where we can have a little more privacy?"

"Yes, of course," David said, and led the way into a very comfortable sitting room. The sunlight filtered through white, frothy, lace curtains. It is a room that reflects both of their tastes, Ashley thought. Two big leather wing back chairs on either side of the fireplace with grained leather-top tables beside both of them that would take heavy glasses or a delicate cup, either way, and look right. His well trained eyes traveled around the room, taking in a comfortable curved window seat that followed the paned, bowed window, covered with crisp chintz of a dark blue background on which was scattered pillows splashed with bright red flowers, big and medium sized ones. Quest thought Peonies and mums. Anyway it was an elegant room. The Chesterfield was made of the same chintz. The big plump pillows filling each corner. A heavy, extra large square coffee table with the same leather covering and just the right balance of magazines, heavy onyx ashtray with a box of cigarettes. He guessed it said a lot about both people, warm and open and sure of themselves and with each other. A room both sexes could be completely comfortable in.

When they were seated, David offered both men a drink, both declined, but wished they hadn't.

"This is a wonderful room." Both men said it almost in unison and for the first time both Margaret and David's faces lost some of the tension and a smile played around the corners of their mouths.

Ronald was right, my God they were a handsome couple. He hoped with all his heart he and Pentecroft would bring a full smile onto their faces and not have to break their hearts.

"Well now," Ronald said, as they settled themselves. "I was wondering if you have a recent picture of Peggy. We would like to circulate it."

David reached over and gave Margaret's hands that were clasped tightly in her lap a quick squeeze and said, "It's all right, love. Why not get the snap we took on her birthday. It's a smashing shot of her."

Margaret nodded and got up. When she returned she handed the picture to Quest who was the closest to her and said, "This is a very good likeness of her, Inspector."

By the Pricking of My Thumb

Quest looked down at the pretty fresh face that was laughing up at him. The likeness to her mother was startling, like sisters. He was staring at the picture of Peggy, trying to remember, and it came to him like a flash. "Look here, Pentecroft. Isn't this the young lady that you collided with in the Grand?"

Ronald took the photo from Ashley's hand and looked down at it. "Would you credit it! I didn't recognize her. She has grown into a beautiful young lady."

"You saw Peggy?" Margaret asked.

"Yes, I did. We collided, actually. I wasn't watching and she was looking for something in her purse and seemed to be in a hurry."

Quest asked, "Did she happen to say anything to the two of you that she was meeting someone special or going somewhere?"

"Well no, not exactly. She had to leave early saying something about having to pick up some things at the stationer in York for the Grand that had been delayed—new memos or billings or something—and if she stayed talking any longer she'd miss her train and that we would all have a lovely natter over Sunday breakfast and if Daddy felt better go to the commons and watch the match. It seems to me now that she said it in one sentence, so fast I scarce had time to put the coffee pot down. A peck on the cheek and she was out the door before I could question her about anything. That was the last time I saw her."

Quest sighed, and finally said, "Please understand the next question I must put to you. There is no intention to malign, I just must ask you if Peggy is likely to tell you something to spare your feelings, and then do something else. What I mean is, would she go to York like she said and then meet someone here in St. Gilliam?"

Margaret seemed to wince. David just pulled himself up straight, squared his shoulders and looked straight in Quest's eyes, "Chief Inspector Quest, Peggy has never lied to us. She was brought up to know the truth is the only way and we would back her no matter what. But if we were ever to catch her in a lie, to either of us, then we would never trust her again. She has always been a good lass. Always home at night, not always on time, but never out all night, I'll wager."

"Thank you, Mr. Collingwood. Now at least we know she took the early train to York and we can show her picture at this end and send the photo through to York and they will show it there and we should be able to pin her comings and goings down."

He looked over their heads at Pentecroft who nodded and got up and said, "Thank you, you have been most cooperative. We will not take up any more of your time. We understand how difficult it is for you both. Rest assured, we will get right onto it. If we have any news at all, we will send young Terry by with it."

The Collingwoods looked a little relieved, at least they were aware they were no longer alone in this distressing matter. They shook hands all around and left the charming cottage.

Pulling out of the driveway Quest said, "What do you make of this, Ronald? Do you think there is something amiss here or is she just out doing the tiles?"

Ronald had never liked the term "doing the tiles." He conjured up a lass that was pretty easy, and just out for a good time, with never a thought to the worry or the care she might be causing. But, he covered up his feelings and said, "I don't want to think something nasty. It is not in character to treat her folks with such disdain. Twenty-one years of doing things the right way, I somehow can't see her doing something so out of line one night. No, there is a lot more lurking here. We just can't see it yet."

"I'm inclined to go along with you. We have time. Let's swing by the Grand and talk to the staff there. Maybe something will surface. Maybe someone will remember something since David was there."

"Hmmm," Pentecroft said, more to himself than to Ashley.

"What?" Quest said, glancing quickly to Ronald.

"Oh, only I was thinking, that night I collided with her she was flushed and nervous. I put it down at the time to embarrassment, but could it have been something else that got her wind up?"

"Yes, I see what you mean. She definitely was in a tear, whether to get away from someone or to get to someone."

"Exactly."

After making their positions clear to management, they were ushered into the elegant office. "I think you will find this adequate," he said quite sarcastically. "Now what is it you want to know. I am a very busy man and can't be delayed too long," he said while looking down and brushing imaginary flecks from his impeccable black coat.

"Right then Mr... Uh, I don't think I caught your name?"

"Clifton."

By the Pricking of My Thumb

"Yes, well, Mr. Clifton, we are duly investigating the disappearance of a young woman who worked here at the Grand and came under your supervision."

Mr. Clifton sniffed in irritation. "That would be that Collingwood girl I should imagine. Well, I told her under no uncertain terms Saturday night that if she was late again, or up to any more of her tricks, that I would mark her cards for her, and I have done just that. Wait 'till she shows her face here again. Not likely to me anyway, she won't. Probably go winzing and mithering around the day crew and management. Oh, she had them all fooled with those big innocent eyes. But not me. She wore her clothes too tight and flirted with everyone in pants that came across to the reception desk. It was shameful. I had had my full of it, I can tell you. Things will run a lot better here in the future. Oh no, I'm sure she saw the writing on the wall and just couldn't face me again after Saturday night."

Ronald Pentecroft took an instant dislike to this pompous little man. Why did short men have to take on such a high-handed manner and a superior attitude that they were better than anyone else? Was it to compensate for being born short? he wondered. Anyway, he said, "What happened Saturday night to warrant this?"

"She only humiliated me in front of two guests that arrived to check in."

"Oh yes, and how would that have been?" Pentecroft looked up over the cigarette he had just lit and exhaled the smoke in Mr. Clifton's direction.

Quest had to suppress a smile as the thin aquiline nose quivered in distaste as the smoke reached his nostrils. Clifton whipped a grey silk handkerchief from his breast pocket and waved it under his nose.

"Well, well," he was sputtering. He started to say something and abruptly had second thoughts. "Now see here, Inspector, I hardly see what difference it will make and I really can't remember now the exact words. Unless I can help you further I really must get back out front."

"Ah, we're not through here, Mr. Clifton. Anything that would cause you to dress down an employee so resoundingly must have made an indelible impression on your mind. One must remember something.

"Well I don't! As far as my duty to the Grand is concerned I've done it. It's a closed chapter and we are well rid of her."

Ashley could see the anger mounting up in Ronald and indeed he felt it also. What a miserable little weasel of a man, and he injected at this point: "Well then, if, you will be so kind as to get us the name of the two guests that all this took place in front of."

Clifton swung around and was almost spitting he was so angry. "I most certainly will not! I will not have guest's pleasures interrupted by police tramping all over and treating them like common criminals over that cheap little piece of goods."

"You will, you know, or would you like to be escorted down to the station house and help us with our inquiry and investigation there for as long as it takes, or let us have a nice quiet chat with two guests over a nice cup of tea and a crumpet?"

He knew he was going to have to comply. The hard cold eyes of both men told him that.

It was well past tea time when both men had gathered all the statements from the staff and the two guests and were quite satisfied with the conclusion they had reached: that this was an out and out blatant act on Mr. Clifton to discredit the character of Peggy whom by all accounts was an honest, delightful, hard working girl and highly thought of by her peers and to all accounts wouldn't be losing her job, most likely the other way around. Mr. Clifton had not endeared himself to management or to anyone and was himself on the way out, and soon. Pentecroft and Quest breathed a sigh of relief as they left the hotel watching Mr. Clifton's receding back entering the hotel manager's office with a look of satisfaction thinking he is going to be commended, never dreaming it was his cards he was going to get and a resounding dressing down.

Chapter 76

Terry and his partner were about half way through the shed working a few inches apart sifting the fine dirt.

"Bloody hell, Terry, if we don't find this soon we'll have to light torches, sun is almost gone."

"Aye," Terry said as he squinted at the sieve in his hands. He shook it once more and thought he caught a glimpse of something. Aye, there it was. He sifted faster.

His partner, back on his haunches wiping his face, looked at Terry. "Hallo, what is it?"

"I think we've found it mate. Tear a piece of your note pad will you, and slip it under in case there are any marks on it."

The young Bobby sank back to his knees and reached into his shirt for his pad and tore the slip and gingerly slipped it under the glass. "We've cracked it, Terry!"

"Aye, not too soon," as they walked to the shed door, to catch the last of the bright sunshine. Terry jiggled the paper as the last of the fine dirt fell away revealing what was left of the glass. Both men knew that the piece back at the station house would fit and make a perfect circle. What was left of the fine black ribbon hung loosely from the loop that had broken when it had been trampled on separating the pieces.

Terry slipped it into a little plastic bag along with the button with some fabric attached and a few hair pins. All in all, both men were pleased. They finished dusting off their trousers and retrieving their jackets from the hook, they took their helmets preparing to return to the precinct.

A heavenly smell reached both young nostrils and they turned to see Dori Halley starting down the walk with a tray in hand containing two steaming beakers of tea and a plate containing… Terry knew it could be nothing else but sticky buns.

The lads looked at each other. "What do you think, Terry? Will the sergeant have our guts for garters?"

Terry grinned. "Look mate, this is thirsty work and I couldn't half murder a cuppa about now and I can't walk away from Mrs. Halley's sticky buns. None better in all St. Gilliam except Gram's and she's gone, God bless her."

"Hear ya are, laddies," Dori said. "Get yourselves around here and have a proper set down." She had placed a large blue tea towel on the little table and the boys sat on the lawn in the lawn chairs. Each had tucked a big white serviette into the collar of his uniform.

"Tae, very much Mrs. Halley, you're an angel."

Dori placed a hand to catch an escaping burnished curl and pushed it back under her scarf. She grinned with pride and with pleasure at the lad's remarks, making short work of her sticky buns, and tea. "Are you finished in the shed?"

"Aye," Terry said between mouthfuls, "and we were successful and all."

Dori didn't press them about what they were looking for although her curiosity had almost got the best of her. Oh well, all in good time, she supposed. She and the rest would just have to wait and be satisfied with that. They wouldn't reveal anything, she'd be bound.

Terry wiped his mouth and fingers on the serviette and gulped the last of his tea. "Thanks again Mrs. Halley. You saved our lives."

"Aye," said his partner. "Never tasted better." And, not knowing what else to say, shifted on one foot and then the other.

Terry, seeing his embarrassment, said, "Are you all set then, mate?"

"Aye," was the answer. Then they each gave her a broad grin, turned on their heels, and made for the back gate.

Chapter 77

"That's all settled then," she said, gracing everyone at the table with a radiant smile. Suzette couldn't explain, but ever since last Sunday's service she'd had such peace. It was as if she had come out of a black, heavy storm and into the clear light of day, with the sunshine drying up all the damp gloomy places in her heart with warmth and abundant calmness, peace. She was back to her old self again, as Aunt M. would have wanted her to be. Not gloomy, soppy and all withdrawn into herself. If there was one thing her aunt couldn't abide with it was self-pity, and she had the support of those loved ones and yes, the whole village. she could feel it.

The three of them looked at her. All had the same thought, how good it was to have her back and know that they could all get on with the rest of their lives. The pain and the loss would remain in their hearts for a long, long time, never to be completely forgotten. But the doom and the gloom would not be noticeable to others.

"Aye, that's fine lass, as long as you're sure. I'll open shop Wednesday morning and keep my dickey bird open for word of a good handy man and to help out driving the van."

"Sounds good to me," Robert said, leaning forward on his elbows. "I'll draw the agreement papers up and have them notarized after the service tomorrow."

Dori, was all flushed. True, she had the agreement with Miss Millacent, but nothing as official as thick vellum paper with seal and ribbon making it all real legal. No one could take it from her. Her own business, shared with Suzette, with her getting the lion's share of the profits, she'd be bound. She was that proud she was.

The vicar had called and told them the service was to be held tomorrow at one p.m. and both women knew it was the right thing, too. Much time had gone by and the longer they put it off, the longer the wounds would stay open.

"So, all in all, things are falling into place and that will give us 'till Monday before Rob and I have to be back in London and we can iron out any difficulties that might surface." They were clearing away the dishes from tea. "And if this fiend is ever caught we can come back to the trial. I'm sure the inspectors will let us go. We can contribute nothing more. We are not suspects and we both have demanding jobs, especially Rob, and they have been most kind and understanding to have us away for as long as we have. But it can't go on indefinitely."

"Quite, my love." Rob pecked her on the cheek. "If you lovelies will excuse me I'll get straight on to these papers."

Ed was close on his heels. They grinned knowing Ed was bound for the fire and the evening paper and Sultan was fast on his heels not wanting to pass up the chance of a warm lap to snuggle in never mind that once he established his territory, kneading and squirming his fat silky body into the most comfortable position, it left little space for a paper, or anything else for that matter, but this was a ritual and everyone knew despite his complaints, Ed enjoyed it as much as Sultan.

Both women shook their heads and giggled and plunged into the dishes.

Chapter 78

There was such an air of excitement at the station house it fair crackled. All the computers, teletypes, fax machines came alive. All spitting out dates, places and valuable information so fast they could scarce take it in, with the exception of Chief Inspector Ashley Quest and Rennie, coming from London's New Scotland Yard CID had dealt with murder in a sometimes hourly basis, or daily, were quite used to it all. But, for the rest of them, they were just getting their feet wet in a murder case. The adrenaline was flowing like water through their veins.

Terry was too charged to go back to the little cottage he was raised in by his Gram on the banks of the river Ouse. The back garden led right down through the gate to the riverbank. Many an hour as a lad he had sat fishing from it as Gram shelled peas or peeled potatoes. Terry's father had been killed in the beginning of the war and his mom had died in an influenza outbreak, but Gram had more than made up for the loss. She had enough love for any four people, so he was more than loved, but she wasn't adverse to the paddle either. He had learned so much at her knee: faith and patience, love and forgiveness. His old Gram was so wise, and now she was gone and he was alone.

The cottage and everything in it was his free and clear, in fact everything Gram had was his now. There was no other. Funny that, all only having had one child on both sides of the road. As much as he loved it, he was too charged to go back, at least for now.

He had taken the long way home across the bridge. It was a beautiful soft evening and the sun was going down. As he approached the bridge, he noticed there was no one around. He chuckled, a bit early for courting couples. It was a favorite spot. But as he approached the middle of the bridge he stooped and removed his helmet and loosened his collar and leaned forward looking down at the swift clear moving water. Oh, aye, he spotted a man further along in hip boots casting his line on the dancing water. The sun's reflection was hypnotic. Like looking through a kaleidoscope with bright blues, pinks and lavenders all communing together. It was so quiet, there wasn't even a breeze on this early eve. The only sound was the water bubbling and dancing over the rocks.

Suddenly, a blinding flash struck Terry in the eye. He closed them tight against it with a touch of irritation at having his tranquility so rudely interrupted. He opened them slowly and it was gone. He moved his eyes along the bank trying to find the source of his irritation. Nothing. Oh, heck! It happened again. What the bloody hell was going on, like as? When he was a nipper they thought it was quite a sport to hide in the soft grasses and shrubs and with a piece of looking glass or metal they'd wait for an unsuspecting soul to come along and then blind them full with the sun, bouncing it back into their eyes. He waited, trying to rid the sunspots from his eyes in order to find the little toe rags. Gone.

He was ready to go now, his peace and thoughts thoroughly dispelled when it caught him full in the eyes again. Terry took a visual fix as to where it was, and, pulling on his helmet made for the other side of the bridge. If they could tell he was a bobby they'd be long gone, but with him crouching and creeping along, maybe not. If he was quick he could catch them and put the fear of God in them so as not to do it again. Maybe, just maybe.

By the Pricking of My Thumb

He was over the bridge and was scrambling down the bank. It was a little steeper than he thought and slippery. He couldn't hear anything and there was really no place to hide. In fact, he was almost at the water's edge. Only a large tree was bent over and some of it's upper branches were dangling in the water but it made for an excellent support. He bent down to part the thick grove of rushes and other water grasses.

Blimie, some of them had thick thorns that held fast his fingers. He managed to extract them and begin again. He parted them more carefully. The first thing he saw were thick strands of blond hair wound around the stickers. Bloody hell, he felt sick. And even before the cold bloated face and lifeless eyes came into view, he knew he had found Peggy. He stared at the bloated, lifeless face and body bobbing up and down with the motion of the river. He couldn't take his eyes from her. His throat ached as he tried to swallow over the huge lump in it. Oh, Peggy, my poor lass. Who ever did this to you will pay.

It was quite evident, even with the water damage, that she had been strangled. He was afraid to leave her to summon help for fear she would break loose and float away.

Think, Terry. Remember, you're a policeman. No matter that the victim was a dear friend. He remembered the man he had seen from the bridge fishing, and reaching into the upper pocket of his tunic withdrew his whistle and prayed the man was still on the river. He gave three sharp blasts and stopped, and then repeated it. He felt he had been hours standing at the water's edge with his boots half submerged in it, but he knew he couldn't have been there more than minutes when he heard the man's voice calling out. Terry answered and told him who he was and to get to the phone as quickly as he could and call the station house and ask for Inspector Pentecroft or Chief Inspector Quest. "Tell them Constable Simms needs assistance at the far end of the bridge. Direct them here and tell them to bring Dr. Dundee with them."

Terry wiped his face with his free hand and dropped his whistle back into his tunic pocket. He brought a branch forward to cover her face. He could no longer stand to look at that once beautiful, laughing girl. All he could think about was David Collingwood, how he had looked at the station house when he was frantically looking for news of his daughter. My God, he's going to go spare when they have to tell him. One of them will have to make the positive ID even if Terry knew it was her. Law made it. One family member must make the ID.

God help them. They were such a wonderful family, so close to each other, but something must have happened to bring Peggy to this tragic end. Something or someone got between her and her folks.

He heard the running on the bridge before he first heard his name being called out. "I'm down here. Mind the bank, sir, it's steep and slippery." All three of them had scrambled down the bank in such haste as to almost push him into the river.

Pentecroft was the first to speak. "What is it, Corporal?"

Terry turned and pulled back the branch.

"Bloody hell, it's not... It can't be!" But from the look on Simms' face, he knew.

Terry and Doc pulled her in as gently as they could and drew her up on the bank. Pentecroft had never seen Doc react like this before. He was white. All colour was drained from his face and his hands shook as he loosed the scarf from her neck. The purple markings were still quite visible.

"Ach, my poor wee bairn. I can no believe it's you."

None of the four men standing there could believe that wretched body was Peggy Collingwood's. But yet they knew it was. Quest could only remember that beautiful, vibrant girl in the photo. Two more lives were about to be shattered. He could see also Margaret, her mother. My God, this was a grim business.

He touched Pentecroft's arm and Pentecroft jerked like he had received a charge of electricity. "What!"

Quest's eyes traveled to young Constable Simms face, which was also a sickly shade with traces of green around his mouth. Sweat was evident on his upper lip and under his eyes. Both men wanted to get him away, for he was going to be sick and he wouldn't do so with his superiors looking on.

They sent him to fetch the lab boys and the photographer. But before he could move, Dr. Dundee grabbed him by the arm. "Here, laddie. I want ye to take a good dram of this." It was a small silver flask Doc had drawn from somewhere.

"Sir, I..." he looked at Pentecroft.

"Go ahead, laddie. We're all in need of it."

The two men were standing at the top of the bank when Terry returned with the boys from the crime lab.

"No need to go back down, Simms. They will find Doc any road without you."

Terry came to stand with his superiors, his feet a little apart, shoulders squared, his hands clasped behind his back. "I want to thank you, sir. I felt like a right birk when you first came."

"Don't be daft, lad. We all have been in that place in the start of our career. Some are lucky and never have to pull a body from a river. But, Terry, you'll make a better copper if you don't forget it and become too calloused to death."

"Yes sir, thank you, sir."

"Terry, what brought you here today?"

Terry was silent for a few seconds. He didn't want to sound too immature but he wanted to be truthful too. "Well, sir, I was pretty keyed up, way thing were going with Miss Lang's case and I didn't feel right going with my mates for a pint and a bite. So, I decided to walk home the long way to think things over. I stopped in the middle of the bridge. It was a soft evening and there was a bloke stream fishing and I was watching when I was struck in the eyes by an abrupt ray of the sun. I was blinded for a second and I couldn't see where it came from. When it happened again I spotted where it was coming from and I thought it might be some lads with a piece of glass or mirror."

"Aye, I know where you're coming from," said Pentecroft.

"Well, sir, I made straight for the spot. But when I got down on the bank I realized there was no place for the nippers to hide, but I looked anyway and that's when I found her."

"What do you suppose caught the sun?"

"Sir, the sun, it was almost set and lay almost even with the water. Can't say sir, but Doc should be able to tell us something."

My God, St. Gilliam has been on the map for a hundred years and nothing like this has happened in centuries. Now two senseless murders. One in the sunset of her years, and the other just beginning hers. It couldn't be possible that these two murders were connected in any way. That meant they were going to be looking for two cold blooded, bloody bastards. If the CID hadn't already been called in from New Scotland Yard, they would have come in force. Pentecroft was somehow relieved that Chief Inspector Quest and Rennie were already here. He felt Quest was one who, like himself, didn't like too much interference from the top brass. And a few handpicked men could accomplish just as much as half a dozen men falling over each other in such a small hamlet. The fine folk here were disrupted enough without that and he didn't want them to hit the panic button. It was hard enough to get these Yorkshire folk to open up. They didn't take to strangers, to say nothing of a half a dozen bobbys with size twelve boots tramping all over their gardens. Heck as like, they would retreat behind closed doors and to peeking out from behind lace curtains.

He was brought back from his wool gathering abruptly by the pressure of a firm hand on his shoulder, his name being called repeatedly in his ear. "Ronald, Ronald, where in the world are ye laddie?"

"Hmmm? What? What's that Doc? Are you talking to me?"

"Don't be so daft, man. No one else here is called Ronald. Of course I was talking to you." Doc was standing in front of him with his arm outstretched and palm closed.

"What have you got?"

"Rather expensive baubles for a young hotel receptionist, would you no be sayin'?"

Pentecroft extended his hand and two shining objects fell into it. Quest had been talking to one of the photo men from forensics. When Pentecroft caught his eye he gave a quick nod of acknowledgement and gave the forensic man another quick word, and with a pat on his shoulder sent him back down to where they were putting Peggy into a black plastic body bag.

My God, what a waste. So young, everything to look forward to and suddenly some sod ended it all, and for what? Where did it lead to? What had happened to these two women? Who in the world would or could be threatened by them, one quite old and the other so young? He shook his head and turned and walked towards Pentecroft.

"What do you make of these? One is so delicate and the other big and ugly. Where have I seen a ring like that before?"

Quest took it and held it up to the fading light. The two interlaced little hearts on the gold chain danced in the fading rays of the sun. This little beauty could have come from her parents as a birthday gift. She just had one not long back didn't she?"

Pentecroft nodded, "But this is a brutish ring, by the looks big hands as well. Yes, I've seen it before, but where in the devil was it?"

Both men looked at the dangling ring on the delicate chain too heavy to carry it. "What is the design on the darn thing anyway?" Both heads bent closer.

"Well I'll be damned, bloody hell!" Pentecroft cried. "I knew I had seen it. Remember? It was in that faded press release we had blown up."

"Herr von Heusen was wearing one just like it," Quest said.

"Right mate. Too right I do. But what would Peggy be doing with a man like that? And where would she have met him?"

"Well we all know Miss Millacent met him and met a similar fate." His raised voice made the three men turn their heads in time to see one of the coroner's men slip to his knees on the slippery bank, losing his grip on the body bag, and Doc running down, being a little less than kind to the young man who was scrambling to get his footing.

"Ronald," he shouted. "We are leaving now. Meet you back at the station house in thirty minutes. You'll no be going to the Collingwood's without me, laddies." Both men nodded, neither man wishing to go at all. One of the grimmest parts of police work was informing the loved ones. Accidents were bad enough, but murder was the grimmest.

They looked at Simms standing a bit apart. "Poor beggar. Dropped right in the thick of it." Well, it would be the making of his career or he would never be anything but a small village bobby. He was destined for more than that and Pentecroft prayed he had the mettle to do it.

They bagged the evidence into plastic bags and walked back to the waiting car. At the car Inspector Quest said, "Ronald, we are overlooking something here." Shouldn't she have a purse? She had one last time we saw her."

"Too right you are. We had better detail some men to do some poking around in the bushes and that area where young lovers do their cuddling, up river a bit to that flat area where the path bends down to the grassy knoll. If she was dumped there or from the bridge on either side, the killer probably thinks she is long gone by now. If it hadn't been for those thorns catching her hair and that damned scarf she would have been. A point in our favor. The killer most likely feels quite safe as no one had discovered the body. And if Simms hadn't come this way tonight we might not have ever found her." Details aside, they pulled away.

Chapter 79

It had been just an hour since he had walked into Heindrich's room. His voice was buzzing around in Kurt's head like a swarm of angry bees. "What's that?" He wished the buzzing would stop, it made it hard to hear.

"Look here, let's stop this wrangling. It makes my face ache and my head pound. We are both after the same things and there is enough for both of us. If we work together instead of against each other, it will be finished, really finished. You can go your way and I mine. We don't ever have to see each other again. Haven't I always taken care of you?"

Kurt looked up, and he thought, Why the sudden change? Why was he even suggesting the split? The crafty old bastard, he was lying to him, trying to win him over. Trying to get him so bedazzled by the thought of so much wealth that he'll let his guard down. And then, when he least expected it he would circle around and pounce. The real jackal on to the kill.

Heindrich was thinking along the same lines. That's right my greedy friend. Step a little closer to the trap and I will have you, and it really will be over for good. He'd go his way to Rio and Kurt to an unmarked grave. No one to grieve for him.

Both men looked hard and long, across the room at each other. Kurt, ready and willing to play along knowing he must never let his guard down, not for one second, was the first to answer.

"I'm listening. Tell me how, where, and what my split is."

Got you, thought Heindrich. But instead said, "Well, my friend, here is the how and the way and your split. Now listen, listen carefully. You have a great deal to accomplish and very little time to do it in."

Both men crossed the room to the coffee table. Heindrich was hideous to look at. Poor devil, the pain must be terrific, thought Kurt. He almost felt sorry for him. He could see well out of one eye but the other was almost closed. But when he got close to him he felt an ice cold chill down his spine. So wild was his good eye he felt it was burning a hole in his brain.

He looked down at the paper on the table in case Heindrich would catch the fear. Heindrich started to speak and Kurt reached for the bottle. This was going to be a long, long day.

Chapter 80

David reached her just before she hit the floor. Crouched there, cradling her in his arms tears flowed down his face and hard sobs racked his body.

Quest thought, My God, she looks even more like Peggy crumpled up than her mother. He looked at Pentecroft and then at Doc. The pain in their eyes told the story. This was the part of their job they all hated. It made them physically sick the way you had to tell people about a death, that a loved one was never coming back. The death of a child was the cruelest of all. To never see them complete their lives, fulfill their dreams, or even reach the goals they had set for themselves. All their dreams and love for that child shattered like glass.

It was so difficult, they could do nothing. Cruel, because they had to poke and pry at an open wound, dig for clues. They all hated it, but they had to turn their already broken and shattered world upside down before they could even begin to know and piece together the whole picture. Doc was speaking softly and slowly to David, words he couldn't make out, but David responded. He gathered Margaret in his arms and with Doc Dundee following, walked slowly to the staircase.

Pentecroft's eyes followed after them. "Might as well wait here, and when David comes down we will ask him about these baubles. Maybe he can shed some light on it all and we will have to go through her room and all her personal things. I hate doing this to them, sir."

Quest noticed the reference to his rank at this time. Not out of anger but out of respect for him and his long time experience at things like this. And he didn't want to be flippant.

Chief Inspector Quest noticed and admired him for it. He was even more certain that this decision to add him to his crew was the right one. "It is a painful time for them, and for us, Inspector," he returned him the same respect, "but a necessary part of our jobs. If it helps to put the cold blooded bastards where they belong it will somehow make it settle better with them and us. We'll do her room ourselves. I think it will be best, don't you?"

"Yes, I do, and if we find anything we can keep it to ourselves and only what they need to know and what is relevant to the case we will tell them."

"Right you are."

Both men lit cigarettes and gazed about the room through their smoke.

Upstairs Doctor sat on the bed holding Margaret's cold hand in his and waiting for her sobs to ease a bit. The injection would take hold any time now.

"It can't be true. Oh God, no, no. It can't be true. They must have made a mistake. Dr. Dundee, please tell me that it's all a horrible mistake." The words tumbled out between her sobs and trembling body.

"Nay, nay, lassie. I'm afraid it's the truth, for I saw her for myself. Oh my dear Margaret, I'd give all I have in the world to tell you different. I've given you an injection and you will be asleep, and sleep the night through, but, I'll be around in the morning, my girl, first thing. We can talk then and you can tell me what you don't think you can tell David."

Her eyes were barely open and she tried to lift her head from the pillow, in a shaky voice, "But how? I didn't..."

"Nay, nay, lassie," he gently pushed her head back and stroked the blond, silky head. "Sleep Margaret, lass. Dinnae you worry. We'll sort it all out in the morning. Sleep now."

Quest and Pentecroft had been in Peggy's room about thirty minutes and had turned up nothing. They had sifted through the drawers of neatly piled stacks of pretty feminine underwear, panties slips, bras, nylons and nighties, and found nothing. They had looked through the bed and between the springs and mattress, and then acting quite out of character, they remade it. They couldn't explain their actions, only they did it in embarrassed silence. Quest lifted his eyes slowly.

Pentecroft was contemplating the ruffled pillow in his hands trying to remember where it was placed on Peggy's bed. He patted it into place and looked up with a sheepish look on his face and said, "Let's try her closet. Can't believe she didn't keep a diary or a journal. Or, am I showing my age and girl's don't do that any more."

"I'm surprised myself. You would have thought she would have had to tell someone, or write it down. Her folks sure don't know anything about the jewelry or anyone who was likely to have given her those baubles. It's funny," said Quest, looking through a hat box he'd taken from the shelf, "they were so close to each other. But Peggy guarded this relationship and played it out in silence. Maybe she thought her folks wouldn't understand, or even like this bloke."

Pentecroft picked up a pair of very dressy high heels and something caught his eye. "'Allo, 'allo. What's this then?" He pulled from the toe of one of the shoes a small prescription bottle. He held it up to the light and Quest looked over.

"What is it?"

"It's a bottle of pills, and not from Dr. Dundee either. It's from a chemist shop in York."

"Do you know what they are?" Quest asked.

"Not really. Not much up on this sort of thing, but Doc can tell us right enough. Maybe this will lead us to something. That's all there is here."

Both men agreed not to mention the bottle of pills to David or Margaret. As they were hidden they most likely didn't know anything, and besides, they had enough on their plate. This was a right doodle, leading them nowhere but York. Maybe the bloke's from York? But then why strangle her here in the little hamlet of St. Gilliam when her death would go unnoticed for much longer in the city of York.

"We've got to find her purse and we had also better pray that bastard didn't take it with him and clean it out and toss it miles from here."

"Too right," Pentecroft said.

They were making their way down the stairs when the phone rang. They could hear David but not understand what he was saying. They reached the bottom of the stairs when David's white and haggard face appeared around the corner. "Oh, Inspector Pentecroft, it's for you. Terry," he said almost as an after thought.

"Thank you."

"You can take it in here and you won't disturb Margaret."

"Yes, yes, of course," Pentecroft said.

He walked into a small room walled with bookcases, which were filled with books on one side and the other side held some trophies. Three big winged backed chairs and a very large desk where the receiver was laying beside a tumbler. David must have been sitting here having a drink and waiting for Doc to come down when the phone rang.

"Please, sit here," David said, picking up his drink and heading for the door.

"Yes, thank you." Pentecroft picked up the receiver and sank into the huge chair that cradled his whole body. "Pentecroft here. Oh, yes Littlejohn. When? Oh, well done. Yes, you know what to do. Meet you at the station house. We're almost finished here. Good work, Sergeant and pass that onto the lads," and hung it up.

Quest was standing with his back to him looking at the books, his head cocked to one side looking at the titles, but Pentecroft knew that he had heard and took in what he had said.

"A break for us, they found her purse. And without handling it too much, figure the contents are all there."

Both men were anxious to get to the station house and examine it for themselves. Almost five minutes later Doc appeared in the doorway looking tired and upset.

"I've done all I can here 'till morning. Are you laddies ready to go? I've no time to stand around waiting," he said crankily.

Both men looked up, surprised, and raised their eyebrows. "Right, we'll be off soon as we have said good-bye to David."

"No need to bother him. I've said everything and he is sitting with Margaret and I've given him something to settle him. It's best to leave him to try and work out his grieving. The poor lass will need all the help and support he can give her. Aye, this is a rum business, and he'll have to get it all out of his system before morning. Not that he won't grieve, mind. Nay, nay, only he will have to have the extra strength. Ach, the wound to their hearts in loosing their only child will never heal. Only crust over. But in time it will be easier to bear." He was talking more to himself than to them, and they followed him like obedient schoolboys out the door and down the path to their cars.

Suddenly Pentecroft turned around. "Oh, Doc. Before you go, we found these in Peggy's room. Can you tell us what they are?"

Doc took the small bottle and his jaw dropped open. "Well bless my kilt! It dinna can be!"

"What can't be? What?" both men said together.

He raised his head and said, "Birth control pills."

"What? Are you...?"

"Aye, you heard me."

"But I thought..."

"Aye, and so did I." He slammed the car door and took off in a cloud of dust and flying gravel.

"Well would you credit that!" They got into their cars and made a much quieter withdrawal down the drive way and back to the station house.

Chapter 81

David had crawled up on the bed beside Margaret's still body and gathered her to him. Her head cradled in the crook of his arms, she clung to him with her small hands. Her long shapely fingers clawed the folds of his shirt and dug into his flesh and he clung as tightly to Margaret. They both seemed to have a need to hold something warm and alive. He looked down at that lovely face. The lines of tension were beginning to ease as she sank deeper into sleep and the tears were flowing down his strong handsome face.

He spoke quietly to Margaret even though she could no longer hear. "Oh, Margaret, my dearest love. What ever shall we do? I want with all my heart to shield you. To be strong for you and make it all go away. Remember six months ago when we had our anniversary, the bottle of bubbly, the big fire, the things we talked about, going back to Peggy's first Christmas, that first holiday at Scarborough and how she squealed and jumped up and down when she saw the donkeys on the sand giving kiddies rides. Her first Christmas pantomime, how grown up she thought she was at six. Too grown up to hiss and boo, and the look she gave us when we did. She finally broke down in hysterical laughter at the appearance of the widow Twankey. Those years just flew by. How I said to you half joking, 'Let's have another baby,' and the look of astonishment on your face, 'You never mean it, and besides, what would Peggy say if we informed her someday over tea, 'by the by, we're going to have a baby.'

"How we giggled as we imagined what she would say. You sprang to your feet pretending you were Peggy. My God, you both look so much alike. I was explaining to her we were not too old and no we would not embarrass her and didn't much care what her friends would say, when you couldn't contain your laughter any longer and I realized it was you and not Peggy. I felt so daft.

"You sank to your knees and cradled my head to your breast saying, 'Oh David, I do love you so. We have been so very lucky with Peggy right from the first night at home. Could we be so lucky twice?'

"'Hmmm, that does bear some thinking. Up half the night with a cranky baby isn't exactly what we want, is it. We would both be so cranky and you would begin to grudge my cricket matches and practices saying I was leaving you to handle everything while I was swooning off with my mates for fun and frolic. Where on the other hand you were trapped, tired and left with a baby who did nothing but cry. No love, you're probably right. We couldn't be that lucky with another one. Might have been fun trying, though.'

"That was only six months ago. What could have happened? What kind of a bloke would do such a thing to a beautiful young girl, our girl. Where would she meet a bastard like that? That jewelry. That ring was an awful big ugly thing, but those hearts were delicate and beautiful and cost a quid or two."

He was so angry it churned and bubbled and boiled and rolled around in David's stomach, working its way up to his throat until he thought he would explode. He sunk his head into the top of the pillow. A long, pitiful, agonizing half moan, half scream broke the silence of their room, until finally it stopped and he was wet with sweat and tears and he dropped into a merciful sleep still holding Margaret in his arms who mercifully had slept through it all.

V.E. Sullivan

Chapter 82

Sergeant Littlejohn, Corporal Simms, and Pentecroft and Quest all stood looking at the contents of Peggy's purse. Quest took his pen and started to separate the contents. They had not been dusted for prints yet. There was a train stub, some kind of receipt, a slip of paper with a list on it.

Pentecroft bent sideways trying to read it. "Train stub is a return, first class, from York. Wait a minute. Isn't that where that prescription came from?"

"Right. But it wasn't for that," Quest said, taking the bottle from his pocket. "This is almost full."

The folded piece of paper, wadded, couldn't be opened by the pencil. It was too closely pressed. The list had: birth certificate, picture. An alarm was going off in Quest's head. Picture, birth certificate… and the next word that came to him was passport.

"Ronald, what do you make of this?"

"What have you found?" he bent his head in order to read: birth certificate, picture. He looked quickly up and met Quest's eyes. "Passport. Now what do you suppose the lass was going to do, or go?

What, or who was the motive behind it. That's the needle we're going to have to find in this haystack of evidence."

"Let's get on to the passport office in Croydon and see where she was heading and the dates shouldn't be too difficult. Not all that much time has passed yet." Turning to Littlejohn Quest said, "Get these dusted for prints. There is a chance there will be a print on it that doesn't match Peggy's that is, if he wasn't wearing gloves. I want a composite sketch taken to the train station here and in York and to be shown to the platform conductor and to the ticket agent. Also cover all the jewelry stores in York and in St. Gilliam and find out who bought those gold hearts. A piece as fine as that is going to cost a few quid, no danger."

"Yes, sir. Is there anything else?"

"Oh, one thing," Pentecroft said. "Check the daily reports from Saturday night on the Bobby that had that patch. There might be something, anything. Some other couple out for a cuddle might have heard or spotted something. It is a popular spot."

"Aye," Littlejohn said, and turned muttering to himself "chance would be a fine thing."

"Did you say something Sergeant?"

"No, sir. I'll be at my desk if you want me. I'll detail the foot work sir."

"Thank you, Sergeant," Quest said, smiling at the big man, for how many times had he asked Rennie the same question only to get the same answer. He turned and looked at Pentecroft. "I'm nackered. I know you must be. What do you say to a little breakfast and talk over the developments and then grab a couple of hours kip back here at the station house."

Pentecroft said, "You're on, mate." Shouting at Littlejohn where they could be reached he hurried after Quest out the door.

Chapter 83

Kurt sat, turning the swizzle stick between his hands at the Fox and Hounds, a popular pub in St. Gilliam with the younger folks from the big manors outside of town. Mein Gott, they are all in jodhpurs, tweed jackets, and riding boots. As he looked around he noticed he was not the only one there in casual dress, expensive like his own. He fit in rather well he thought.

His eyes met those of a stunning redhead. She looked back, interested like. The full lips were moist and slightly parted showing white, even teeth. As she looked at him they broke into a wide, beautiful smile. But after that night with Peggy, he didn't dare get even slightly involved. He looked hard at her and watched the rather puzzled look on her face as the smile faded. Anyway, he didn't have time.

He had to keep all of his wits about him and try and stay one jump ahead of Heindrich. He was going to try to kill him. Never has Heindrich offered to give anyone anything and all this talk about working together and sharing 50/50 was just that, talk. No one knew it better than Kurt. The Jackal didn't intend to do more than to kill him and leave him in some God forsaken place with no marks of identification on him or his clothes. Ja, he was going to have to out smart him or he would surely die.

He felt the band of cold steel on his forearm and it gave him comfort and a sense of security. In the old days, it would have been quite noticeable that he had something up his sleeve because of the cheap clothing he was forced to wear. But today, in his cashmere sport coat, it was undetectable. This was the first day he had worn it since he had picked it up last Saturday and he was only wearing the sheath to get used to the feel of it again. He wouldn't load it with the stiletto until they left the hotel together and his muscles would be ready. He could practice how much he had to flex his forearm before it fired with deadly aim, just as quick as a bullet but no noise at all.

He liked that, liked that a lot. The look of surprise on his victim's face. They never knew what hit them. A faint smile twisted around his mouth. Ja, a complete surprise for Colonel Heindrich von Heusen. Laying the five pound note on the bar, he got up and walked out.

Chapter 84

Dr. Dundee stood at the foot of the bed looking at the pair of them. They looked wretched. Ach, his own heart was heavy. He knew the load they were carrying, but still, things had to be done and matters settled and the sooner the better for both of them.

"Did you no sleep last night, Margaret lass?"

She looked at him through heavy eyes. "I must have, I don't remember anything after..." her voice faltered. "After..." She put her shaking hand up to cover her mouth as if she could hold back anything and her eyes welled and tears spilled down her cheeks.

David drew her to him. "There, there, lass. Doc said all will come right. You'll see."

"David, go down and brew some tea and make two slices of thin toast." Margaret opened her mouth to protest. "Go now, there's a good laddie. I want to look over the lassie."

David bent and kissed the top of Margaret's head and left the room. Margaret looked down at her hands. They were clutched in tight fists over the down duvet, as if some invisible person was trying to take it from her.

"Well lassie, I know what it is that's troubling you, but I'd rather hear it from your own lips." He sat on the side of the bed and gently released her fingers from the cover. She raised her head and looked at him. Her eyes were very large and very blue, awash with tears. Ach, they're like the bonnie highland bluebells, he thought as he waited for her to speak.

"I'm pregnant," she blurted out.

"Aye, and are you sure, Margaret lass?"

"Yes, very, at least two months gone or more. Whatever can I say to David with our Peggy not even laid to rest yet? What will this do to him, to us?" She was sitting bolt up, almost on her knees. "We have always been so close, so much in love. Our lives were perfect, maybe the Lord thought too perfect. I couldn't stand it if this came between us in any way. I can't lose them both."

Her voice was getting higher with each word, and before he could say anything she flung herself at him, twining her slender arms around his neck. "Help me, Dr. Dundee! Help me tell him."

"There, there, lassie." He held her and patted her back. "Do you no see, lass. This is the finest thing that could be happenin'. The Lord has sent this baby to you as a comfort, something warm and helpless to hold to you. You both can gain from this. Dinna you see? Nay, nay, not to take Peggy's place. No one can do that. Her memory will burn bright and this bairn will make your lives complete again. Come full circle. Not broken, with that half you've built your two lives around, missing. You have a second chance with this one. It may come as a shock to David when he first hears, but I know David and he'll no resent it. And when this business is over there will be much to do in preparation. I dinna know what you've got from Peggy's baby years, but do ya no think in time you could rummage in the attic?" He reached behind his head and loosened her arms. "Lay back, lass. I want to take your blood pressure and have a wee listen. David can bring you to the surgery later for a proper exam."

He was just closing his bag when there was a soft rap on the door. Margaret looked like a startled hare ready to escape from the cabbage patch. Doc shook his head from side to side and opened the door.

David stood with the tray in his hands. A steaming pot of tea, three cups, toast and a small pot of marmalade.

"Mmmm, just what we need, laddie."

David didn't say anything. He looked frozen in time. It had hit him hard and fast. A baby! He couldn't have heard right. He was dreaming. Everything was a dream. He'd wake up in a few minutes. Margaret's voice pulled him through the dim haze of his mind.

"I knew it!" she shouted, bouncing up and down on the bed on her knees. "You hate me, don't you! You think I'm trying to erase Peggy, or eradicate her from your heart. Oh David, love, don't you see? I didn't even know for sure myself. I've been half out of my mind with worry for Peggy and then this nagging at the back of me like some angry dog nipping at my heels."

This was getting out of control and Margaret was almost at the end of her tether.

"My God, man. Say something. Can you no see what you're doing to her?"

David jumped like he was hit with a cattle prod and was by her side a second later. He took her in his arms and lifted her out of the bed. He swung her around and around. He still hadn't opened his mouth but Dr. Dundee had a mind that his actions spoke louder than words.

By the Pricking of My Thumb

Their arms were entwined around each other as they twirled around the room. Laughing and crying, their emotions on a roller coaster. Up at the highest peak one minute, and down, down in the deepest darkest pit the next. It was like watching a tragic opera like Madame Butterfly.

He wiped his eyes with a large handkerchief. His own emotions were in a tailspin for he had brought Peggy into the world and now he was going to have to find what took her out of it. He was going to loathe that, cutting, poking, examining. Ach, it's a rum job at the best of times. They didn't even notice him as he left the room. He'd call them later and set up an appointment. He had left some prescriptions with plenty of instructions for Margaret. They were over the first hurdle but there was a long, long road before them, with a lot of grieving to do. But this would take some of the bitterness out of it. Ach, it is indeed an ill wind that blows well.

He opened the front door and took a big, deep breath of fresh air and walked towards the car.

V.E. Sullivan

Chapter 85

Heindrich was finding it harder to keep his thoughts together and to remember the things he had to do. He had taken to keeping notes but the same thing applied. He would forget and he couldn't afford to leave them lying around or in the pockets of his clothing.

He paced back and forth across the room and he knew that time was running out. What day is it? He crossed quickly to the big desk and on the top was a large desk blotter. Up in the right hand corner was a calendar big enough for him to read even with his impaired vision. He had taken to putting an X through the day so if he had got off track he'd still know, that is if he'd remembered to do it. But if all else failed, the daily paper came in on his breakfast tray.

Oh, it was Tuesday, Tuesday morning. That left two days, actually a day and a half. Everything had to be finished on Thursday evening. He had to be on his way out of the country Friday. He walked to the bedroom, looked longingly at the bed. Mein Gott I'm so tired. But there would be all the rest he needed on Friday.

Instead, he went to the closet and took out his jacket and felt for his wallet in the inside pocket. Empty. The same with the rest, and he

By the Pricking of My Thumb

broke out in a sweat. Where was it? He had to find it. Think, think! But thinking made his head pound and his face hurt. The hurt went way beyond hurt, past pain into agony beyond belief. He threw the jacket onto the bed and frantically searched the clothes in the closet.

As he was rummaging through the hangers one got twisted and caught him full in the face with the infected wound side getting the worst of the stinging blow. He fell to his knees in the closet bent double with arms wrapped around his head. He couldn't move, he was frozen in pain. It tore through the side of his face, breaking open the crusty scab. His heart was pounding. With each beat it sent more blood pounding into his face and head. He could feel his hands sticky and the smell made him wretch. His pride wouldn't let him be sick on his shoes or on the closet floor. He reached for the first thing he could find. It was soft and it smelled fresh.

He had no idea how long it all lasted, but it seemed like hours. He rose slowly to his feet. He was wringing wet. His head and hair were dripping. As the perspiration trickled down his face it stung his eyes. His shirt and pants stuck to his body. The soft thing he was holding turned out to be a silk shirt. Standing, shaking from head to toe, he slowly made his way to the bathroom dropping his shirt into the wastebasket as he passed. He would take care of it preferably later.

He returned to the bedroom trying to remember what had brought on this violent attack. He threw down the towel and tightened the sash on his dressing gown. He looked in the mirror, the face staring back at him he hardly recognized. It was swollen and an unhealthy colour of grey except where it was twisted by the sutures that should have been removed long ago. His eye was almost useless to him. Those stitches were all covered over with a messy scab which was oozing a smelly, sticky substance. Death was staring at him.

He thought, Mein Gott, if I don't finish this up and get to my doctor soon there will be no new life in Rio, and all possessions and money will be of no use.

His hatred boiled to the surface. That Lang woman! None of this would have happened if she had sold me that desk. This trouble started with Jason, her brother. The sooner that name was finished with the better. Silly old bitch. Well, she, like her brother, were both dead now. And that girl, Jason's girl, had better not stand in my way or she'll be dead too. That would finish that line off. He laughed at the

By the Pricking of My Thumb

thought of it and jammed his hands deep in his dressing gown pocket. His hands came in contact with the soft leather. He drew out his secretary wallet and it came flooding back. This. This is what he couldn't find that he was so frantically searching for.

He walked over to the bar and poured himself a drink. With shaking hands he laid it before him and opened it. Yes, there it all was. His reservations for first class on the boat train to Calais France from London. He had worked it right down to the very second: pick up the Madonna and child from the desk, tidy up loose ends such as Kurt, then clear sailing. He planned to turn the car in at London. The late drive would help clear his head and the less people saw of him the better. He had made arrangements, as soon as his bill was paid, his baggage was to be picked up and put on the York train straight through to the boat train and this life would be over and a new life with a new face would await him in Rio. Nothing must stop him, nothing. He had worked too long for this, had gone through so much to have it all snatched away from him now.

He refilled his glass and raised it to his lips. Nothing. There wasn't anyone living or dead strong enough to stop the Jackal. But now he must rest. He swallowed some pills, gulped the last of his drink, and walked unsteadily to the bedroom.

Chapter 86

Suzette tightened the sash on her light cotton robe about her slim waist. Maybe Rob was right and she had lost at least a stone. Picking up the towel and starting down the hall, rubbing her hair to get most of the moisture, the scent of roses swirled up around her. Tossing back her hair she realized the sweet smell was coming in her auntie's windows, which were open. A shaft of sunlight beckoned to her and she stepped into the room. A pang of loneliness swept over her so fresh it was as if someone had cut across her heart.

She looked at the four-poster bed and remembered as if it were yesterday. As a child, sitting cross-legged on that bed, in her robe and Auntie Millacent towel drying her hair. A wistful smile crossed her beautiful face briefly. She walked to the windows, those beautiful bays with the window seat built all around and so enticing with the plump colourful pillows piled every which way. She curled up and drew back the curtain.

By the Pricking of My Thumb

Sultan was playing with something, probably a shrew, poor little thing. He was batting it back and forth between his huge paws. Rolling over, he noticed Suzette staring down at him. For a second their eyes locked, and as if he could read her mind, released his paws and the little shrew almost lost in his thick fur scurried away into the shrubbery. "You are an old darling," Suzette said to him. And, as if to say, I know I am, he started methodically to clean himself.

The garden was so lovely this time of year. It really is a beautiful old cottage and Auntie had been so happy here. They all had been. She glanced up at the overhang, no sign of rust on the wire mesh that covered the thatch. Auntie, just this spring, had a new thatch roof done, and it should be good for another twenty-five years or more. It was in prime condition inside and out. No cracks in the walls or foundation. No leaks or termites, a prime piece of property for sure.

Listen to you, you sound like an ad from the Country Gentleman. Anyway, I would never part with this place. She had so many happy memories here of her parents and her aunt. The first time she remembered meeting Ed and Dori was as a very small child. Such a happy cottage, until someone destroyed it when they killed that gentle soul. Tomorrow, Auntie would be laid to rest in the church she had loved so much, and they could start to put their lives together again, and get on with living, as she would have wanted them to do.

The shop was ready to open. Rob had the books up to date and the Inland Revenue paid. Ed had new pieces in and was advertising for a new handy man and driver. The small cottage business was Dori's, with papers all proper and legal and she was acting as the silent partner, but all proceeds were Dori's. She didn't need the money. They would be going back to London soon, and returning for weekends and holidays as they always had, or sooner, if that sod was ever caught. Ed and Dori would move in here when they were gone and let their own place. All in all, their lives would be more secure and they could build a nice nest egg for themselves for the future.

She felt a calmness inside, yes a nice restful calmness. A kind of happiness. It felt right and things were going to come right. She dragged herself away and left the room to get ready for tea.

Chapter 87

A rap on the office door received no answer. Sergeant Littlejohn, balancing a tray of sandwiches and tea things in his huge hands and turning the doorknob poked his head around the door and looked into the dim office. Both men were dead to the world, sprawled on the cots. They had removed their shoes and jackets, trousers and ties. He hated to wake them, but orders were orders. He set the tray down and walked to the small closet that was just big enough for a small sink and a loo. Yes, towels and soap and shaving gear all at the ready. He walked back and gently shook both men awake.

"Thanks, Sergeant."

"Aye, sir. Tea and sandwiches on the table. We will be waiting in the evidence room when you are ready. Doc sent a report—not final—he's gone home for some kip himself, asked that you meet him at the pub around seven."

"Thanks again, Littlejohn. We'll be around shortly."

He brought a steaming beaker of tea and a sandwich to Quest who was lying on his back with his arms across his face.

"Bloody hell, can't get my eyes open."

"I know, this will help."

He sat up and swung his long legs to the side of the cot. "Thanks, Ronald. God, what a night, and morning. What time is it?"

"Gone past three. Wonder what the boys have dug up for us. Maybe the same like as not. Clues leading us up the garden path to the same dead end."

Quest took a gulp of hot tea, "My gosh, my mouth feels as if it's lined in wool. This tea's great. What are the sandwiches?"

"Ham and cheese," Pentecroft said around a mouthful. "And mighty tasty, I might add." They had both freshened up and had a go at shaving with an electric razor. They both were feeling better and had polished off the pot of tea and all the sandwiches.

Quest, pulling on his jacket, looked over at Pentecroft who was doing the same. "I didn't realize how hungry I was."

"Nor did I. They went down a proper treat, though," and jerked open the door for Quest. He stopped long enough to light a cigarette and tossed the empty package in the wastebasket and walked out after the Chief Inspector.

"All right lads, look sharp. Here they come."

Chapter 88

Margaret strolled through the back garden picking off the dead flowers. How peaceful it was. The garden looked so beautiful, she felt so strange, consumed with sorrow over the loss of Peggy. There was so much she wanted to tell her, to share with her. They had always been so close to each other. They had talked about everything. She never thought they had any secrets. But now she was dead, murdered. It was impossible to think about. Heaven only knows where David and she would be in their relationship, lost in their own sorrows, not really talking. Afraid of what they might say. Afraid of hurting each other but for this baby. This blessed little baby gave them a common ground on which to meet. She folded her arms across her stomach as if to hug this new life.

How can two people be so devastated, and at the same time have a happy, quiet peace within them? It didn't make any sense to either of them, but there it was. It was almost as if Peggy was still with them. They talked to her, and about her just as they had always done. This little one, this miracle that God had given them, was going to be a special child. She prayed that it would be a boy. She turned and shielding her eyes against the sun, watched David coming towards her.

"All right, love?" he said.

She nodded and lifted her face to receive his kiss. "Doctor Dundee just called and said he thought it would be best if we didn't attend the inquest. And I must confess, I'm thankful."

"Me too, darling. There was a part of our daughter, a part of herself, she didn't share with us, David. And I'd rather not hear some stranger tell us something we would be better off not knowing. It can't bring her back to us and it might even do more harm to us and our wonderful memories of her."

"I agree, my sweet," and putting his arm around her waist, he felt her trembling. Drawing her close to his side he said, "Come on, love. Let's go in and have a cuppa."

Chapter 89

They had finished their drinks when Dr. Dundee came into the pub.

"Poor old boy," Pentecroft said. "He looks knackered. He looks like he didn't get as much kip as we did, and he has years on us."

He raised his hand to him and Quest caught the barmaid's eye and ordered a double Scotch on the rocks for him and a menu.

"Thanks, laddie, this will warm the cockles of my heart and my blood. Aye, a big plate of hot food. Good old pub fare. Bangers and mash and mushie peas."

"Sounds good, Doc. Make that three of the same. And Liz, bring three pints of your best bitter."

Doc set his glass down on the table and let out a long sigh. "I've been on the phone to David Collingwood telling him I dinna' think they should come to the inquest. This is a really hard time for both of them and I dinna' want any more stress on Margaret than Peggy's death has already brought. We have no need the loss of another child for them to bear."

Both men looked at him.

"Oh, did I no tell ya? The lass is pregnant. Oh, aye, about five months."

"But that's wonderful news," Quest said. "Give them something to build on. Oh I know, it's bloody awful to have a child of yours brutally murdered, but this will give them something to live for. Not the constant pain of a wasted life every time they pass Peggy's door."

"Oh aye, there will be a fair bit of grieving. She'll no be forgotten, but in a few months they'll be so busy with the wee bairn the wounds might not be so open and painful. Aye, there's a time for laughing and there's a time for crying and a time for birth and death. There's time enough for everything and everything in its time. I'm sure the master of us all knows what's best for us."

Ronald sat and looked at both men. He never had thought of Doc as being a religious man, but then the subject had never come up. It touched something in him. Being a policeman, you're either a believer or you're not; seeing all sorts of crimes, and it was certain he was brought up chapel, no danger. He just hadn't had time to go. His hours didn't always permit on a Sunday, but it gave him a reassuring feeling to know his beliefs were still there no matter how deep or covered up they were.

He looked at them and said quietly, "I pray it's a boy, and they will need all the strength they can muster to get through this. I think you did the right thing telling them not to come."

"Aye, there's no need for them to know the lass was sexually active shortly before her death, and no she was not assaulted. She was quite willing I would guess."

The three men, their voices soft, went over everything. Passing papers back and forth and taking notes. They talked about Collingwood's inquest and they all knew the verdict on that one, and also Miss Lang's service in the afternoon the next day. They decided to all attend. Doc and Pentecroft because they knew her and respected and liked the old girl. And Quest just out of respect, wishing he had known her.

Ronald said, "I was going to give Simms leave to attend. He's known the whole family for donkey's years, unless you have an objection." He directed his question to Quest as his superior. He felt he had to clear it.

"I've no objections."

"Right then. I'll leave a message with Sergeant Littlejohn for him."

Chapter 90

Terry was sitting, staring at the hundreds of bits and pieces of the evidence that was now mounting by the hour, the consequences being that both crimes were committed not necessarily by the same person.

Peggy's photo had been identified by the ticket agent early Saturday morning and also by the platform agent in York. It was indeed a passport she had been in York to get and a visa for Switzerland. Terry found that almost impossible to take in, knowing Peggy as well as he did. Someone had been certainly playing a fiddle on her. This would never have come about without outside influence. And from the jewelry found on her person it was a man. All they needed was one really good break and everything would fall into place.

Tomorrow Miss Lang's service would be held. He really missed her. She had been there all his life from a slip of a lad he had known her. And she had known his Gram. They did the well dressings together until his Gram could no longer get about to do it. And when Gram was gone, Miss Lang had been there for him. Those cold rainy nights on his bike doing his patch, she always watched out for him with a hot cuppa and a sit by the fire. Saved him many a night. And then Suzette, and Robert, and the Halley's. They were like an extended family. A family he never had. He desperately wanted to attend the service, but he knew it was out of his hands. Ah, a policeman's lot was not always a happy one. But he would do what was expected of him. A shadow crossed the table in front of him and he looked over his shoulder up into the face of his Sergeant.

Littlejohn said, "Well, me fine bucko. I have been asked to relay a message to you. Inspector Pentecroft expects to see you spit and polished tomorrow at Miss Lang's service."

"Yes sir! I'll be there," and he felt that relieved to know that he could say good-bye to his dear old friend.

Chapter 91

Kurt was reading the local paper in the lounge trying not to look frantic. Ever since Friday night he had looked everyday to see if Peggy's body had been found and he was relieved to see nothing of a young woman's body being found anywhere. He only had two more days, or a day and a half if his luck held. He would be out of the country, free of this mess and of Heindrich, and he would have everything: money, and a good life.

Heindrich still hadn't told him what he was after. He knew it had to do with the desk but he couldn't move that heavy desk. Ja, there was something in it, concealed somewhere, somehow. It had to be something very special, and priceless for him to have traced it all these years into this little village in Yorkshire. Who would have thought so much violence could happen here in this gentle place? St. Gilliam probably hadn't changed all that much in a hundred years.

He had gotten to know the village well and he had become quite fond of it. The way the mist rolled between the hills and the lush green pastoral lands with the sheep grazing and the farmers working their fields. Ja, some even walking behind a team of shires. Mein

Gott, what was happening to him? Next thing I know I'll be bursting into song. He tossed the paper aside in disgust and ordered another drink.

He was lighting a cigarette when his eyes caught a small paragraph on the tossed paper and what he read made his blood run cold and he broke out into a sweat. He gathered the paper closer to himself with trembling fingers. Another inquest held in the town hall at three p.m. today. How could you have missed that, you dumkopf?

He knew he shouldn't attend another after what happened at the old lady's inquest. But he just had to chance it. He had to know what they knew, or thought they knew, so he could plan accordingly. Just as well they were finishing up here, so he could get away. And get away he would. He looked at his watch. Three hours.

Chapter 92

Heindrich wiped his mouth tenderly and picked up the paper. It was the local St. Gilliam paper. Now, why after all these weeks of getting the London Times did they send up this rag? He threw it down. He went to the phone to call the desk. Turning, he moved slowly back to the table and picking up the paper, he walked to the window for better light and read, "Second inquest to be held at the town hall at 3:00 p.m. with Dr. Dundee giving medical evidence."

He let the paper slowly drop to his side. Second? And he turned back to the table for his cigarettes and slowly walked back to the window. He knew of the Lang inquest, of course. He had sent Kurt to that one. But what was this one? And what was even more interesting was that Kurt had said nothing. Because he never left his suite any more he depended on Kurt for all the village news. He wondered what else Kurt hadn't told him.

He looked down at the street below, at the flowerbeds, but not really seeing them. His mind was racing. A figure passed across his line of vision. It was Kurt rapidly descending the steps that ran between the flowerbeds. He stopped to light a cigarette, and for a moment he though Kurt might look up and see him. But no, he walked briskly away towards town. Damn this face! And damn that cat. Confined to his suite. There was no telling what Kurt was doing. He needed to know what he was up to, every day. Gott in Himmel. If that dumkopf did anything to spoil his plans at this late stage he would kill him with his bare hands and not wait until it was all over and he was out of the country. Damn! If only he didn't need him for Thursday he would be tempted to do it now. He had had about all he could take from that infuriating, overbearing bastard.

V.E. Sullivan

Chapter 93

Kurt stood under the tree watching the people enter the building. He hoped he could merge with the people in the back, able to exit quickly without being seen or drawing too much attention to himself. He entered the packed building with the last few latecomers. He listened as Corporal Simms gave full details, how he found Peggy's body, her handbag, all of it.

He was sweating. He felt very short of breath. He had been listening so intently, he hadn't noticed, until he turned to go, that his way was blocked by a dozen or so people who had entered after him. Steady, steady. Don't bolt. Take some deep breaths. Just when he thought he couldn't stand another second of this close airless room, the gavel came down with a resounding crack and the Judge's deep voice uttered, "Murder, by person or persons unknown."

Immediately, murmurs were heard, starting at the front, and it seemed to Kurt to be gathering momentum and getting louder. It was rolling like a wave over him but he was caught in the crush of people, some wanting to move as he did and others that were in tight circles and in no hurry to move. And the more he tried to go forward, the more he seemed to be pushed back. And he felt out of control. He was loosing it. Why did he come here? It had been a stupid move on his part.

It was so hot. He was sweating like a pig. He could feel it trickling down his back and over his ribs. Why had he chosen a turtleneck today? Even if it was the softest of cashmere, under the leather jacket it felt like a hair shirt. He pushed harder. It was no good. Someone had opened the door and he caught a whiff of clean fresh air. It was going to be all right. The air was coming back now. He would just wait and not push any more, but let the crowd thin and quietly make his way out.

Chapter 94

Ed had hung back waiting for a chance to talk to Terry. They wanted him to come to the house after the service. They had something for him. As he waited, he turned to face the crowd as they left. He wondered why so many people had come. Of course, David Collingwood was one of their own, and he was getting quite well known for his bowling on the Cricket field. But he wondered how many had known Peggy and how well.

He was there because Peggy was a lass they had known since she was a little 'un running barefoot in the grass and as a pretty teenager following Terry around with those big blue eyes. Aye, they had been stepping out for a short while, but nothing came of it but they were still good friends and had remained that way. Aye, this must be hard on young Terry, finding her body and all. He remembered how hard it had been on Dori when she had found Miss Lang.

Sommat's going on in that crowd of people. Wait, wait a minute. He knew that face. What in all that's holy was he doing here? He didn't like him any more than the first time he had met him at the shop door reading the closed notice. He wasn't from these parts, those clothes and those manners. What was he trying to do any road? He looked like a trapped animal fighting for his life. But why? What could be so threatening for him here? And what was he doing here in the first place? First at Miss Lang's inquest, then at the shop, and now here. Nay, nay. Sommat was not right here. But what?

"Waiting for me Ed?"

"Aye, laddie."

"What is it, Ed? What's wrong?"

"Don't right know. See that bloke what's pushing and shoving?" Terry looked in the direction that Ed was talking about and looked at the huddle in the middle of the room. "That be him, well dressed bloke."

"Oh, aye, he does stand out a bit."

"Aye, you ever see him before laddie?"

"Can't say I have, Ed. But I've been really busy what with two unsolved crimes of murder. Blimey, a bloke would be lucky in a village the size of St. Gilliam to have one murder, to say nothing of two. Haven't had much time to go to the places I'd see him, any road. What's so interesting about the bloke, Ed."

"Well, only that he turned up at Miss Lang's inquest and pushing on the door of shop looking in windows and asking questions he did, and now he is here and seems to be in a hurry to leave."

"Yes, I see what you mean. He's been in the village a few days, then. I'll ask about and tell Inspector Pentecroft what you have said, Ed. Thanks a lot. Any information, however small or seemingly unimportant at this stage is worth a look," and patting Ed on the shoulder, he turned to go.

He stopped Terry, "By heck, lad. I was supposed to ask you by house after service if you can make it or after your duty's up."

"Thanks, I'd like that." Terry was surprised. "You know how much I though of her, Ed. I'll miss her a lot, an awful lot." He raised his eyes and saw Sergeant Littlejohn beckoning. "I've got to go, Ed, before Sarge has me guts for garters."

"Aye, laddie. See you on morrow then."

Chapter 95

Suzette studied her reflection in the mirror. The day had started like any other, bright, cloudless skies, sweet scented breeze and warm sunshine. But, it wasn't just another day. It was the day she said good-bye to her last and only blood relative. There was just Robert, Dori and Ed now, all of whom she loved. But Auntie Millacent, she felt, as long as she had Auntie she had her parents, or part of them. Now all was gone, only memories. It would have been just as hard if Auntie had died of natural causes but she hadn't. She was so cruelly murdered. She never hurt anyone, so why was she, a tiny defenseless little lady? She couldn't bring herself to say old, little old lady, it just didn't fit her Auntie. She could hold her weight with the best of them. Her tongue could scald the wallpaper off the wall if she so desired. So it had to be something she had, or had known, or both.

She suddenly realized she was dressed and putting on her lipstick. She felt she hadn't moved, but there it was, she was ready. She had to put her thoughts aside and think of saying her good-byes and remembering all that Aunt Millacent had meant to her and all she had done over the years for her since her darling parents had died.

She smoothed her skirt and reached for her jacket and hat and left the room. She passed by her aunt's door. Her eyes took it all in and there was Sultan, sitting bolt upright with his green eyes bright and flashy, his tail swishing back and forth. He was something to fear. He had looked like he was ready to spring at her. Surely not, he must know me. "Sultan, darling, what is it?" She walked towards him. She was trembling. He looked so fierce, so big. This is what he must have looked like the night Auntie died and Suzette knew he could do considerable damage with those claws front and back and his sharp teeth.

"Sultan, it's all right. If you could only talk, and tell us what happened that night, to Auntie, and to you, Sultan. Please you're scaring me. She slowly stretched her hand out and he sank to the bed and was the old darling they knew and loved. She gathered him to her and said, "Yes, we all miss her, but it will be all right. We'll all take care of you and we all love you and you will be staying right here where you've always lived in your own well-tended home and you'll have the run of the cottage as always."

He wrapped her hand in his huge front paw, no claws showing, and hung on to her. "You stay here, we will be back soon." Her eyes caught hold of the small prayer book and the lace hankie on the table by the bed. She picked up the prayer book and gave the hankie to Sultan. "Now then, we both have a part of her."

Sultan gathered the delicate hankie to him without a snag and started to purr. "Good boy, you'll be all right and so will I. We'll both be all right." Clutching the prayer book, she made her way down to the three people below the stairs who were waiting for her. Their support and love would carry her though this day.

Sitting in the pew with Rob's hand holding hers tightly, Suzette heard Ed start at the back of the chapel, his tribute to his friend. And, at each pull of the change his mind went back to the days he and Dori came to St. Gilliam and went to work for Miss Millacent Lang and the happy years that followed. The long summers when Mr. Jason and Miss Amelia came for months to be with his sister and to write his books and then Suzette was born. What happy days they all had had together. Then Mr. Jason and Miss Amelia had been struck down. Those were black days, seem as same as these. They saw them

V.E. Sullivan

through, and by heck, they'd see these through, an all, and live to see that bastard caught.

Chapter 96

Kurt stared across the small table in disbelief at how much Heindrich had deteriorated. The once handsome face was grey and twisted. No, more pulled back to his left ear. His lips were no longer able to completely close on that side and the whole left side of his face from temple to the tip of his chin was all matted and bumpy and the infection was worse than he remembered. He almost felt sorry for the poor bastard. He could see the look of pain in his eyes. He could only see out of his right eye. There was no way he could use his monocle and he didn't know how much clear vision Heindrich had out of his good eye.

"Well, what are you staring at you dumkopf? Do I have to do everything?"

"You haven't done much of anything," Kurt replied tartly. "And before you say anymore..."

"Ja?"

"The Daimler is topped off with petrol and all checked out."

"Well, that's something. You know what you have to do."

"Ja. I call the Lang's cottage at six thirty and ask for Robert Nevil, et cetera."

"Good. Right after you will take your bags down and make sure you have left nothing behind in your room. I'll take care of mine."

"Thank you, you're too kind," Kurt said. Bitter sarcasm fell on deaf ears.

"You will stop by the desk and pay the bill."

"Ja, ja."

"For both our suites with a draft I will have ready for you. And at exactly six forty-five you will have the car on the side street and I will be there. Don't be late, you dumkopf. I warn you, don't be late! Now go. I have some things to do and I will rest for awhile."

Kurt was pleased to be dismissed. He had a few things he wanted to do himself, work with his stiletto and make sure it released. He didn't want to give Heindrich a chance to kill him because he missed. It had to work the first time. It was going to be kill or be killed. There was so much at stake for him as well as for Heindrich. They both had committed a crime punishable by death. So far they had gotten away

By the Pricking of My Thumb

with it. But tonight, tonight had to go off without a trace of trouble for them to get away.

His mind was in a turmoil, racing around ahead of him, only why did he feel so anxious, as if something was about to happen. Mein Gott, of course something was going to happen. We're going to return to the Lang's cottage for one, and two, he was going to do away with Heindrich before Heindrich got the chance to do the dirty on him. That had to be it. There wasn't anything to connect him to the old lady's murder and nothing to link him to Peggy.

He had to calm himself. His hands were shaking. At this rate he had a better chance of stabbing himself and saving Heindrich the trouble.

V.E. Sullivan

Chapter 97

Ronald Pentecroft looked over his crockery mug of steaming tea. My God, you could cut the tension in this room with a knife. Picking up his not so delicate ham and pickle sandwich, his eyes settled on the large table as he bit into the crusty bread. His eyes wandered over bits and pieces of evidence. Bits and pieces of two women's lives, one elderly and tiny, and still quite beautiful in the way older women can look, and one young and strikingly beautiful. What did these two women know or have that could cause them to meet such violent deaths? They knew each other, of course, as all village people did. But how else were they connected or by whom?

They had worked very hard, all of them and he was proud of his officers. They had gathered so much evidence, valuable evidence. They needed just one small piece of a missing puzzle and they would be able to bring these two cases to a close because he believed, as Quest did, they were tied together. As yet, it was not clear to them how.

Quest interrupted his thought with a rhythmic tip, tap, tip, tap of his pencil on the table. Pentecroft looked at him. He was lost in his own thoughts. My God, everyone in this room is, this is crazy. The phone at one end of the table rang and every Jack man of them jumped. It was Doc.

"He wants to speak to either one of you, Sir."

Pentecroft got up and took the receiver from the PC. "Hello, Doc? Have you found something?"

"Nay, nay, laddie. But it's no for the trying. Would you and Ashley care to have a wee dram and a bit of a supper at the Black Swan?"

"Anything for a break. We are all dizzy trying to break this thing. I feel we are so close. Hang on, and I'll ask him... He says it's a go. Oh, hang on Doc. Where is the place?"

"Oh, aye. About ten minutes out of St. Gilliam. You no can miss it, a nice wee place. Give ye a chance of a bit of a change. See you at six."

"Right you are, then."

Chapter 98

Terry replaced the lid on the boot polishing box, picked it up, put the brushes and cloths in it and returned it to it's place. He had never mastered the art of not getting his hands mucked up.

That taken care of he buttoned the last two buttons on his uniform and felt for his note pad and whistle in his breast pocket. The gentle sound of chimes making the half hour made Terry smile and look up at the deep windowsill. Fancy them remembering all these years how much he had loved the little ornate clock. It used to sit on the window sill in Miss Lang's kitchen when he was a little lad doing chores, and then as he got older, the yard. He could see it as if it was yesterday, cutting the hedges and clipping the edge of lawn after he had mowed, and the smell of the roses and heather wafting through the air as the breeze stirred them. All the while at the hour and on the half he would hear the little clock chiming through the open kitchen window. Either Dori or Miss Lang would come out with a cold drink and sandwiches and plate of cookies or sticky buns. He wasn't going to half miss her. He had loved her and for her to end her days in such a cruel and heartless manner made his blood boil.

She had never hurt anyone, only had helped people when she could. There wasn't any person in the village, young or old, that hadn't known her kindness at some time or other in their lives. They had all known they had lost a benefactor and a friend when she died, they were so close the heavy air was making him uneasy, almost as if something was in the air. He could almost taste it. He stopped at the kitchen door, looked around, lights out, cooker off, and then he picked up his keys and his bicycle clips from the peg by the door, and was off.

Terry was making for the incident room when he heard his name being called out. He turned to see young PC Ross hurrying towards him. "What's up, Ross?" The young bobby looked flustered and embarrassed.

"It's this, Terry." He palmed a small jewelry box over to Terry.

"What's this?"

"Well, well, I found it, Saturday night when I stopped for a smoke."

"Saturday night! Flamin' Nora, Ross. Do you have cloth ears or sommat? Don't you remember what they said about finding anything, anything at all that night?"

"Give over, Terry, and just listen to me. Hear me out, any road. When I got to the station after my beat it was six a.m. Sunday. I meant to turn it in then, but the place was like a beehive. Sergeant told me to take a couple of hours kip and then to get back to where you found the body and look for clues. Her purse, anything. Well, after another six hours I was knackered. Pentecroft told me to go home and to take Monday off. Well, when I came back it I just completely forgot about it until now, and when it fell out of my locker I just didn't know what to do. I knew Sergeant Littlejohn would have my head on a platter."

"But, why me, Ross?"

"Well, you seem to be working rather closer to the top brass than most and maybe you can help me. I did everything wrong. I picked it up; I put it in my pocket. I smudged any prints that may have been on it.

"Oh God, Terry, this is just such a mess! But maybe I can tell them something that will help. Just as I was cycling up I could just make out a large black car. When the driver saw me he stepped on the accelerator and sprayed dust and gravel getting out of there. You know what a popular place that spot is for young couples wanting a cuddle. I thought it was just a young courting couple that didn't want to be recognized by me. I put my bike against the tree and walked down to the grassy knoll by the water, and I either saw it, or I stepped on it."

"Don't say anything else. I'll tell the inspector."

"Ah, which one?" Ross asked cautiously.

"Who do you think, ye daft pellick? Keep your head down and your mouth shut and stay out of Sergeant Littlejohn's way."

"Thanks, Terry."

"Well, we'll see how much you thank me later."

When Terry walked into the room he found both men poring over pictures and papers and reports. "Might I have a word with you, sir?"

Pentecroft looked up, "Right now, Simms?"

"Yes, sir, I think it is important."

"Excuse me, Quest. This won't take long." Quest nodded and watched the two men move away.

Pentecroft moved to the table in the corner. It was covered with heavy crockery mugs and there was a hot plate and a big old kettle on the boil. "Care for a cuppa while we talk?"

"Thanks, sir."

Inspector Pentecroft sat himself on the corner on the table and put his last cigarette in his mouth and looked at Terry through a cloud of smoke.

Terry took a quick gulp of hot tea. It burned going down but it was good. "It's this, sir." Terry took the small box from his uniform pocket and handed it to his superior and related Ross's story to him.

"Where is he?"

Terry said, "Waiting out of Sergeant's way. He's scared sir. Didn't know what to do. Knows he bunged it up, so's to speak, and he's afraid Sergeant will put him on report."

"You did the right thing, Terry. Well done. Go and see if you can find him and tell him not to worry, this time. But it had better be his last."

"Right, sir. Thank you."

"That's all right Simms. Off you go."

Quest had been watching the two. He could tell by Ronald's face it was serious. And as Terry moved quickly from the room Ronald made his way back to him. "What's the lather all about?"

By the time Terry had found Ross and made his way back, both men were waiting. It wasn't long after that, that the activity in the small room was at a fever pitch. They all knew that this was the missing piece of the puzzle. Quest, Pentecroft and Terry prayed they were not too late.

Chapter 99

It had gone past six, Dori and Suzette were finishing up the dishes. Robert and Ed were still talking at the table and Sultan was cleaning himself on his stool. It was Ed and Dori's night for choir practice and bell ringing, and they usually left about six forty-five and were home at eight. Suzette and Rob didn't have any particular plans for the evening, just relaxing.

Kurt had finished packing and was checking the bathroom for anything he might have left behind. Clean. Out in the bedroom the closet door stood open. Empty. He ran his hands across the shelf. Nothing. Over to the bed, it was neatly made, on to the bedstand table. He slid open the small drawer and checked it. He had been trained to be thorough. He glanced at his watch. He had time for one last visit to the Grand's bar, felt he was going to need it and all of the nerve he could get.

Margaret and David had finished their tea and were sitting in front of the fire. David was reading and Margaret was knitting. The inquest was over and a strange calm had settled upon them. David looked up slowly. As always, he almost caught his breath. She was so beautiful.

He felt the same way each time. Just like the first time he had ever seen her. She had changed so little. A small wrinkle crossed her brow and she stared down at the small white piece of knitting. Maybe she's made a mistake. No. All was well.

He smiled and then a stab of pain ran across his heart. Peggy, his darling child. How could she have gotten so caught up in anything so evil that it took her life away from them? It was like reading a cheap thriller; only this was real and not so cheap. It came at a great cost to them. He quickly lowered his gaze behind his book so Margaret wouldn't see his tears. But Margaret couldn't have seen through the blur in her own eyes.

Kurt placed his glass back on the bar and, putting a five pound note under it, got up and went to the kiosk outside the lounge and called the Lang's cottage. It was exactly six-thirty.

When Dori picked up the phone, she listened and set the receiver down. "Robert," she called down the hall, "it's for you."

As Robert came down the hall, he looked puzzled, and picking up the receiver said, "Hello?"

"Mr. Nevil? Robert Nevil?"

It was a voice he didn't recognize. "Yes, this is he."

"Mr. Nevil, this is Mr. Jenkins from the museum. There has been a break-in and you are needed as soon as you can get back to London, Sir."

"I'm sorry, I don't know you. Are you with the museum?"

"Yes sir, I'm with the security. And the artifacts missing are very old and rare. They need you to help itemize them for identification. They're calling me, sir. Can I say you are returning tonight?"

"Ah, well... yes, of course. I'll start back immediately."

"Thank you, sir," and the wire went dead.

He slowly replaced the receiver and rubbed the back of his neck with his hand as he returned to the kitchen.

"Rob, what's the matter? What is it, love?"

"The phone call was from the museum. There's been a break in and they need me tonight."

"Of course." Suzette crossed the floor and slid her arm through his. "I'll help you pack a few things."

"Thanks, Petal. I'll only be gone for a day. I'm sure I'll be back by this time tomorrow night."

"My goodness Ed, look at time. We must be off else we'll be late. You be all right Suzette, love?"

"Of course, Dori. And you'll be back by eight."

"Maybe sooner. I won't need my pint and Dori won't need her natter. Isn't that right, Dori?"

"Aye, Ed. And it's only gossip any road. See you soon ducks."

"Bye, don't worry about me. I'll be fine, Dori. Come on, Rob."

Dori smiled as she watched them ascend the stairs arm in arm.

Rob opened the car door and glanced at his watch. "It's a quarter to seven so if the traffic is light I'll make good time and by this time tomorrow I'll be on my way back." He encircled her waist and drew her to him.

"Please be careful, Rob darling. I love you so much. I couldn't stand..."

He stopped her words with a tender kiss and held her close. "I'll call you from the office, love, as soon as I can. Suzette, you know how much you mean to me and how very much I love you, don't you?" She smiled and he was off.

Suzette went slowly back to the house picking a few roses and deadheads as she went. She was going to leave the door open, it was a soft evening, but suddenly she felt a chill run through her and she shuddered. Sultan was at her feet looking up at her.

"You know, Sultan. If Auntie were here she would have said, 'Someone just crossed over my grave.' Come on old dear, let's have a cuppa."

With tea tray in her hands she made her way back to the front room. Setting down the tray, she knelt to light the fire wondering if this is what Auntie had done the last night of her life.

Chapter 100

Terry burst through the door of the jewelry shop and up to the car, thrust a piece of paper into Pentecroft's hand. Both officers looked at it.

"Get in, Terry. Sergeant, call for back up. Seal off all of the driveways front and back of the Grand, and post officers at all the doors. Set up roadblocks and get on to York. We will need their help. You know the drill, Sergeant. They will get on to London, to the ferrys, airport, rail stations, and they'll get through to Interpol."

Kurt pulled the Daimler into the side and out of nowhere Heindrich appeared. Kurt reached across and opened the car door. He stepped in and they were off almost without stopping. They were making good time. Everything was going as they had planned. They would be at the Lang's almost at seven. Neither man spoke. Each was consumed with their own thoughts.

Detective Chief Inspector Quest turned and looked at Inspector Pentecroft.

"Bloody hell," Pentecroft said. "If we had been just fifteen minutes earlier we would have had them."

"We're still not that far behind," Quest said. He had been there before, but he remembered his first time and knew what Pentecroft was thinking and the frustration he felt. "We have everything covered. They can't get out of St. Gilliam, and if they do get by, they will not get out of York. Come on, we had better get back to the station house and see what's coming in over the wire. We'll get them."

Suzette sat and licked her middle finger. She set her teacup down. How quiet the room was. She could hear Sultan purring. It was such a pretty room and had not changed much over the years. A few good pieces added. A painting changed here and there. Small things. Her glance came back to the desk. It really was a handsome piece of work and the way the last rays of the sun danced across the surface, it took on a life of its own.

"Oh, Sultan. If only it could tell us, or you could talk." As if he knew what she was saying, he rolled over, his massive head tilted to one side and eyes glowing, and a deep-throated mew came from his throat.

"Oh, look, there's a thread from Dori's polishing cloth." She uncurled her long legs and walked over to the desk. "Cracky! This is really stuck in there." She wrapped the thread around her index finger and jerked. She heard a crack or a creak and a piece of wood came away in her hand. "Oh no! Look what I've done! This precious old thing Auntie loved so much," and she was on her knees in front of it with the damaged piece in her hands. "I'll just fit it back in place and get Rob to fix it, or Ed. What in the world? There's something in here." She could only see a piece of material.

She reached in and drew the soft bundle out. It was small and she went towards the fireplace for a better look. She sat down and unwrapped the bundle. Sultan sat up and came quickly to her. "Oh, you want to see too, do you?" The last fold was lifted and there it lay. Suzette sucked in her breath. It was exquisite. The most perfect icon she had ever seen. It seemed to be on fire in her lap. The gold and silver and the jewels. The Madonna and Christ child. She didn't touch it, just sat spellbound. Then it hit her, like a blow from an invisible hand to her midsection. This is why Auntie Millacent died. This is what they were after but somehow never found.

"Oh, Sultan! What am I going to do? I've got to think." It was going on seven. Dori and Ed said they would be home early. She was trembling. She rose slowly to her feet and walked back to the desk. How clever someone had been. You would never have known that the secret compartment was there, or how to get into it unless someone had told you or, like herself, and her aunt, had found it by accident. She was going to put it back but she couldn't. She couldn't make it fit. Her hands were trembling so.

Gathering it back up, she turned and ran into the hall and took the stairs two at a time. She hadn't realized until she got to the top of the stairs that Sultan had beat her to the top. She turned and looked down, and the only light was coming from the front room fireplace and the small lamp by the chair. She passed her aunt's room and started in, but something stopped her. Backing out she went to her old room that looked out over the back garden. Crawling up onto the old high bed, she sank into the big eiderdown. Clutching the precious bundle to her chest and crying, she felt so alone, so vulnerable.

"Oh, Rob. Here it is! This is the answer to all this maddening mess." She sat up, tucking her legs under her and opened it once again and laid it before her. Rubbing the tears from her eyes with the back of her hand she heard the clock in the hall strike seven.

By the Pricking of My Thumb

Kurt pulled the car into the same spot as the first time they were there and he turned and looked at Heindrich. It was like looking at a death mask. He sat staring at the house.

"Well? It isn't going to come to us, is it? This thing you're looking for."

"Shut up! Dumkopf. And don't talk unless I ask you to." He drew a small leather pouch from the inside pocket of his coat and a heavy torch from the other. "Come on. And close the door quietly."

He fell in beside Heindrich as they walked softly up to the gate. Kurt watched as Heindrich opened the pouch and withdrew a small syringe and put a few drops from it onto the old gate hinge. It swung open silently. He stood just inside it for a few seconds looking at the house. Kurt felt his arm under the expensive sports coat. It was there and he felt calmer.

"How do we know there's no one home?" He spoke softly at Heindrich's back. Before he knew what happened, Heindrich turned, and with his open palm, hit him hard across the face. He fell back a pace. He put his hand up to his throbbing jaw.

"I told you to shut up and not speak unless I said so, you Sweinhund."

And Kurt knew at that moment that Heindrich had crossed that fine line between sanity and madness and he would be twice as hard to get the better of now. His only chance was to make him think he had won.

"Ja, mein Colonel."

Heindrich never winced. Thinks he's back in command of his storm troupers.

They moved to the door. Once more the pouch came out. Kurt couldn't see much but once more the door swung open without a sound and they were in the hall. He motioned Kurt forward. He closed the door as silently as it opened. He moved as quiet as a cat to the front room and he stood in the middle of the room listening.

When he was satisfied they were alone he walked to the tray, felt the teapot. It was cold. Heindrich picked up the untouched sandwich and started to eat it. Kurt knew there was something wrong. He was more alert and in tune with his instincts than he had ever felt before. No one would go away and leave a fireplace going without putting up the screen for fear a large ember might start a fire spreading in a thatched cottage as old as this one.

Heindrich turned and walked towards the desk. Kurt already saw the opening in it but he also knew Heindrich's condition and that he only had the sight of one eye and the light wasn't that good from the dying fire and the small lamp cast lots of shadows. Heindrich still hadn't noticed. He was busy finishing the sandwich. He stopped short, his hand dropped, the crusts fell to the carpet and he ran forward. He fell on his knees. He just knelt there, looking into the hole and he started to pound the top of the desk with his fist and low sobs came from deep within.

Suzette was just pulling on her light dressing gown when she thought she heard something. Can't be eight o'clock yet, surely. She looked at her watch. It was just gone past seven. She froze, almost afraid to breathe. Her mind raced. Had she locked all the doors? She was sure she had. That gate always groaned loudly when it was opened and she had heard nothing. She was barefooted. She crept to the door and listened, nothing. She went softly back to the bed. She didn't know why but she wrapped the icon up in the scarf she had taken off and laid it on the bottom of the bed and turned off the bedside lamp and sat motionless on the bed in the dark.

Her breath was coming fast and her heart was pounding. She felt the pressure on the eiderdown change and she put her hand over her mouth when she felt the silky fur. She gathered Sultan up so quickly and was holding him so close to her, so glad of his warmth and his massive weight. He was struggling. "Oh Sultan," she barely whispered, "I'm so sorry. I was just so glad you were here." She loosened her grip half afraid he would leave her but he didn't. He settled and started purring.

Kurt quickly crossed the room to Heindrich's side. "Mein Colonel. I thought I heard something." Heindrich turned and his twisted face had cracked and puss mingled with blood was oozing out from the dirty scab from his eye to his mouth. He didn't seem to notice.

He grabbed Kurt by the shoulders and shook him and pulling him down to the carpet said "Look, look," as they crouched. "It's gone. My prize is gone. We must search the house from top to bottom."

"Ja. Ja, ja, mein Colonel. But what if they took it with them?" Kurt said.

He froze and Kurt saw the same look on Heindrich's face and the wild, unsteady look in his one eye as he had seen all those years ago in the prison when he was attacking and brutalizing that poor, poor Jew. He swung away from Kurt and in doing so knocked the small lamp off the desk. It crashed to the floor. For a brief instant both men stood frozen.

Suzette knew there was someone in the cottage and she knew what they were looking for. She also knew that she knew every nook and cranny, every squeaky board, every sharp turn, where every window was and every door, which was to her advantage. Whoever was downstairs didn't know all this and they also didn't know where she was or even if there was anyone else in the cottage. She wouldn't be alone much longer. Ed and Dori would be home soon.

Robert was half way to York. He still puzzled over the phone call. Why hadn't Alway called him himself? After all, he was his assistant and had been for more than two years. And he was the one who was in charge while he was away. And why couldn't Alway have assisted them in the itemizing and identifications? No, he had to find a kiosk and call. There should be one in one of these lay bys. He'd have to keep watch.

He had driven another quarter of a mile when he spotted it. He pulled in hastily, getting out of the car praying it was in working order. It was. Dropping in the coin, he waited, and on the third beep he heard the familiar voice.

"Alway, this is Robert. I'm about to York. Fine, fine, but listen. About that break in. Can't you... What? No. Can't you speak a little louder Alway? I can't hear you and the traffic on the A-1 is terrific. My God, Alway, you're telling me it was someone's idea of a joke. Well, they must be having a howl. No, thanks, Alway. I'll see you soon. Bye for now. What's that? Yes, yes, I'll tell her. I will."

Hanging up, he got out more coins to call the cottage and to tell Suzette he would be back as soon as he could. Looking at his watch, he saw it was twenty to eight. Should be back by eight ten at the latest. Funny, where in the world was she? He felt a tightening in his chest. "Oh, no. Oh my God!" and he slammed down the receiver and ran back to the Jag. He didn't care how fast he was going. In fact, he would have welcomed a police panda as he swung about and squealed on to the A-1 and headed back to St. Gilliam.

Suzette started out the bedroom and got as far as the landing at the top of the stairs. She froze, the phone was ringing. It couldn't be Rob. He wouldn't be in London yet, but who? She realized where she was. It was so dark and the phone was just at the bottom of the stairs but she couldn't see it, only hear it.

Both men froze at the ringing of the phone. Kurt grabbed Heindrich's sleeve and pulled him down quickly and silently. The fire was almost out and between the last embers and the small lamp, for miraculously the light hadn't broken, it was shinning, only a small section of the room was lit. Thank God the phone stopped. His heart was pounding so loud he thought it would burst.

He had heard something else, a small thud. Heindrich must have heard it too because he started to make his way on his hands and knees to the far wall. Turning in the dark, Kurt watched him as he made his way around the room pulling the plug from the socket. There was just enough light left for Kurt to see him motion for him to follow.

Barely audible he said, "Hang on to my jacket." He started to move. Kurt couldn't believe he could move so swiftly, so quietly, and not hit anything. His eyes were trying to adjust to the dark. Heindrich stopped and Kurt hit his back. They were against something hard. Kurt put out his hand. It was the banister and Kurt realized they were at the foot of the stairs, just to one side. He felt Heindrich stiffen. There was a sound on the stair. Then he knew. It was the cat. No wonder Heindrich reacted. Wait. There was something else. He felt Heindrich's arm and he was raising it.

Suzette knew Sultan had raced passed her on the stairs but she could do nothing to stop him. She was almost at the bottom now. She stopped to listen and heard nothing. A savage blow took her behind the ear. She pitched forward in a cloud of bright red haze, which was slowly turning into a purple black pit, as she lost consciousness. The last thing she heard was a man's voice, "Silly bitch," and it was blackness.

It had happened so fast, Kurt heard the body hit the floor. Heindrich was laughing. It was high pitched and it was getting louder.

By the Pricking of My Thumb

He was shining the torch on the crumpled body at the foot of the stairs.

"Heindrich, what have you done? Who is this?"

"Shut up, dumkopf. Schwein-hund. Tie up her hands and feet."

"But what do you suggest I use, mein herr?"

Heindrich was on him in a second. He back-handed him across the mouth, drawing blood. "Must I do everything? I've always known just how low you're mentality was. How did you ever expect to be one of us, the chosen? Use your belt to tie."

Kurt could have killed him then and there but knew he had to leave this place and quickly. He also knew this was the last time Heindrich would have the chance to hit him again. He tied her hands behind her back and her ankles very tightly with the cord from the drapes. Heindrich hadn't noticed, or if he did he didn't seem to care. She was bleeding badly. It was matting her hair and running down her neck.

He took a chance and spoke, "What now, Heindrich? We've got to get out of here. It's almost eight."

"Nein, nein. I won't be cheated out of this. It's mine. I found it, I trailed it for years. First it was that Jason Lang and his French whore, then his sister, now his bastard. But I took care of them all, didn't I?" He was ranting and pacing.

"Heindrich, please. They'll come back."

"If we have to take this cottage apart piece by piece, we won't leave 'till I find it."

"But if we stay, we'll be caught."

Heindrich turned his twisted, wretched face to him and he wished he hadn't. It was worse. Why couldn't he feel it? He seemed to be oblivious to everything. He opened his mouth to speak but didn't. He stood with his mouth open. "Mein Gott, what is loust?"

Kurt stood rigid. He heard the high-powered motor. Heindrich was swinging from sanity to madness like the pendulum of the clock. It struck eight.

"Pick her up! Pick her up! We'll go out the back way and we'll pass them on the road. Schnell, schnell."

Kurt picked up Suzette. Her head fell against his chest. He didn't know if she was dead or alive, but he followed Heindrich as fast as he could out the door, down the garden path just as he had done once before with the old lady, past the shed through the gate. Heindrich had the boot open. He dumped her in it. Heindrich was behind the wheel and was rolling before he had his whole body in and he thought for a moment he would fall out. He slammed the heavy door just in time.

The Jag swung into the lane and the headlights blinding each driver, Kurt put up his arm to protect his face from the glass. Robert swung into the lane and was immediately blinded by the high beam light of the oncoming car. How he missed slamming into it he would never know. Running up the walk, he noticed that the cottage was dark. Not even the carriage lamps by the door were burning.

He had a lump the size of a boulder in his stomach as he turned the old fashioned hasp of the door and it opened. Pushing it wide, he reached in for the switch and the lamps came on, flooding the landing.

"Suzette, Suzette! It's Rob. Where are you?" Crossing to the landing to turn on the lamp by the phone. He skidded. "Bloody hell!" The lamp spread a small glow in the hall and his heart almost stopped. It was blood he had slipped on. "Blood! My God, what has happened?"

He took the stairs two at a time, turning on lights and calling as he went. Her old bedroom had her clothes on the end of the bed. It looked like she was getting ready to go to bed. He was halfway down the stairs when Ed came bursting through the house with Dori on his heels.

"What's wrong, laddie? What's happened? Why are you here?"

"Oh God, Ed. Suzette's gone and there's blood on the floor."

Dori sank to her knees looking at the large smear on the hardwood floor and she saw Sultan. He was laying in the darkened doorway of the front room. "Oh, Ed!"

Robert and he walked swiftly over. "It's all right, he's just stunned."

Chapter 101

Sergeant Littlejohn burst into the room. His huge bulk filling the doorway. "It's Robert Nevil from the Lang's cottage, Sir. Miss Lang is missing and the cottage has been rummaged and there's some blood on the floor. Terry was the first one on his feet with Quest and Pentecroft following.

"Let's go. Terry, you come with us. Sergeant, you stay by the phone. Every exit in St. Gilliam is covered. That only leaves the back roads leading to the moors," Pentecroft went on. "I've lived here for years and I wouldn't go out there alone on a night as dark as this. Very dangerous, the moors, unless you know exactly which toe path to take. Even with experience some have met with disaster on those moors."

Minutes later they pulled up in front of the Lang cottage and were bolting up the walk only to collide with the distraught Robert. They made a quick check of the cottage, realizing the blood did not come from Sultan, they determined it had to be Suzette's.

"Ed and Dori, I want you to stay here by the phone. I don't expect our caller to call but he might. Robert, I want you to come with us."

They were met at the door by Dr. Dundee. "Aye, laddies. When you didn't a show for tea I called the station. Sergeant told me. I've got my bag. Am I needed here?"

"No," Quest said, "but we might need you later on.

Suzette was slowly coming around. Her head felt like it was exploding. The throbbing came in waves like the tide coming in and going out. She was in a cramped space. Her arms ached. She tried to move but couldn't. Where am I? What's that smell? She tried to raise her head but was overcome with waves of nausea and dizziness. She was being thumped and jostled. Every movement caused her excruciating pain.

That smell, it was rubber, a rubber tyre smell. She was in the boot of a car. And through the daze of pain she forced her mind back trying to remember. Then it all slowly came in bits and pieces. The icon, someone in the house. The decent down the stairs, the pain. Suzette slipped into unconsciousness again.

She was playing hopscotch outside of Aunt Millacent's house and she was singing, "Doctor, doctor, will I die? Yes, my child, and so will I." A phone was ringing, loud, and louder. She opened her eyes.

Oh God, what's happening to me? I'm dying. Rob, Rob, where are you? Oh, Rob, you've come. She felt herself being lifted from the boot of the car and was being carried along. Why wasn't Rob talking to her?

"There, right there, dumkopf. Prop her against the tree. She'll either be found or she will die and be found later. In any case I'll be gone."

Kurt turned to face Heindrich for an explanation. It must have been the impact of the bullet that caused Kurt's muscle to tighten and the stiletto imbedded itself into the fatty tissue just above the left pectoral muscle of Heindrich's chest. He let out a wild howl like a wounded dog. The Luger fell to the ground and he turned and tried to extract the stiletto but he couldn't, he couldn't stand the pain. His head, face and shoulder were all throbbing with each beat of his heart. And with each beat he felt the warm sticky blood oozing between his fingers. Heindrich ran howling straight out onto the moor.

Quest had taken the call on the car phone. The Daimler had been spotted heading out of St. Gilliam on a little used back road.

"I know that road, sir," and he directed them to it. "This is it. And sir, it's a bad place for a stranger to be heading into for it ends abruptly and it's very boggy to go further. And if they're out there we have them for sure, sir."

"Right. Glad to have you with us, Terry," Quest said. "Can you guide us if we have to take up chase on foot with just our torches and lamps?"

"Yes, sir. Used to hunt rabbits here. I know all the bogs and the safe places and all the dangerous drops like the back of my hand."

Doctor Dundee suggested that an ambulance be called to follow them just in case. He didn't finish. Looking at Robert, he didn't want to. Poor laddie. He said a silent prayer for Suzette.

By the Pricking of My Thumb

Chapter 102

They heard her screaming a good few minutes before they found her propped against the tree. Her hands were bound behind her back, her legs bent at the knees, and her ankles bound tightly. Her blood was trickling to mix with Kurt's who lay across her lap, his lifeless eyes staring up at her. His blood saturated her thin cotton robe and gown; the bullet had gotten him squarely between the eyes. Bits of bone and brains were spattered all over her.

Robert was beside her, his arms encircled her. "Suzette, Suzette. Darling it's me, Robert. You're safe now. I never will forgive myself for leaving you alone." He kissed her forehead. She knew it was Rob. He had come for her. She wanted to tell him how much she loved him and how proud she was of him. To tell him, if she had her life to live over again she would change nothing. But all she seemed to be able to do was to stare at him and clutch at him with swollen blue hands. Oh no, not yet. Her head slumped onto his shoulder. He could feel her blood soaking his shirt.

"Doctor"

"Nay, nay laddie. Dinna you fear now. I've given her a strong injection for pain. And can you no hear the ambulance coming?"

"Yes, yes I can. Will she be all right?"

"Aye. She'll have a terrible headache for some time and she has a concussion, she's badly shaken and bruised, but aye, she's a grand lassie. Young and strong. A good few stitches behind her ear and she'll be good as ever with rest and time"

The ambulance was there and they were putting her in when they all heard the terrible howling. Then it stopped. The sudden silence was eerie. It was black. The night closed in on them as if it were a velvet cape, thick and heavy. The mist covered them with beads of moisture, making them cold and clammy.

Robert was hard pressed to keep up to Terry and was very mindful of his warning to follow closely and to step in his steps. So black was the night Robert ran right into Terry's back almost knocking him off his feet. But he was like a brick wall.

"Quick, sir. Shine your torch with mine down there, sir."

What met Rob's eyes was straight out of a Gothic horror story. "My God, Terry. I could have sent you to your death."

"Shine it to your left a bit sir."

Robert sucked in his breath. There he was, hanging in the craggy branches of a tree growing out of the sides of the rough granite. It was grotesque. He looked like a giant puppet whose strings had been suddenly cut, setting him free. His head lay right back. His one eye was wide open with a look of wild surprise frozen on his disfigured face.

"Do you think he's dead?"

"Quite, sir."

The rest had caught them up and stood shining their torches on the gruesome sight. They were standing in a small group with the light of their lamps making them all look like big, wet, black ravens.

"I agree," Chief Inspector Quest said. "Too dangerous to do anything tonight and he's not going anywhere and we can do much more in the daylight. And you, sir, must be anxious to return to see how your young lady is doing."

"Yes, please. I'd like that very much."

Chapter 103

It was their last night in the cottage. Everything was settled. She lay across Robert's lap, cradled in his arms. Only the fire was burning and cast such a lovely warm glow. She loved this room.

She looked up at Rob who had fallen asleep. Poor darling. He had been her rock through all of this. He had the strength when she had none and she loved him for that. He had identified the icon. It had once hung in the small chapel of Catherine, the Empress of all Russia. Peter the Greats granddaughter-in-law. It had been lost for years and found again during the war. The holy church of Russia was afraid it would not be safe to send it back to St. Petersburg and suggested to the Russian Orthodox Holy Fathers in Poland where it had surfaced that they hide it in that wonderful old desk made by a Polish Jew who had given his life to protect it. And it was on its way back to its rightful home to hang in the Hermitage and rightfully so. As her aunt had given her life to protect it also and she had almost given hers.

Ed and Dori would keep the cottage and the shop and the cottage business would be Dori's alone. It was the way she and Rob wanted it.

It would be in safe and dear hands and Rob and she would be back in the spring to be married in the chapel. She was so happy.

Sultan lay on his back soaking up the warmth of the fire. Auntie would be so pleased he would be staying in his own home, loved and cared for by the Halleys and so was she.

One day, years down the road, this would be her home, Rob and hers. She was content and pleased the way everything had turned out. She was suddenly very sleepy herself. She turned her head and through eyes closing in sleep stared at the fire and dreamed about the happy days to come when Robert and she would walk hand in hand along the tree lined streets of St. Gilliam growing old together. For after all, wasn't the best yet to come?

~The End~

ABOUT THE AUTHOR

V. E. Sullivan was born in Regina, Saskatchewan and educated in British Columbia. She lived in the United States for a number of years, but then took up residence in Great Britain. She fell in love with the English village life and her mysteries revolve around the places she knows so well and loved. After her marriage to an Irish citizen, they traveled all over Europe for research and relaxation. They now reside in British Columbia close to family and friends, some of whom reside in the United States. She loves spending time with their children and grandchildren meeting people, going to quaint places and antiquing.

Printed in the United States
837000001B